D0392621

ifferisms

Also by Dr. Mardy Grothe

I Never Metaphor I Didn't Like

Viva la Repartee

Oxymoronica

Never Let a Fool Kiss You or a Kiss Fool You

ifferisms

AN ANTHOLOGY OF APHORISMS
THAT BEGIN WITH THE WORD *IF*

Dr. Mardy Grothe

COLLINS REFERENCE
An Imprint of HarperCollins*Publishers*
www.harpercollins.com

For information, address HarperCollins Publishers, 10 East 53rd Street, New York, NY 10022.

HarperCollins books may be purchased for educational, business, or sales promotional use. For information, please write: Special Markets Department, HarperCollins Publishers, 10 East 53rd Street, New York, NY 10022.

FIRST EDITION

Designed by Emily Cavett Taff

Library of Congress Cataloging-in-Publication Data

Grothe, Mardy.
Ifferisms: an anthology of aphorisms that begin with the word "if" / Mardy Grothe.—1st ed.
p. cm.
ISBN 978-0-06-167230-9
1. Aphorisms and apothegms. I. Title.
PN6271.G76 2009
082—dc22

2008053948

09 10 11 12 13 OV/RRD 10 9 8 7 6 5 4 3 2 1

To my wife, Katherine Robinson.
If I could change one thing about her . . .
I wouldn't.

contents

introduction

Do you know what an aphorism is?

When I began work on this book a few years ago, I asked hundreds of people this simple question. I'm not quite sure what I expected, but I was surprised by the large number of people who hesitated, and then hemmed and hawed before saying something like, "I know what it is, but I'm having trouble putting it into words." Try the question on some of your friends. You may be surprised.

Technically, an *aphorism* (AFF-uhr-IZ-uhm) is a brief observation that attempts to communicate some kind of truth about the human experience:

Contact with the world either breaks or hardens the heart.

NICOLAS CHAMFORT

To measure the man, measure his heart.

MALCOLM FORBES

The human heart is vast enough to contain all the world.

JOSEPH CONRAD

He has the right to criticize who has the heart to help.

ABRAHAM LINCOLN

The heart has reasons that the reason knows not of.

BLAISE PASCAL

The American Heritage Dictionary defines an aphorism as "a tersely phrased statement of a truth or opinion; an adage." Like so many dictionary definitions, though, this is a bit of a yawner. But—appropriately, I think—some of the best descriptions of aphorisms have been expressed aphoristically:

An aphorism is the last link in a long chain of thought.

MARIE VON EBNER-ESCHENBACH

The aphorism is a personal observation inflated into a universal truth, a private posing as a general.

STEFAN KANFER

A slightly longer—but equally memorable—description comes from James Geary, who wrote in *The World in a Phrase: A History of the Aphorism* (2005):

Aphorisms are literature's hand luggage.
Light and compact, they fit easily into the overhead compartment of your brain and contain everything you need to get through a rough day at the office or a dark night of the soul.

While *aphorism* is the noun, *aphoristic* is the adjective. A person who creates aphorisms is called an *aphorist*, and writers who pen them are said to write *aphoristically*. Many literary giants—such as Mark Twain, Oscar Wilde, and George Bernard Shaw—have been drawn to the writing of these little gems. Friedrich Nietzsche, another master of the form, hinted at the motivation of many aphorists when he said, "My ambition is to say in ten sentences what everyone else says in a book." And if you think terse and pithy sayings are trivial, consider what Samuel Taylor Coleridge had to say on the subject:

The largest and worthiest portion of our knowledge consists of aphorisms.

A synonym for aphorism is *epigram*, and they are also known as *maxims* and *adages*. They were once commonly called *apothegms* (APP-uh-thums), but that word has completely dropped out of favor. Many aphorisms have gained such a widespread currency they are called *proverbs*, *axioms*, or *truisms*. Some have a guide-your-life quality, and are given the honorific title of *precept* or *dictum*. And some are so popular they become victims of their own success and are dismissed or disparaged as platitudes, bromides, or clichés. Whatever they're called, succinctly phrased sayings have an honored place in intellectual history.

At the beginning of the chapter, I presented five aphorisms on the subject of the human heart. Below are five more. Notice the one thing they have in common:

If a good face is a letter of recommendation, a good heart is a letter of credit.

EDWARD BULWER-LYTTON

If your heart has peace, nothing can disturb you.

THE DALAI LAMA

If it were not for hopes, the heart would break.

THOMAS FULLER, M.D.

If you haven't any charity in your heart, you have the worst kind of heart trouble.

BOB HOPE

If the heart be right, it matters not which way the head lies.

WALTER RALEIGH

All of these observations, of course, begin with the word *if*. I have coined the term *ifferism* for this kind of aphorism, and I intend to celebrate them in this book. While most aphorisms do not begin with the word *if*, there are many thousands that do—and they are among history's most compelling quotations:

If you can put the question,
"Am I or am I not responsible for my acts?"
then you are responsible.

FYODOR DOSTOYEVSKY

If you want to lift yourself up, lift up someone else.

BOOKER T. WASHINGTON

If you do not tell the truth about yourself
you cannot tell it about other people.

VIRGINIA WOOLF

The following ifferisms—some of which will be explored in more detail in a later chapter—have achieved a classic status in popular culture:

If it ain't broke, don't fix it.

If anything can go wrong, it will.

If life hands you lemons, make lemonade.

If momma ain't happy, ain't nobody happy.

If it sounds too good to be true, it probably is.

Some others are enormously thought provoking:

If merely "feeling good" could decide,
drunkenness would be the supremely valid human experience.

WILLIAM JAMES

If man does find the solution for world peace it will be
the most revolutionary reversal of his record we have ever known.

GEORGE C. MARSHALL

If you can talk brilliantly about a problem,
it can create the consoling illusion that it has been mastered.

STANLEY KUBRICK

Some of the most famous biblical passages are ifferisms:

If the blind lead the blind, both shall fall into the ditch.

MATTHEW 15:14

If a house be divided against itself, that house cannot stand.

MARK 3:25

And, finally, some are among the world's most popular proverbs:

If you give a man a fish, he will eat for a day;
if you teach a man to fish, he will eat for a lifetime.

CHINESE PROVERB

If a man deceives me once, shame on him;
if he deceives me twice, shame on me.

ITALIAN PROVERB

At the beginning of my quotation-collecting career many decades ago, I noticed that a fair number of my favorite observations were introduced with the word *if.* I didn't give the matter a whole lot of thought back then, but I did think it was of enough potential interest that I created a manila folder—and later a computer file—to store what I was calling at the time *iffy* quotations. The number of quotations in that file has mushroomed over the years, and my thinking about them has evolved. I now understand the critical role that this simple two-letter word plays in human discourse, and I have come to believe that *if* is the biggest little word in the English language. It is an essential tool when people engage in hypothetical or counterfactual thinking and when they make conditional statements.

Hypothetical Thinking

At one level, *ifferism* is simply a playful pun on the word *aphorism.* But at another level, the term points to one of the most fascinating aspects of the human experience: the ability to use our imaginations to perform thought experiments. Aristotle maintained that the mark of an intelligent person was to entertain an idea without actually believing it—and this is exactly what people do when they engage in "what if?" thinking.

Hypothetical thinking involves the formulation of some kind of hypothesis, which *The American Heritage Dictionary* defines as "something taken to be true for the purpose of argument or investigation." When people formulate a hypothesis or imagine a hypothetical scenario, they operate *as if* something is true, even when they know that what they are imagining is fanciful or far-fetched.

In 1978, Gloria Steinem wrote a *Ms.* magazine article titled "If Men Could Menstruate: A Political Fantasy." In answer to the hypothetical question "What would happen if suddenly, magically, men could menstruate and women could not?" she wrote: "The answer is clear—menstruation would become an enviable, boast-worthy, masculine event." In one of the decade's most provocative essays, Steinem helped readers imagine a world in which men bought Paul Newman Tampons, bragged about how long they menstruated, and said things like "I'm a three-pad man."

When people create a hypothetical scenario in their minds, and then express the thought ifferistically, they are often trying to make a point or advance an argument:

If we were to wake up some morning
and find that everyone was the same race, creed, and color,
we would find some other causes for prejudice by noon.

GEORGE AIKEN

If the aborigine drafted an IQ test,
all of Western civilization would presumably flunk it.

STANLEY MARION GARN,
on cultural bias in IQ tests

If all mankind were to disappear, the world would regenerate
back to the rich state of equilibrium that existed ten thousand years ago.
If insects were to vanish, the environment would collapse into chaos.

EDWARD O. WILSON

Occasionally a hypothetical thought is combined with a flight of fantasy to forge a delightful—and absolutely unforgettable—observation. Some years ago, the actress Candice Bergen offered this gem about pregnancy and childbirth:

If God were a woman, She would have installed
one of those turkey thermometers in our belly buttons.
When we were done, the thermometer pops up,
the doctor reaches for the zipper
conveniently located beneath our bikini lines,
and out comes a smiling, fully diapered baby.

While many hypothetical observations imagine how things in the future might look if some present condition of existence were changed, still others imagine what the present world might look like if some aspect of the past were changed.

Counterfactual Thinking

When the hypothetical imagination looks backward, it engages in counterfactual thinking, the notion being that what is imagined runs counter to the actual facts of history.

Counterfactual thinking shows up in a wide variety of ways in everyday life, but it is at the core of one of the most poignant aspects of the human experience—the tendency to deal with regret or remorse by engaging in what is called *if only* thinking. After almost every blunder or misfortune or tragedy, it is common for people to engage in a kind of mental revisionism:

If only I had stopped after that second drink.

If only I had kept my big mouth shut.

If only I had decided not to take that shortcut.

The tendency to think in such a way is as pervasive as it is futile. The American writer Mercedes Lackey described the phenomenon this way:

"If only." They must be the two saddest words in the world.

In another type of counterfactual thinking—commonly called *what if* thinking—people speculate about how things might have turned out differently if certain aspects of the past were changed:

What if the South had won the Civil War?

What if the colonists had lost the Revolutionary War?

What if John F. Kennedy had survived the assassination attempt?

As with hypothetical observations, when people engage in counterfactual thinking, they often construct an imagined scenario in order to further an argument or drive home a point. At a conference in the 1970s, W. Karl Kapp, a professor of economics at Switzerland's Basel University, attempted to capture the hazards of making predictions by relying solely on computer models:

If there had been a computer in 1872, it would have predicted that by now there would be so many horse-drawn carriages that the entire surface of the earth would be ten feet deep in horse manure.

Some counterfactual observations provide a fascinating glimpse into modern history's most important developments. In a chapter on "The Counterfactual Imagination" in her 2005 book, *The Rational Imagination*, Ruth Byrne describes a speech that Martin Luther King, Jr. made in 1968 in Memphis the night before he died. Exactly a decade earlier, King had another brush with death when he was stabbed in the neck by a demented woman at a Harlem book signing. The letter opener was still lodged in Dr. King's neck when physicians began attending to him, and a hospital spokesperson later told journalists that the tip of the instrument came so perilously close to King's aorta that if he had sneezed, the aorta would have been punctured and he would have drowned in his own blood. In his 1968 speech, the thirty-nine-year-old preacher reported that he, too, was happy he didn't sneeze. Using the familiar oratorical device of repetition, he went on to say:

If I had sneezed, I wouldn't have been around here in 1960 when students all over the South started sitting at lunch counters . . .

If I had sneezed, I wouldn't have been here in 1963 when the black people of Birmingham, Alabama, aroused the conscience of this nation . . .

If I had sneezed, I wouldn't have had the chance later that year in August to tell America about a dream that I had.

Forty years later, many people are still wondering what America would look like if Dr. King hadn't been killed the next day. The capacity to think about what might have been is a powerfully important human ability, and the results of such thinking are often serious and sober. At other times, though, the results can be hilarious.

In the late 1980s, when Mikhail Gorbachev's policies of glasnost and perestroika began to open up the former Soviet Union to the freewheeling journalistic tendencies of the West, a reporter asked Gorbachev an unexpected counterfactual question: "What effect on history do you think it would have made if, in 1963, Chairman Khrushchev had been assassinated instead of President Kennedy?" Clearly, this was not a question for which Gorbachev could have been prepared, but he proved himself as adept as any witty Western politician when he answered with a straight face:

I don't think Mr. Onassis would have married Mrs. Khrushchev.

In all counterfactual thinking, people look to the past and then alter it in some way. The process has resulted in many provocative observations:

If one looks with a cold eye at the mess man has made of his history, it is difficult to avoid the conclusion that he has been afflicted by some built-in mental disorder which drives him towards self-destruction.

ARTHUR KOESTLER

If the American Revolution had produced nothing but the Declaration of Independence, it would have been worthwhile.

SAMUEL ELIOT MORISON

If some really acute observer made as much of egotism
as Freud has made of sex,
people would forget a good deal about sex
and find the explanation for everything in egotism.

WALLACE STEVENS

So far, we've briefly examined hypothetical and counterfactual thinking. If you were to go back and take another look at all the observations featured, you would notice that they're also characterized by one other quality of interest: They are examples of what is commonly called *if-then* thinking. In the world of intellectual discourse, there is a term for such observations.

Conditional Statements

Conditional statements, sometimes called *if-then statements*, reveal yet another aspect of ifferistic thinking: the attempt to establish a direct connection between one thing and another.

If you lose the power to laugh, you lose the power to think.

CLARENCE DARROW

If I create from the heart, nearly everything works;
if from the head, almost nothing.

MARC CHAGALL

We call such statements *conditional* because they make a connection between a condition and a consequence. Structurally, all conditional observations make the same point—if a certain condition occurs, a consequence will then result.

In conditional statements, the *if* portion is always stated, but the word *then* is optional. Sometimes it formally appears:

If you can't feed a hundred people, then feed just one.

MOTHER TERESA

But more often than not, it is only suggested:

If you obey all the rules, you miss all the fun.

KATHARINE HEPBURN

In many if-then statements, the condition is stated first and the consequence second:

If you work hard, you will get ahead.

In yet other examples, the consequence is stated first and the condition that must be met is offered at the conclusion:

If you want to lose weight, you must eat less or exercise more.

Conditional statements are an integral aspect of human communication and are often used to provide inducements or to offer advice. A little later you'll see an entire chapter devoted to *advice conditionals*, but for now let me simply assert that some of history's best advice has been offered in a conditional manner:

If you want to live a happy life,
tie it to a goal, not to people or objects.

ALBERT EINSTEIN

If a small thing has the power to make you angry,
does that not indicate something about your size?

SYDNEY J. HARRIS

Simple conditional observations have also given birth to some of the modern era's most important ideas. In a 1956 interview in *Life* magazine, John Foster Dulles, the secretary of state during the Eisenhower administrations, said:

If you are scared to go to the brink, you are lost.

This remark, originally offered in almost an offhand manner, is now regarded as the origin of the term *brinkmanship*, the practice of convincing an enemy that one is willing to pursue a dangerous course of action to the brink of catastrophe. In the interview, Dulles explained himself by stating that "the ability to get to the verge without getting into the war is the necessary art" of all heads of state.

In the remainder of the book, I will present approximately 2,000 additional ifferisms in chapters on such topics as Wit & Wordplay, The Human Condition, Gender Dynamics, Stage & Screen, Politics & Government, and Sports. As you may have noticed when you perused the table of contents, I've given each chapter an ifferistic title.

In each chapter, I will provide a wide variety of quotations that fit within the theme of the chapter, arranged alphabetically by author. If you want to locate observations from a particular person, consult the index.

I was professionally trained as a psychologist, but I have been a voracious reader all my life, and for many decades have been a serious quotation collector. I currently have hundreds of thousands of quotations in my personal collection, all organized into many different categories. Some of them—like my metaphorical and oxymoronic quotations—have already made it into my previous books. And now my decades-old file of *iffy* quotations has been retitled and has provided the bulk of the quotations to be found in these pages.

In addition to my intrinsic love of beautifully crafted or eloquently expressed quotations, I also get a thrill when I discover something special about a remark or an observation (as in that story about brinkmanship). If I were to provide an anthology of quotations without sharing some of what I've learned about them, I believe I would be shortchanging you as a reader. So after many of the quotations in this book, I will provide information about the author or offer some brief commentary about the meaning or the context of the quotation. I will also occasionally present similar observations that have been offered on the same subject.

While I am committed to accuracy, I'm sure I've made some mistakes. If you discover any errors or would simply like to offer some feedback, please write me in care of the publisher or e-mail me at DrMGrothe@aol.com.

I also have a Web site where you can delve into the topic a bit deeper, learn about my other books, or sign up for my free weekly e-newsletter, *Dr. Mardy's Quotes of the Week*. Come up and visit sometime: www.DrMardy.com.

1

If Anything Can Go Wrong, It Will

CLASSIC IFFERISMS

In 1911, the American writer and publisher Elbert Hubbard—best known as the author of the inspirational story "A Message to Garcia"—aroused controversy when he suggested that he was the original author of a popular American sentiment:

> **If a man can write a better book, preach a better sermon,**
> **or make a better mousetrap than his neighbor,**
> **though he builds his house in the woods,**
> **the world will make a beaten path to his door.**

Quotation researchers were quickly on the case and discovered that, in an 1855 journal entry, Ralph Waldo Emerson had written something similar: "If a man has good corn, or wood, or boards, or pigs, to sell, or can make better chairs or knives, crucibles or church organs, than anybody else, you will find a broad hard-beaten road to his house, though it be in the woods." You will notice, though, that there is no mention of a mousetrap.

In 1889, seven years after Emerson's death, two California women, Sarah Yule and Mary Keene, compiled a book of quotations, titled it *Borrowings*, and arranged for the First Unitarian Church of San Francisco to publish it. The book attributed the mousetrap observation—exactly as it appears above—to Emerson. In 1912, a year after Hubbard's claim of authorship, Sarah Rule said that she heard Emerson make the remark in an 1871 lecture he delivered in San Francisco. She was sixteen at the time and had attempted to faithfully record the observation in a notebook. We'll never know with certainty how Emerson phrased the thought, but it is generally agreed that Emerson, and not Hubbard, was the sentiment's original author. The saying enjoys exalted status in the world of quotations—a classic homage to American ingenuity. As often happens with quotations, it got simplified over time and most people today are familiar with this more streamlined version:

If a man can make a better mousetrap,
the world will beat a path to his door.

The dictionary defines *classic* as "belonging to the highest rank or class." And just as there are classic cars and classic books, there are also classic quotations—a surprisingly large number of which are ifferisms. The most famous of all may be a saying known all around the world as *Murphy's Law*:

If anything can go wrong, it will.

Millions of words have been written about this observation, including at least three books, so I'll discuss it only briefly. The saying originated with Captain Edward A. Murphy, Jr., a U.S. Air Force engineer stationed at Wright Air Development Center in Ohio. In 1949, he was assisting on a research project at Edwards Air Force Base in California. The project, headed by Air Force Major John Paul Stapp, was examining the effect of rapid deceleration on human beings—as when a pilot ejects from a supersonic aircraft. In one of the first-ever uses of crash-test dummies, a rocket sled would speed down a long track at over 600 miles per hour and come to a halt in less than two seconds. Some courageous human subjects—including Major Stapp—also rode the rocket sleds, serving as human guinea pigs in one of the riskiest research projects of all time.

A 1949 test run revealed that a complete series of sensors designed by Murphy to measure the extent of gravitational forces—or g-forces—had been wired incorrectly. There were only two possible ways of doing the wiring and, in every single case, a technician had done the job in the wrong way. There are differing reports about what Murphy said when the problem became apparent. In his version offered years later, a distraught Murphy took responsibility for the error because he hadn't been absolutely clear in his original instructions. He recalled saying, "If there's more than one way to do a job, and one of those ways will result in disaster, then somebody will do it that way." Another version, also offered years later, came from George Nichols, another Air Force engineer present at the time. In the Nichols version, a frustrated Murphy blamed the mistake on the technician by saying, "If there is any way to do it wrong, he will." Whatever Murphy's exact words, the people in attendance were taken with the observation. Somebody in the group—possibly Major Stapp, but it is not certain—even suggested that it might be called *Murphy's Law*.

Captain Murphy's observation quickly made the rounds among the engineers on the project and was transformed into more general principles like "if anything can go wrong it will" and "if it can happen, it will." The basic idea behind the cleverly worded remark was extremely serious: If the engineers were to reduce the risk of a disastrous outcome for Major Stapp and the other subjects strapped to the rocket sled, they must anticipate every single thing that could go wrong.

Murphy's observation was introduced to the world a few days later. At a press conference, a reporter asked Major Stapp if he could explain why nobody had been injured or killed in the project's series of extremely risky tests involving human subjects. According to one version, Stapp replied, "We do all our work in consideration of Murphy's Law" (another version says "with due regard to Murphy's Law"). When curious reporters asked for an explanation, Stapp offered the first public utterance of the law: "If anything can go wrong, it will."

Stapp explained the observation by saying that the best way to avoid disaster was to imagine every possible thing that could go wrong, and then design with that thought in mind. The saying almost immediately began appearing as Murphy's Law in engineering and aerospace publications. It soon began to show up in newspapers and popular magazines, and by the mid-1950s was a part of popular culture. Murphy never said the exact words *if anything can go wrong, it will*, but they will always be associated with him, and it is unquestionably one of the most famous conditional observations of all time.

In the rest of the chapter, I'll present many more classic ifferisms. Let's begin with a few anonymous gems before moving on to those whose authors are known.

If you want something done right, do it yourself.

If you play with fire, you're likely to get burned.

If guns are outlawed, only outlaws will have guns.

If you don't make any mistakes, you don't make anything.

If you can't beat 'em, join 'em.

This last saying, which originated in the political arena in the early twentieth century, is now popular all over the world (only in America, though, will you see the "if you can't lick 'em" variation). If you are unable to defeat an adversary, the saying suggests that the best course is to make peace and form an alliance. An early modification was "if you can't beat 'em, cheat 'em." And George Carlin cleverly quipped: "If you can't beat them, arrange to have them beaten."

If it sounds too good to be true, it probably is.

This warning about being bamboozled by something that appears unbelievably good is a modern alteration of the ancient saying, "It's too good to be true."

If at first you don't succeed, try, try again.

In 1841, the G. & C. Merriam Company of Springfield, Massachusetts, published *The Village Reader*, a compilation of literary selections to be used in the instruction of primary school students. The book never enjoyed the success of *McGuffey's Readers*, the most popular of such early textbooks, but it earned an important footnote in history because it included a poem from Thomas H. Palmer:

'Tis a lesson you should heed,
Try, try again;
If at first you don't succeed,
Try, try again.

Educators at the time routinely engaged in what is called *moral instruction*, and a poem lauding the values of persistence would have been a typical part of the elementary school curriculum. Was Palmer the original author? We don't know for certain; he may have been poetically expressing a saying that was popular at the time. One thing is certain, though; it went on to become one of history's most popular admonitions. It also inspired many parodies, or as I prefer to call them, *altered ifferisms*:

If at first you don't succeed, you're running about average.

If at first you don't succeed, skydiving's not for you.

If at first you don't succeed, destroy all evidence that you tried.

If at first you do succeed, try to hide your astonishment.

The saying has also been creatively altered by many well-known people:

If at first you don't succeed, failure may be your style.
QUENTIN CRISP

If at first you don't succeed, try reading the instructions.
EVAN ESAR

If at first you don't succeed, try, try again. Then give up.
There's no use in being a damn fool about it.
W. C. FIELDS

If at first you do succeed, try, try not to be insufferable.
FRANKLIN P. JONES

If at first you don't succeed, lie, lie again.
LAURENCE J. PETER

If you always do what you always did,
you will always get what you always got.

This modern proverb—which also has a number of variant forms—is reminiscent of another popular saying: "Insanity is doing the same thing over and over again and expecting different results." The point of both is that doing something over and over again will never lead to a desired change, and might even reflect stupidity or a lack of mental health. In a 2008 column, Thomas L. Friedman applied the saying to George W. Bush's decision to lift the executive order banning off-shore drilling. Drawing an analogy between addiction to oil and addiction to crack cocaine, Friedman said the appropriate response was not to lower the price of the drug, but to get rid of the addiction. He wrote: "There is an old saying in Texas that goes like this: 'If all you ever do is all you've ever done, then all you'll ever get is all you ever got.' Could anyone possibly come up with a better description of President Bush's energy policy?"

If it bleeds, it leads.

This maxim of television broadcasting means that sensational and lurid stories are generally the ones chosen to lead off the evening news broadcasts.

If the shoe fits, wear it.

The message here is that you must accept an unflattering assessment if it is true. The admonition, which first appeared in a 1773 New York newspaper, is based on an earlier English proverb with the same meaning: "If the cap fits, wear it."

If it moves, salute it;
if it doesn't move, pick it up;
if you can't pick it up, paint it.

This saying was extremely popular with GIs in World War II. It also inspired several variations, including a profane one that ends this way: "If it doesn't move, paint it; if you can't paint it, fuck it!"

If you've seen one, you've seen 'em all.

The meaning of this saying is that all things in a given class are pretty much the same. Often called upon by men to describe women, and vice versa, it is also often used by members of both genders to describe the sexual organs of the opposite sex. In 1968, Richard Nixon's vice presidential running mate Spiro Agnew drew criticism when he said, "To some extent, if you've seen one city slum, you've seen them all."

If you can't be good, be careful.

This aphorism has been popular in America for at least a century. It was the title of a 1907 song "If You Can't Be Good—Be Careful," written by B. Scott, but the saying was already in common use at that time. It is an alteration of an earlier European proverb, "If you can't be chaste, be cautious."

If life hands you lemons, make lemonade.

This American adage about dealing with adversity now enjoys the status of a modern proverb—or a hackneyed cliché, according to some. The observation that may have started it all came from the American writer Elbert Hubbard, who was quoted in 1927 as saying, "A genius is a man who takes the lemons that fate hands him and starts a lemonade stand with them."

If you build it, they will come.

This saying has become so popular in recent years it might also be considered a cliché. The point is that chasing your dreams, no matter what the doubters say, will ultimately lead to success. The saying was inspired by a line from *Field of Dreams*, a 1989 film that was nominated for three Academy Awards, including Best Picture. In the film, Kevin Costner plays the role of Ray Kinsella, an Iowa farmer whose deceased father was a great fan of "Shoeless Joe" Jackson, the Chicago White Sox baseball star who was accused of throwing the 1919 World Series and banned from baseball for life. When Kinsella hears a mysterious voice whisper the words "if you build it, he will come," he becomes convinced that building a baseball field in his cornfield will resurrect the ghosts—and the reputations—of Jackson and other disgraced teammates implicated in the infamous "Black Sox" scandal. The film was adapted from *Shoeless Joe*, an award-winning 1982 novel from the Canadian novelist W. P. Kinsella (yes, the author gave his protagonist the same last name). On the first page of the novel, the fictional Kinsella says, "I was sitting on the verandah of my farm home in eastern Iowa when a voice very clearly said to me, 'If you build it, he will come.' "

If you're not part of the solution, you're part of the problem.

This modern proverb maintains doing nothing during difficult times is equivalent to supporting the status quo. The saying is often attributed to Black Power activist Eldridge Cleaver, but he never said it in this way. In a 1968 speech, Cleaver said, "You're either part of the solution or you're part of the problem." Phrased in this way, however, the observation was not original, for similar formulations had appeared as early as the mid-1950s. Nobody knows the author of the now-classic ifferistic line, but many fondly recall the George Carlin parody of it: "If you think there's a solution, you're a part of the problem."

If I've only one life, let me live it as a blonde!

ADVERTISING SLOGAN *for Clairol*

If you've got it—flaunt it!

ADVERTISING SLOGAN
for Braniff Airlines, 1969

This slogan was inspired by a line from the 1968 Mel Brooks film *The Producers*: "That's it, baby! When you've got it, flaunt it!" That remark became an instant classic shortly after it was unforgettably delivered by Zero Mostel as the original Max Bialystock. The basic sentiment was entrenched in pop culture when in 1982 Sidney Sheldon wrote in his novel *The Master of the Game*: "Old money's motto was, *if you have it, hide it*. New money's motto was, *if you have it, flaunt it*."

If the doors of perception were cleansed, everything would appear to man as it is, infinite.

WILLIAM BLAKE

This line from Blake's 1793 classic *The Marriage of Heaven and Hell* occupies a special place in literary as well as pop culture history. In 1954, Aldous Huxley wrote a book on the mind-expanding effects of mescaline, titling it *The Doors of Perception*. Slightly more than a decade later, in 1965, Jim Morrison was studying film and poetry at UCLA when he and a keyboard-playing friend named Ray Manzerek formed a friendship fueled by their love of rock music and fascination with hallucinogenic drugs. After reading Huxley's 1954 book, they decided to call their newly formed band The Doors.

If you think education is expensive, try ignorance.

DEREK BOK

This was a signature observation of Dr. Bok, the long-time president of Harvard University. The saying became extremely popular in the 1970s and is still occasionally seen on the bumper stickers of people who support greater funding for education. It was likely inspired by a line from *Poor Richard's Almanack*: "The only thing more expensive than education is ignorance."

If it doesn't fit, you must acquit.

JOHNNIE L. COCHRAN, JR.

Cochran made this remark in his closing statement to the jury in the 1995 trial of O. J. Simpson. Earlier in the trial, Simpson appeared to struggle when he was ordered to try on a pair of bloody gloves that were found at the murder scene.

If you can keep your head when all about you
Are losing theirs and blaming it on you;
If you can trust yourself when all men doubt you,
But make allowance for their doubting too . . .

RUDYARD KIPLING

These are the first four lines of Kipling's "If," one of history's most popular poems. The entire poem, which was written in 1895 and first published in 1910, consists of four eight-line stanzas. The full poem is too long to include here, but can be found on the ifferisms page of my Web site (www.DrMardy.com). In survey after survey, "If" has been routinely named Britain's favorite poem. If you ever visit Wimbledon's All England Lawn Tennis Club, you will notice that a couplet from the poem is inscribed above the entryway to Centre Court:

If you can meet with Triumph and Disaster
And treat those two imposters just the same

In the past century, "If "has inspired millions of people, and in the past several decades it has become a staple of inspirational literature. In *Wisdom of the Ages* (1998), Wayne Dyer hailed Kipling's poem, writing: "The lofty ideas in his four-stanza poem inspire me to be a better man each time I read it and share it with my children, students, and audiences." In many ways, the poem is one long ifferism. It is also a magnificent tribute to many of humankind's great virtues: staying composed under stress, remaining humble when victorious, never despairing when defeated, and always retaining honor and authenticity. The poem has been much parodied, perhaps most memorably by the American humorist Jean Kerr, who wrote in her 1958 book *Please Don't Eat the Daisies*:

If you can keep your head when all about you are losing theirs,
it's just possible you haven't grasped the situation.

If it ain't broke, don't fix it.

BERT LANCE, *quoted in a 1977* Nation's Business *article*

Bert Lance, a Georgia banker and advisor to Jimmy Carter, was director of the Office of Management and Budget in the late 1970s. The saying is now routinely used as a warning about the dangers of trying to improve something that already works. In a 1992 column, William Safire said the maxim "has become a source of inspiration to anti-activists."

If the only tool you have is a hammer,
you tend to see every problem as a nail.

ABRAHAM H. MASLOW

This is the most popular observation from the man responsible for such familiar psychological concepts as the hierarchy of needs and self-actualization. You've probably seen several versions of the saying, which Maslow offered in slightly different ways in his many speeches and books. No matter how it is phrased, the point remains the same: If you have one idea that dominates your life, you approach every problem from that point of view. This problem was eloquently captured in an observation by the French philosopher and critic Émile-Auguste Chartier who under the pen name of Alain wrote: "Nothing is more dangerous than an idea when it is the only idea you have."

**If I have seen further,
it is by standing on the shoulders of giants.**

ISAAC NEWTON

Newton wrote this—one of the most celebrated aphorisms in intellectual history—in a 1676 letter to the English physicist Robert Hooke. The metaphorical notion that we can see further by standing on the shoulders of others was well established when Newton wrote his letter. The idea was first offered six centuries earlier by the French philosopher Bernard of Chartres: "We are like dwarfs on the shoulders of giants, so that we can see more than they." In a 1965 book, *On the Shoulders of Giants,* the American sociologist Robert Merton put on a dazzling display of scholarship and erudition as he traced the history behind the famous line.

If you scratch my back, I'll scratch yours.

AMERICAN PROVERB

If a thing is worth doing, it is worth doing well.

ENGLISH PROVERB

It's often difficult to trace the exact origin of proverbial sayings, but not in this case. This one comes from a 1746 letter that British nobleman Philip Dormer Stanhope (better known as Lord Chesterfield) wrote to his son. By writing "Whatever worth doing at all, is worth doing well," he was warning his son about the dangers of a halfhearted effort. Lord Chesterfield is best known as the author of *Letters to His Son*, a compilation of thousands of private letters written over a period of more than thirty years. Not originally intended for publication, the letters were published in 1774, a year after Chesterfield's death. They contain everything from instructions on etiquette and good manners to observations about life, love, and many other topics.

If you give a man enough rope, he'll hang himself.

ENGLISH PROVERB

This centuries-old proverb is often used to describe how guilty people incriminate themselves when they're given the freedom to talk about their actions. The point is that people who behave badly often get caught up in a web of lies and contradictions, unintentionally revealing their guilt. It is also sometimes used to describe what happens when people are allowed to do exactly as they want, despite the cautions of other people. It has also been humorously altered in many ways, but my favorite is: "If you give a man enough rope he'll hang himself, thereby saving you the job."

If wishes were horses, beggars would ride.

SCOTTISH PROVERB

This proverb about the foolishness of indulging in wishful thinking was first recorded in a 1628 book of Scottish proverbs. In the 1800s it was incorporated into a popular nursery rhyme:

If wishes were horses, beggars would ride;
If turnips were watches, I would wear one by my side;
If "ifs and ands" were pots and pans,
there'd be no work for tinkers' hands.

If it walks like a duck and quacks like a duck, then it just may be a duck.

WALTER REUTHER

This is the original version of a popular sentiment that, in a number of variant forms, refers to the process of identifying the true nature of people on the basis of their words or actions. The saying is often used to rebut the argument that something is not the way it appears to be. William Safire, who's been tracking political catchphrases for many decades, says that Reuther, a prominent American labor leader, originally used the expression as a surefire way to identify a Communist.

**If you can't be with the one you love,
love the one you're with.**

STEPHEN STILLS

Stills, who arrived on the musical scene in the mid-1960s with Buffalo Springfield, went on to achieve fame with the rock group Crosby, Stills & Nash (and a few years later Crosby, Stills, Nash & Young). In 1970, this chiastic lyric from his smash hit "Love the One You're With" became a virtual anthem for the "free love" generation. Stills may have been influenced by a similar lyric from a song in the 1947 musical *Finian's Rainbow*. Written by E. Y. "Yip" Harburg (music by Burton Lane), the song "When I'm Not Near the Girl I Love" included the line, "When I'm not near the girl I love, I love the girl I'm near." Harburg's lyric, in turn, may have been inspired by a French proverb that goes back to the mid-nineteenth century: "If we cannot get what we love, we must love what is within our reach."

If you can't stand the heat, get out of the kitchen.

HARRY S TRUMAN

This political axiom is almost always attributed to President Truman, and he did say it this way in 1952 when he announced he was not seeking reelection to the presidency. Truman said he got the remark from an old friend, Missouri judge Eugene "Buck" Purcell. The meaning is clear: People who can't handle the pressure should exit the scene. In January 1953, as Truman was leaving the White House to make room for President-elect Eisenhower, he quipped, "If I'd have known how much packing I'd have to do, I'd have run again."

If God did not exist, it would be necessary to invent him.

VOLTAIRE *(François-Marie Arouet)*

Voltaire was one of history's most quotable writers, and this 1768 epigram is one of his most famous observations. He also had a great fondness for it, once writing in a letter to Frederick the Great: "I am rarely satisfied with my lines, but I own that I have a father's tenderness for that one." In earlier centuries, other writers had expressed the same idea, but nobody as memorably as Voltaire. Many people have piggybacked on the sentiment, but none more famously than when the nineteenth-century German chancellor Otto von Bismarck said, "If Italy did not exist, it would be necessary to invent her."

If we don't end war, war will end us.

H. G. WELLS, *first written in 1936, and later much imitated by others*

2

If It Bends, It's Funny; If It Breaks, It Isn't

WIT & WORDPLAY

U.S. presidents and other heads of state have long struggled with the behavior of their adolescent children, but none more famously than Theodore Roosevelt did with his only daughter, Alice. "Princess Alice," as she was dubbed by the press, was seventeen when her father was inaugurated in 1901. Shortly after her father took office, she became America's first presidential wild child, and a true media darling. Newspapers all over America chronicled her many antics, which included smoking on the White House roof, placing bets with a Washington bookie, keeping a pet snake, going on unchaperoned dates (shocking at the time), and once, jumping into a swimming pool fully clothed. She became so popular in the general culture that her favorite color, a shade of blue and green, became known as *Alice blue*. A popular song of the era, which first appeared in the 1919 Broadway musical *Irene*, was titled (In My Sweet Little) "Alice Blue Gown."

After marrying Ohio congressman Nicholas Longworth in 1906, Alice became formally known as Alice Roosevelt Longworth. Despite a shaky marriage, the couple's Washington home became a virtual salon for politicians, writers, movie stars, and other celebrities. After her husband's death in 1931, Mrs. L (as she was popularly known) became such a fixture in the nation's capital that she was called "Washington's Other Monument." A colorful woman with a caustic wit and an acerbic tongue, she once said about herself, "My specialty is detached malevolence." She was also a notorious gossip, and many visitors to her home got a great chuckle when they walked into her drawing room and saw a velvet cushion embroidered with the saying:

If you haven't got anything good to say about anyone, come sit by me.

In *The World in a Phrase* (2005), James Geary laid out the Five Laws of Aphorisms. They must, he said, be *brief*, *definitive*, *personal*, *philosophical*, and *have a twist*. If you examine Mrs. L's saying, you will see that it meets all five criteria. In addition to its brevity, it is definitively—as opposed to tentatively—stated. It is both personal and philosophical in the sense that it takes us directly into Mrs. Longworth's mind and reveals something special about her philosophy of life. And finally, it ends with a neat and unexpected twist, cleverly altering the old bromide: "If you can't say anything good about somebody, don't say anything at all." It also begins with the word *if*, making it a perfect ifferism.

Ifferisms have been especially favored by humorists. After graduating as an English major from the University of Dayton in 1949, Erma Fiste took a job at a local newspaper. She soon married her college sweetheart Bill Bombeck and, like so many women at the time, quit her job in order to raise a family. She never lost her desire to write, however, and a quarter of a century later, in 1964, began writing "At Wit's End," a wry and witty newspaper column about her life as a wife, mother, and homemaker. In one of her columns, she captured the frustration of many women who are married to football fanatics:

If a man watches three football games in a row,
he should be declared legally dead.

Bombeck's column was nationally syndicated in 1965 and eventually appeared in more than 700 newspapers, making her one of the most popular humorists of her time. She wrote many best-selling books, including a 1971 effort cleverly titled:

If Life Is a Bowl of Cherries,
What Am I Doing in the Pits?

While many humorous ifferisms—like these two from Bombeck—represent good, clean fun, others have a slightly edgy quality, as when Ed Bluestone said:

If God wanted sex to be fun,
he wouldn't have included children as punishment.

In the 1970s, Bluestone was a stand-up comedian and a frequent contributor to the humor magazine *National Lampoon.* He had a dark and abrasive comedic style that often bordered on the tasteless, once writing an article titled "23 Ways to Be Offensive at the Funeral of Someone You Didn't Like."

Bluestone had a routine that included a bit about a deadbeat customer's refusal to pay a long-overdue bill. After exhausting all the usual collection procedures, the company finally sent the customer a photograph of his pet cocker spaniel with a gun to the dog's head. The routine inspired what many regard as the most famous magazine cover in publishing history. The January 1973 issue of the *National Lampoon* shows a picture of an adorable dog with a gun pointed at his head. The headline declares:

If You Don't Buy This Magazine,
We'll Kill This Dog.

More than three decades later, *Texas Monthly* reprised the sentiment in a January 2007 cover that featured a picture of Vice President Dick Cheney holding a smoking shotgun. It was eleven months after the celebrated hunting accident in which Cheney shot his friend Harry Whittington in the face, but the event was still very much in the public mind. It was the most successful cover in the history of the magazine and, at the end of the year, was named Best Cover of 2007 by the American Society of Magazine Editors. The message next to the photograph of Cheney and his gun said simply:

If You Don't Buy This Magazine,
Dick Cheney Will Shoot You in the Face.

Both magazine covers illustrate how often humor walks close to the edge of offensiveness. But when it is done well, as in these two cases, humor gets close but doesn't cross the line. In his 1989 film *Crimes and Misdemeanors*, Woody Allen chose a slightly different metaphor to express the idea when he had the character played by Alan Alda say:

If it bends, it's funny; if it breaks, it isn't.

In the rest of the chapter, I've tried to include only those observations that bend. All are attempts at wit or wordplay, and all are phrased ifferistically.

If it weren't for the fact that
the TV set and the refrigerator are so far apart,
some of us wouldn't get any exercise at all.

JOEY ADAMS

If only God would give me some clear sign!
Like making a large deposit in my name at a Swiss bank.

WOODY ALLEN

If a pig loses its voice, is it disgruntled?

ANONYMOUS

Many humorous hypothetical questions have been authored by anonymous sources and spread around the world in e-mail attachments—often with the subject heading *ponderisms* or *imponderables.* Here are a bunch more:

If a cow laughed, would milk come out of her nose?

If a turtle doesn't have a shell, is he homeless or naked?

If a parsley farmer is sued, can they garnish his wages?

If you don't pay your exorcist, do you get repossessed?

If you spin an Oriental person around several times,
does he become disoriented?

If you can speak three languages—you're trilingual.
If you can speak two languages—you're bilingual.
If you can speak only one language—you're an American.

ANONYMOUS

If it tastes good, it's bad for you.

ISAAC ASIMOV, *citing*
"The First Law of Dietetics"

If there are any of you at the back who do not hear me,
please do not raise your hands because I am also nearsighted.

W. H. AUDEN

Auden said this at the beginning of a 1946 lecture, demonstrating that the wittiest remarks often come from people not typically associated with humor.

If you want to recapture your youth, cut off his allowance.

AL BERNSTEIN

If Shaw and Einstein couldn't beat death, what chance have I got? Practically none.

MEL BROOKS

If anyone corrects your pronunciation of a word in a public place, you have every right to punch him in the nose.

HEYWOOD BROUN

If President Nixon's secretary, Rose Mary Woods, had been Moses's secretary, there would only be eight commandments.

ART BUCHWALD

Rose Mary Woods occupies a footnote in history as the woman who erased—accidentally, she said—eighteen minutes from secret White House tape recordings in the Watergate era.

If you know the average person is stupid, then realize that half are stupider than that.

GEORGE CARLIN

In his five-decade career, Carlin was famous for hilarious hypothetical questions and quirky conditional observations. You'll find other Carlin quotations in later chapters, but here are a half-dozen more for your enjoyment:

If a safe is unlocked, is it still a safe?

If you mail a letter to the Post Office, who delivers it?

If you get cheated by the Better Business Bureau,
who do you complain to?

If no one knows when a person is going to die,
how can we say he died prematurely?

If crime fighters fight crime and fire fighters fight fire,
what do freedom fighters fight?

If you have a perfectly DNA-matched identical twin,
technically, it's possible to go fuck yourself.

If life were fair,
Elvis would be alive and all the impersonators would be dead.

JOHNNY CARSON

If airline travel is so safe,
how come the flight attendants sit right next to the emergency exits?

JOHNNY CARSON

Jerry Seinfeld said similarly: "If airline seat cushions are such great flotation devices, why don't you ever see anyone take one to the beach?"

If the witty backbiter is blamed and condemned as obnoxious,
he is nonetheless absolved and praised as a clever fellow.

MIGUEL DE CERVANTES

This 1617 observation describes a fascinating human reality: Many witty people are not particularly nice, but are still admired for their wicked wit.

If we don't change direction soon, we'll end up where we're going.

PROFESSOR IRWIN COREY

Corey was a popular twentieth-century comedian who adopted the demeanor of a zany college professor. His schtick consisted of observations that initially appeared inane but, on second thought, often seemed meaningful or even profound.

If your eyes hurt after you drink coffee,
you have to take the spoon out of the cup.

NORM CROSBY

If we're not supposed to eat animals,
how come they're made out of meat?

DOUG DOTY

This line appeared in a letter that Doty, a resident of Helena, Montana, wrote to *Harper's Magazine* in 1998. The observation might have died in obscurity, but it was resurrected by John Leo in a January 1999 *U.S. News & World Report* article titled "You Can Say That Again." Leo's article was his annual "roundup of the year's best aphorisms and most memorable sayings."

If you have a DVD player, it's rude to watch porn in coach.

ADAM FERRARA

If you can look back on your life with contentment,
you have one of man's most precious gifts—a selective memory.

JIM FIEBIG

If you can't dazzle them with brilliance, baffle them with bullshit.

W. C. FIELDS

If there is anyone to whom I owe money,
I am prepared to forget it if they are.

ERROL FLYNN

If you think a quarter horse is that ride in front of Kmart,
then you might be a redneck.

JEFF FOXWORTHY

After graduating from Georgia Tech in 1979, Foxworthy worked on mainframe computers at IBM before winning an Atlanta comedy competition in 1984. He burst on the national scene in 1993 with a successful comedy album titled, "You Might Be a Redneck If . . ." The album introduced a series of *if A, then B* propositions in which the A portion varied and the concluding B portion was always the same: "then you might be a redneck." Here are a few more of the lead-in lines:

If your ironing board doubles as a buffet table, then . . .

If your underwear doubles as your bathing suit, then . . .

If you think 'N Sync is where the dirty dishes go, then . . .

If you think a weakness can be turned into a strength,
I hate to tell you this, but that's another weakness.

AL FRANKEN, *a "deep thought" from Jack Handy*

If all else fails, immortality can always be assured by spectacular error.

JOHN KENNETH GALBRAITH

If *con* is the opposite of *pro*, and progress is good, what is Congress?

GALLAGHER

If you water it and it dies, it's a plant.
If you pull it out and it grows back, it's a weed.

GALLAGHER

If you ever see me getting beaten up by the police,
put down the video camera and come help me!

BOBCAT GOLDTHWAIT

If you don't like a parade, walk in the opposite direction.
You'll fast-forward the parade.

MITCH HEDBERG

If You Can't Live Without Me, Why Aren't You Dead Yet?

CYNTHIA HEIMEL, *title of her 1991 book*

Heimel, an American feminist writer and for many years a columnist for *Playboy* and *The Village Voice*, had a gift for coming up with snappy and attention-grabbing book titles. A 1995 collection of essays was titled *If You Leave Me, Can I Come Too?* Perhaps her best, though, was *Get Your Tongue Out of My Mouth, I'm Kissing You Good-Bye* (1993).

If you can't answer a man's argument, all is not lost;
you can still call him vile names.

ELBERT HUBBARD

If the English language made any sense,
a catastrophe would be an apostrophe with fur.

DOUG LARSON

If a day goes by and I haven't been slain, I'm happy.

CAROL LEIFER, *on life in New York City*

If your wife wants to learn to drive, don't stand in her way.

SAM LEVENSON

If we see light at the end of the tunnel
It's the light of the oncoming train.

ROBERT LOWELL

From the early twentieth century, the expression *light at the end of the tunnel* was used to express optimism about coming to the end of a lengthy and difficult endeavor. The saying was used so frequently during the Vietnam War that many people began to view it with suspicion and cynicism. In his poem "Since 1939," published in 1977, Lowell simply offered this parody.

If you've heard this story before,
don't stop me, because I'd like to hear it again.

GROUCHO MARX

If you think you have it tough, read history books.

BILL MAHER

If you're saying you didn't know cigarettes were bad for you,
you're lying through the hole in your trachea.

DENNIS MILLER

If you are sure you understand everything that is going on,
you are hopelessly confused.

WALTER MONDALE

This observation first appeared in a March 1978 issue of the *Poughkeepsie Journal*. A decade earlier, Edward R. Murrow made a similar quip about the Vietnam War: "Anyone who isn't confused doesn't really understand the situation."

If you run after wit, you will succeed in catching folly.

CHARLES DE MONTESQUIEU

The point is that wit, to be successful, must come naturally. When people try too hard to be witty, it becomes forced, and they only succeed in looking foolish.

If you see a shark, you don't have to swim faster than the shark. You only have to swim faster than the person you're with.

KEVIN NEALON

If all the girls who attended the Yale prom were laid end to end, I wouldn't be a bit surprised.

DOROTHY PARKER

In this observation, Parker was likely inspired by a George Bernard Shaw remark about the inability of economists to make decisive recommendations: "If all economists were laid end to end, they would not reach a conclusion." The underlying concept has been picked up by many others over the years, including Doug Larson, who wrote, "If all the cars in the United States were placed end to end, it would probably be Labor Day weekend." Perhaps my favorite spin-off, though, comes from an anonymous college professor who once observed, "If all the students who slept through lectures were laid end to end, they'd be a lot more comfortable."

I'm Jewish. I don't work out.
If God wanted us to bend over, he'd have put diamonds on the floor.

JOAN RIVERS

If dogs could talk,
it would take a lot of the fun out of owning one.

ANDY ROONEY

Rooney suggests here that we love pets in part because we don't have to listen to them. Roy Blount, Jr. wrote similarly, "If a cat spoke, it would say things like 'Hey, I don't see the *problem* here.' " And both of these men might have been inspired by an observation from the English critic Philip Gilbert Hamerton (a remark Cleveland Amory hailed as the most memorable comparison ever made about cats and dogs): "If animals could speak, the dog would be a blundering, outspoken fellow—but the cat would have the rare grace of never saying a word too much." The philosopher Alfred North Whitehead also weighed in on the difference between the two most common household pets: "If a dog jumps in your lap, it is because he is fond of you; but if a cat does the same thing, it is because your lap is warmer."

If you're Black, you got to look at America a little bit different.
You got to look at America like the uncle who
paid for you to go to college, but who molested you.

CHRIS ROCK

If I had a hammer, I'd use it on Peter, Paul, and Mary.

HOWARD ROSENBERG

The folk music trio known as Peter, Paul, and Mary was one of the most popular groups of the 1960s, and the Pete Seeger song "If I Had a Hammer," released in 1962, was one of their biggest hits. The song received so much airplay it quickly became a signature song for the group. Rosenberg, a television critic for the *Los Angeles Times*, grew weary of hearing the ubiquitous song every time he turned on the radio.

If you were a bigot and wanted to drive a Unitarian out of your town, you'd burn a question mark on his lawn.

MORT SAHL

**If no one ever took risks,
Michelangelo would have painted the Sistine floor.**

NEIL SIMON

**If America leads a blessed life,
then why did God put all of our oil under people who hate us?**

JON STEWART

**If you see a white man running, you think,
"He must be late for a meeting."
When you see a black man running, you think,
"I'm calling the cops. Hey, somebody stop his black ass!"**

WANDA SYKES

**If I have any beliefs about immortality,
it is that certain dogs I have known will go to heaven,
and very, very few persons.**

JAMES THURBER

**If I'd known what it would have been like to have it all,
I might have been willing to settle for less.**

LILY TOMLIN *(written by Jane Wagner)*

This line comes from Tomlin's critically acclaimed one-woman Broadway show *The Search for Signs of Intelligent Life in the Universe*. Many of Tomlin's best lines were written by her long-time professional collaborator and life partner, Jane Wagner. Here are several other Wagner-authored ifferisms delivered by Tomlin:

If love is the answer, could you please rephrase the question?

If the formula for water is H_2O*,*
is the formula for an ice cube H_2O *squared?*

If you read a lot of books, you're considered well read.
But if you watch a lot of TV, you're not considered well viewed.

If the desire to kill and the opportunity to kill came always together, who would escape hanging?

MARK TWAIN, *from his 1897 book* Following the Equator

If alcohol is a crutch, then Jack Daniel's is the wheelchair.
Eight glasses and you forget the English language.
You just have one massive vowel movement.

ROBIN WILLIAMS

If you don't think too good, don't think too much.

TED WILLIAMS

If you look like your passport photo, in all probability you need the holiday.

EARL WILSON

If you think nobody cares you're alive, try missing a couple of car payments.

EARL WILSON

If it's true that we are here to help others,
then what exactly are the others here for?

TOM WILSON

This bit of whimsy from the creator of the comic strip *Ziggy* was almost certainly inspired by a line from the poet W. H. Auden, who parodied "the conceit of the social worker" in an essay in *The Dyer's Hand* (1962): "We are all here on earth to help others; what on earth others are here for, I don't know." *Ziggy* also provided several other memorable ifferisms:

If it wasn't for wrong numbers, I'd get no calls at all.

If they ever have a series about me on TV,
it'd be a situation tragedy.

If I ever managed to "get it all together,"
I have a feeling I wouldn't know what to do with it.

If everything seems to be going well,
you have obviously overlooked something.

STEVEN WRIGHT

With his deadpan persona and monotone delivery, Wright's stand-up comedy routine is not to everyone's taste. But for those who love the exploration of life's little absurdities through witty wordplay, there's nobody better. Here are a number of additional ifferisms from the master of the conditional question:

If God dropped acid, would he see people?

If a mime commits suicide, does he use a silencer?

If you tell a joke in the forest, but nobody laughs, was it a joke?

If a word in the dictionary were misspelled, how would we know?

If you are sending someone some Styrofoam,
what do you pack it in?

If one synchronized swimmer drowns,
do all the rest have to drown too?

If Dracula can't see his reflection in a mirror,
how come his hair is always so neatly combed?

If I'm not in bed by eleven at night, I go home.

HENNY YOUNGMAN

3

If It Is to Be, It Is Up to Me

WORDS TO LIVE BY

In a 1904 letter to a friend, Franz Kafka asked a powerful rhetorical question:

If the book we are reading does not wake us, as with a fist hammering on our skull, why then do we read it?

He then answered the question with an even more powerful assertion: "A book should serve as an ice-axe to break the frozen sea within us." I experienced the full truth of Kafka's observation during my junior year of college, when I experienced a full-blown identity crisis. In the middle of that very difficult time, I came upon a book that broke the frozen sea within me. That book was *Walden*, Henry David Thoreau's 1854 classic about his "experiment in living" at Walden Pond.

First, a little background. When I entered college as a freshman, I knew what I wanted—to become a psychologist one day—but after my first semester, I was completely seduced by the Joe College lifestyle that was so prevalent at the time. I studied just enough to get by and devoted almost all of my time to what are quite accurately called *extra*-curricular activities. At the time, I saw myself as a leader-in-training, but in an illustration of Blaise Pascal's dictum that "the heart has reasons that the reason knows not of," I was more likely motivated by a desire to extinguish some deep-seated doubts I had about myself.

By the middle of my junior year, I was so overly involved in campus activities that my grades began to suffer and I was constantly feeling overwhelmed. I was, to use a popular metaphor, dancing as fast as I could, but I was not enjoying the music that was playing. When I had arrived at college two and a half years earlier, I knew where I was going, but I had lost my way.

I'm not exactly sure what precipitated the realization, but I suddenly concluded I couldn't take it anymore and abruptly walked away from everything that, up to that point, had been so important to me. I moved into a dark and dingy off-campus apartment and began to contemplate a very uncertain future. I brought with me a copy of *Walden*. I had not read the book, but it had been suggested by a professor who was familiar with my situation—and who had once cleverly disparaged the behavior of college students as "lives of noisy desperation."

After reading the first few pages of *Walden*, I deeply resonated to Thoreau's central idea, which was to "live deep and suck out all the marrow of life." The entire book was filled with many mind-expanding ideas, but the final chapter had a passage that was so powerful it almost exploded in my head:

If a man does not keep pace with his companions,
perhaps it is because he hears a different drummer.
Let him step to the music he hears, however measured or far away.

I had already begun to think of Thoreau as a valued new friend, but here he was, eloquently describing my very own recent situation. If I ever had any doubts about the wisdom of my decision to walk down a different path from my former companions, they completely evaporated in that moment. I immediately wrote the passage on a three-by-five index card and thumbtacked it on the wall above my desk.

Like Kafka, Thoreau clearly understood the importance of life-altering books. Indeed, he had written earlier in his classic work, "How many a man has dated a new era in his life from the reading of a book!" Now the same thing had happened to me. Reading *Walden* marked a new era in my life, and I soon went back through the book to record some of his other thoughts on my index cards:

**If one advances confidently in the direction of his dreams,
and endeavors to live the life which he has imagined,
he will meet with a success unexpected in common hours.**

**If you have built castles in the air,
your work need not be lost; that is where they should be.
Now put the foundations under them.**

As I began reading the works of other authors, I continued this simple ritual of recording great observations on index cards and tacking them up on the wall. After six months, my dingy apartment was transformed into a space that was alive with great ideas posted all around.

When I graduated from college, I retired my Wall of Quotes and placed all of the index cards in a manila folder that I labeled "Words to Live By." As the years went by, I continued to add inspirational quotes, and when I bought my first Apple IIE computer in 1984, I transferred all of the quotations from my index cards into a computer file I designated by the initials *WTLB.*

While almost all of the observations in my collection have been authored by specific people, some come from people whose names will never be known with certainty. Many years ago, I came across an anonymous saying that so captured my own view of self-reliance that I immediately adopted it as a motto:

If it is to be, it is up to me.

The saying has been attributed to many people, including the artist William H. Johnson, but the original author has never been conclusively identified. If you do a Google search under "ten two-letter words," you will see that the saying enjoys a legendary status among word and language lovers.

For the past few decades, my regimen has been the same. When I find an inspiring quotation, I immediately record it in my *WTLB* file. All the quotations in the file have inspired or challenged me in some important way and, while many are examples of some of my other favorite literary devices—like chiasmus, paradox, and metaphor—a significant number of them are ifferisms. And that is what you shall find in the remainder of the chapter.

If you're willing to fail interestingly, you tend to succeed interestingly.

EDWARD ALBEE

If you are not failing every now and again, it's a sign you're playing it safe.

WOODY ALLEN

If you find it in your heart to care for somebody else, you will have succeeded.

MAYA ANGELOU

If the highest aim of a captain were to preserve his ship, he would keep it in port forever.

SAINT THOMAS AQUINAS

**If you are distressed by anything external,
the pain is not due to the thing itself but to your own estimate of it;
and this you have the power to revoke at any moment.**

MARCUS AURELIUS

**If your happiness depends on what somebody else does,
I guess you do have a problem.**

RICHARD BACH

**If you want to learn something, read about it.
If you want to understand something, write about it.
If you want to master something, teach it.**

YOGI BHAJAN

This is the most elegant version of a sentiment that has appeared in almost every culture of the world. Yogi Bhajan was a Sikh spiritual leader who moved from Pakistan to the United States in the 1960s. He became widely known as a master of Kundalini Yoga and the founder of the nonprofit organization 3HO (for "healthy, happy, holy"). In an earlier version of the same idea, the nineteenth-century American theologian and writer Tryon Edwards wrote, "If you would thoroughly know anything, teach it to others."

**If you're alive, you've got to flap your arms and legs,
you've got to jump around a lot, you've got to make a lot of noise,
because life is the very opposite of death.**

MEL BROOKS

**If, after all, men cannot always make history have a meaning,
they can always act so that their own lives have one.**

ALBERT CAMUS

If what you have done is unjust, you have not succeeded.

THOMAS CARLYLE

If we can't turn the world around,
we can at least bolster the victims.

LIZ CARPENTER

This comes from Carpenter's 1987 autobiography, *Getting Better All the Time*. A similar thought has been attributed to Marlon Brando: "If we are not our brother's keeper, at least let us not be his executioner."

If you limit your actions in life
to things that *nobody* can possibly find fault with,
you will not do much!

LEWIS CARROLL
(Charles Lutwidge Dodgson)

If I have learned anything in my life,
it is that bitterness consumes the vessel that contains it.

RUBIN "HURRICANE" CARTER

Carter, a promising middleweight boxer with a troubled past, was arrested in 1966 for three murders in Paterson, New Jersey. Despite his protestations of innocence, he was convicted in 1967 and sentenced to life in prison. In 1975, the Bob Dylan song "Hurricane" helped bring Carter's case to the public eye. The resulting publicity helped win Carter a new trial in 1976, but he was convicted a second time and once again sentenced to life in prison. The complex and convoluted case came to an end in 1985, when a federal district court judge overturned the conviction, ruling that the prosecution's case had been "based on racism rather than reason and concealment rather than disclosure." Carter's story inspired the 1999 Norman Jewison film *The Hurricane*, with Denzel Washington in the title role.

After being released from prison in 1985, Carter moved to Canada—where he still lives—and devoted his life to working on behalf of wrongly convicted people.

If a man would allot half an hour every night for self-conversation, and recapitulate with himself whatever he has done, right or wrong, in the course of the day, he would be both the better and the wiser for it.

LORD CHESTERFIELD *(Philip Dormer Stanhope), in a 1763 letter to his son*

If you would convince others, seem open to conviction yourself.

LORD CHESTERFIELD *(Philip Dormer Stanhope), in a 1763 letter to his son*

If we are not ashamed to think it, we should not be ashamed to say it.

MARCUS TULLIUS CICERO

If a man wants to be of the greatest possible value to his fellow-creatures, let him begin the long, solitary process of perfecting himself.

ROBERTSON DAVIES

If we want to change our lives, we need to stretch our minds.

WAYNE DYER

Dyer, a psychologist and popular self-help writer, also once wrote, "If we are to have magical bodies, we must have magical minds."

If the only prayer you said in your whole life was "thank you," that would suffice.

JOHANNES ECKHART

Eckhart (1260–1327) was a German theologian who is known to history as Meister Eckhart, after an academic title he received in Paris (*Meister* is German for "master"). His humanistic leanings, which angered the papal hierarchy, led to a trial for heresy shortly before his death. (Eckhart's story inspired Martin Luther, so it may be said that he helped to lay the foundation for the Reformation.) His writings and sermons were characterized by a directness of style, highly unusual at the time.

If we take care of the moments, the years will take care of themselves.

MARIA EDGEWORTH

If you are out to describe the truth, leave elegance to the tailor.

ALBERT EINSTEIN

This is a widely quoted observation, but Einstein never said it in this exact way. It is, however, a nice summary of what he believed. In the preface to *Relativity* (1916), he did suggest that the truth of ideas was more important than the elegance with which they were expressed. Referring to the Austrian physicist Ludwig Boltzmann, he wrote: "I adhered scrupulously to the precept of that brilliant theoretical physicist L. Boltzmann, according to whom matters of elegance ought to be left to the tailor and the cobbler."

If men as individuals surrender to the call of their elementary instincts,
avoiding pain and seeking satisfaction only for their own selves,
the result for them all taken together
must be a state of insecurity, of fear, and of promiscuous misery.

ALBERT EINSTEIN, *appealing to a higher instinct*

If you would lift me, you must be on higher ground.
If you would liberate me, you must be free.

If you would correct my false view of facts—
hold up to me the same facts in the true order of thought.

RALPH WALDO EMERSON,
in Society and Solitude *(1870)*

If you're strong enough, there *are* no precedents.

F. SCOTT FITZGERALD,
in The Crack-Up *(1945)*

If err we must, let us err on the side of tolerance.

FELIX FRANKFURTER

If thou hast Knowledge, let others light their Candle at thine.

THOMAS FULLER, M.D.

This is the original version of a saying that is commonly misattributed to both Winston Churchill and the American transcendentalist Margaret Fuller: "If you have knowledge, let others light their candles at it." Thomas Fuller was an eighteenth-century London physician and preacher who is remembered by quotation lovers for *Introductio ad Prudentiam*, a 1731 collection of aphorisms about leading a prudent life, and *Gnomologia*, a 1732 anthology of quotations.

If you don't find God in the next person you meet,
it is a waste of time looking for him further.

MOHANDAS GANDHI

If you want to keep on learning,
you must keep on risking failure all your life.

JOHN W. GARDNER

Gardner, a respected educator and public official, believed that "We pay a heavy price for our fear of failure." He also wrote, "There is no learning without some difficulty and fumbling."

I am told there is a passage in the Talmud that says:
"If you do not know where you are going, any road will take you there."

MARTIN GARDNER

As it turns out, the evidence suggests that this saying does not appear in the Talmud. Gardner was best known for his mathematical and scientific pursuits, but he was also a leading authority on the writings of Lewis Carroll. This comes from *The Annotated Alice* (1960), a beautifully illustrated and exhaustively annotated book. The quotation is often misattributed to Carroll, probably because of this line from Gardner's book.

If you treat men the way they are, you never improve them.
If you treat them the way you want them to be, you do.

JOHANN WOLFGANG VON GOETHE

These words—presented in slightly different ways in different translations—come from a character in Goethe's 1795 masterpiece, *Wilhelm Meister's Apprenticeship*, but they almost certainly represent Goethe's view. In the 1960s, John W. Gardner offered a slightly different perspective: "If you have some respect for people as they are, you can be more effective in helping them to become better than they are."

If you have accomplished all that you have planned for yourself,
you have not planned enough.

EDWARD EVERETT HALE

If a way to the Better there be, it exacts a full look at the Worst.

THOMAS HARDY

This line from the poem "In Tenebris II" may be seen as a reminder that we must be willing to confront the worst aspects of ourselves if we are to have a better future.

If you do not conquer self, you will be conquered by self.

NAPOLEON HILL

If I had a formula for bypassing trouble, I would not pass it around. Trouble creates a capacity to handle it.

OLIVER WENDELL HOLMES, JR.

These are unexpected but very wise words. Holmes added: "I don't say embrace trouble; that's as bad as treating it as an enemy. But I do say meet it as a friend, for you'll see a lot of it and you had better be on speaking terms with it."

If a friend is in trouble,
don't annoy him by asking if there is anything you can do.
Think up something appropriate and do it.

EDGAR WATSON HOWE

If you accept the expectations of others,
especially negative ones, then you never will change the outcome.

MICHAEL JORDAN

If a man hasn't discovered something that he will die for, he isn't fit to live.

MARTIN LUTHER KING, JR.

If the creator had a purpose in equipping us with a neck,
he surely meant us to stick it out.

ARTHUR KOESTLER

If we have not peace within ourselves,
it is vain to seek it from outward sources.

FRANÇOIS DE LA ROCHEFOUCAULD

This appeared in La Rochefoucauld's 1665 classic, *Maxims*. Three centuries later, Henry Miller picked up on the idea in *The Books in My Life* (1969): "If we have not found heaven within, it is a certainty we will not find it without."

If you would win a man to your cause,
***first* convince him that you are his sincere friend.**

ABRAHAM LINCOLN

If you would hit the mark, you must aim a little above it;
Every arrow that flies feels the attraction of earth.

HENRY WADSWORTH LONGFELLOW,
in the 1881 poem "Elegiac Verse"

If you're not sure where you're going, you're liable to end up someplace else.

ROBERT MAGER

This comes from Mager's *Preparing Instructional Objectives* (1962), but it has been misattributed to many more familiar names, including Confucius and Yogi Berra.

If you deliberately plan to be less than you are capable of being,
then I warn you that you'll be deeply unhappy for the rest of your life.

ABRAHAM H. MASLOW

In *Man's Search for Himself* (1953), Rollo May expressed the same idea in an equally compelling way: "If any organism fails to fulfill its potentialities, it becomes sick, just as your legs would wither if you never walked."

If we're growing, we're always going to be out of our comfort zone.

JOHN MAXWELL

If one cannot state a matter clearly enough
so that even an intelligent twelve-year-old can understand it,
one should remain within the cloistered walls of the university and laboratory
until one gets a better grasp of one's subject matter.

MARGARET MEAD

If others do not respond to your love with love,
look into your own benevolence;
if others fail to respond to your attempts to govern them with order,
look into your own wisdom;
if others do not return your courtesy, look into your own respect.

MENCIUS *(4th century B.C.)*

Mencius concluded this thought by writing: "In other words, look into yourself whenever you fail to achieve your purpose." A century after the death of Confucius in 479 B.C., Mencius (the Latinized form of Meng-tzu) emerged as one of the great sage's most popular disciples.

If there is to be any peace it will come about through being, not having.

HENRY MILLER

If others surpass you in knowledge, in charm, in strength, in fortune,
you have other causes to blame for it;
but if you yield to them in stoutness of heart, you have only yourself to blame.

MICHEL DE MONTAIGNE

If we have our own *why* of life,
we shall get along with almost any *how*.

FRIEDRICH NIETZSCHE

This passage, from Nietzsche's *Twilight of the Idols* (1889), is seen in a variety of different translations in different quotation anthologies. This version comes from Nietzsche scholar Walter Kaufmann, who offered it in *The Portable Nietzsche* (1959). When I first came across the saying as an undergraduate, I immediately sensed the implication—if I could construct a meaningful philosophy to guide my life, it would help me endure whatever the future would have in store for me. I later learned that the saying was extremely important to concentration camp survivor Viktor Frankl, who offered a slightly different version in his 1946 classic *Man's Search for Meaning:* "He who has a *why* to live for can bear almost any *how*."

If a person is to get the meaning of life,
he must learn to like the facts about himself—
ugly as they may seem to his sentimental vanity—
before he can lay hold on the truth behind the facts.

EUGENE O'NEILL

If everyone is thinking alike, then somebody isn't thinking.

GEORGE S. PATTON

If you have made mistakes, even serious ones,
there is always another chance for you.

MARY PICKFORD

Pickford added, "What we call failure is not the falling down but the staying down." She might have been inspired by an ancient Chinese proverb: "If you get up one more time than you fall, you will make it through." H. G. Wells said it even more tersely: "If you fell down yesterday, stand up today."

If you do not raise your eyes
you will think that you are the highest point.

ANTONIO PORCHIA

Surely this must be an ancient Proverb:
"If the situation is killing you, get the hell out."

HUGH PRATHER

As it turns out, there is no such proverb, but as Prather suggests, there *should* be.

If you want to go quickly, go alone. If you want to go far, go together.

AFRICAN PROVERB

Al Gore brought this proverb to an international audience when he included it in his Nobel Peace Prize acceptance speech in Oslo, Norway, in 2007.

If you think that you are where you are just because you worked hard,
it is easy to become self-righteous
and make classist moral judgments about others.

COLETTA REID *and*
CHARLOTTE BUNCH

This comes from Reid and Bunch's 1976 book, *Class and Feminism*. It's a nice reminder that, no matter how hard we work, we have a tendency to downplay many of the privileges that fate has granted us. Note also the use of the term *classist*, an extension of terms like *racist* and *sexist* to class prejudice.

If you're not big enough to lose, you're not big enough to win.

WALTER REUTHER

If your daily life seems poor, do not blame it;
blame yourself that you are not poet enough to call forth its riches.

RAINER MARIA RILKE

If I feel depressed, I go to work.
Work is always an antidote to depression.

ELEANOR ROOSEVELT

If you are lonely while you're alone, you are in bad company.

JEAN-PAUL SARTRE

If we let things terrify us, life will not be worth living.

SENECA

If we don't change, we don't grow.
If we don't grow, we are not really living.
Growth demands a temporary surrender of security.

GAIL SHEEHY

If one is a greyhound, why try to look like a Pekingese?

EDITH SITWELL, *on the secret of a successful appearance*

If there were no difficulties, there would be no success;
if there were nothing to struggle for, there would be nothing to be achieved.

SAMUEL SMILES

Smiles, a nineteenth-century writer and political reformer, introduced this observation by writing: "The battle of life is, in most cases, fought uphill; and to win it without a struggle were perhaps to win it without honor."

If a plant cannot live according to its nature, it dies; and so a man.

HENRY DAVID THOREAU

If a man constantly aspires, is he not elevated?

HENRY DAVID THOREAU

**If we wait for the moment when everything,
absolutely everything, is ready, we shall never begin.**

IVAN TURGENEV

**If you are neutral in situations of injustice,
you have chosen the side of the oppressor.**

DESMOND TUTU

Bishop Tutu added: "If an elephant has its foot on the tail of a mouse and you say that you are neutral, the mouse will not appreciate your neutrality."

**If you have no anxiety, the risk you face is probably not worthy of you.
Only risks you have outgrown don't frighten you.**

DAVID VISCOTT

**If you believe you can, you probably can.
If you believe you won't, you most assuredly won't.
Belief is the ignition switch that gets you off the launching pad.**

DENIS WAITLEY

The critical importance of belief is a central tenet of the current success literature, but the idea has been around for some time. In an 1836 essay, William Hazlitt wrote, "If you think you can win, you can win."

If you want to lift yourself up, lift up someone else.

BOOKER T. WASHINGTON

The notion that we best help ourselves by helping others is a well-established theme in philosophical history. Dietrich Bonhoeffer, the German theologian and writer, conveyed the idea in another ifferism: "If you do a good job for others, you heal yourself at the same time, because a dose of joy is a spiritual cure."

**If you will think about what you ought to do for other people,
your character will take care of itself.**

WOODROW WILSON

This comes from a 1914 speech in which Wilson argued that we need to be less self-absorbed and more focused on what we can do for others.

**If you look at what you have in life, you'll always have more.
If you look at what you don't have in life, you'll never have enough.**

OPRAH WINFREY

**If a man has a talent and cannot use it, he has failed.
If he has a talent and uses only half of it, he has partly failed.
If he has a talent and learns somehow to use the whole of it,
he has gloriously succeeded,
and won a satisfaction and a triumph few men ever know.**

THOMAS WOLFE, *from his novel*
The Web and the Rock *(1939)*

If I am through learning, I am through.

JOHN WOODEN

Wooden was the most successful coach in college basketball history. In the 1960s and '70s, he led the UCLA Bruins to an unprecedented ten NCAA championships in twelve years. (During that period, he won a record eighty-eight consecutive games and had two back-to-back 30–0 seasons.) One of only three people to be named to the Basketball Hall of Fame as a player and a coach (the others are Lenny Wilkens and Bill Sharman), he was always ready to offer an inspirational quotation to a player. He also favored these ifferisms:

If you're not making mistakes,
then you're not doing anything.

If you don't have time to do it right,
when will you have time to do it over?

If you can spend a perfectly useless afternoon
in a perfectly useless manner, you have learned how to live.

LIN YUTANG

If you ask me what I came into this life to do, I will tell you:
I came to live out loud.

ÉMILE ZOLA

4

If Men Could Learn from History, What Lessons It Might Teach Us

THE HUMAN CONDITION

In 1930, a thirty-nine-year-old aspiring writer named Henry Miller moved from New York City to Paris, joining a vibrant community of American expatriates and European intellectuals. For several years he lived from hand to mouth, subsisting on part-time jobs and the generosity of friends. Despite his meager circumstances and dim prospects, he found a happiness he had never before experienced. He expressed his joy in a fascinating way: "I have no money, no resources, no hopes. I am the happiest man alive."

Part of Miller's happiness came from his affair with another aspiring writer, the sensual and free-spirited Anaïs Nin. Their relationship took some adjustment on Miller's part, though, for Nin continued to share her bed with the writer Lawrence Durrell *and* his wife June (despite the complexity, Miller and Durrell went on to become friends). In 1934, Nin helped finance the printing of Miller's first book, *Tropic of Cancer*, an autobiographical novel that was so sexually explicit it was banned in England and America. The book was ultimately hailed by Norman Mailer as "one of the ten or twenty greatest novels of the twentieth century," but it wasn't published in America until 1961.

Shortly after the publication of *Tropic of Capricorn* in 1939, Miller decided to leave Paris because of the imminent Nazi threat. He originally planned to return to America, but decided instead to visit his old friend Lawrence Durrell, who was living at the time in Greece. That visit inspired Miller's fascinating account of Greek life and culture, *The Colossus of Maroussi*, published in 1941. The book, equal parts travelogue, personal diary, and philosophical notebook, contains one of Miller's most frequently quoted lines:

If men cease to believe that they will one day become gods then they will surely become worms.

Miller wrote that the Greek gods "were of human proportion," a belief that starkly contrasted with the Judeo-Christian notion of an all-powerful God. By attributing human characteristics to gods, according to Miller, an important link between the human and the divine was established, helping to elevate people and even encouraging them to aspire to divine status. Miller used the literary device of chiasmus to describe the situation: "We say erroneously that the Greeks humanized the gods. It is just the contrary. The gods humanized the Greeks."

Observations about men and their gods have been a staple of intellectual history. In the sixth century B.C., the Greek philosopher Xenophanes wrote:

If oxen and horses and lions had hands,
and were able to draw with their hands and do the same things as men,
horses would draw the shapes of gods to look like horses
and oxen would draw them to look like oxen.

This is an early suggestion that man created God in his image, a belief that is exactly the reverse of the Judeo-Christian view. With the deaths of the Greek and then the Roman civilizations, the Judeo-Christian view was virtually unchallenged in the West for a thousand years. During the Renaissance, however, as the influence of the church began to diminish, unfettered thinkers began to entertain a thought that orthodox believers considered unimaginable: Perhaps man had indeed created God in his image.

Such a belief, however, would have been considered heretical by church authorities. Knowing the risks, but still wanting to remain intellectually honest, some freethinkers began to express the view in carefully phrased terms. In a 1674 letter, the Dutch philosopher Benedict Spinoza wrote:

If a triangle could speak, it would say that God is eminently triangular, while a circle would say that the divine nature is eminently circular.

Spinoza's observation soon began to be whispered in Dutch intellectual circles, and it eventually spread to salons all around Europe. In a 1721 letter, the French diplomat Charles de Montesquieu said that he had recently heard a saying that he greatly admired:

If triangles had a god, he would have three sides.

The saying that Montesquieu admired was almost certainly an adaptation of Spinoza's observation—but it was so much better expressed that it quickly supplanted the earlier one in popularity. It may also have inspired the most famous observation on the subject:

If God created us in his image, we have more than reciprocated.

VOLTAIRE *(François Marie Arouet)*

First written in a private journal entry around 1726, Voltaire's bold assertion was regarded as so controversial that it did not become public until more than a century after Voltaire's death in 1778.

If human beings have created an anthropomorphic God, they have also done the same thing with that other great figure in theological history, Satan. In his literary classic *The Brothers Karamazov*, Fyodor Dostoyevsky wrote in 1879:

If the devil doesn't exist and, therefore, man has created him, he has created him in his own image and likeness.

So far we've explored only one aspect of the human condition: man's search for meaning and his attempt to understand his relationship with the divine. In the remainder of the chapter, you will find hypothetical, counterfactual, and conditional observations on other important aspects of the human experience.

If knowledge can create problems, it is not through ignorance that we can solve them.

ISAAC ASIMOV

If you are to judge a man, you must know his secret thoughts, sorrows, and feelings.

HONORÉ DE BALZAC

This observation comes from Balzac's *Philosophical Studies* (1831). The twentieth-century writer Harry Golden also offered a pithy thought on the same subject: "If you want to judge a man, take a look at his enemies."

If you've ever really been poor, you remain poor at heart all your life.

ARNOLD BENNETT

If we had no winter, the spring would not be so pleasant: If we did not sometimes taste of adversity, prosperity would not be so welcome.

ANNE BRADSTREET,
the first published poet in America

If you're losing your soul and you know it,
then you've still got a soul left to lose.

CHARLES BUKOWSKI

If what pleases some didn't make others miserable,
you wouldn't have a world divided into Smoking and No Smoking.

GEORGE BURNS

If an elderly but distinguished scientist
says that something is possible he is almost certainly right,
but if he says that it is impossible he is very probably wrong.

ARTHUR C. CLARKE

If men could learn from history, what lessons it might teach us!

SAMUEL TAYLOR COLERIDGE

This comes from *Table Talk*, an 1835 compilation of Coleridge observations that was published a year after his death. He added with a metaphorical flair: "But passion and party blind our eyes, and the light which experience gives is a lantern on the stern, which shines only on the waves behind us!" Coleridge may have been influenced by one of history's most famous observations, offered by the German philosopher Hegel shortly before his death in 1831: "What experience and history teach is this—that people and governments have never learned anything from history."

If you want to test your memory,
try to recall what you were worrying about one year ago today.

E. JOSEPH COSSMAN

If a person never contradicts himself, it must be that he says nothing.

MIGUEL DE UNAMUNO

If there were no bad people, there would be no good lawyers.

CHARLES DICKENS, *the character Brass*
in The Old Curiosity Shop *(1899)*

If there is no struggle, there is no progress.

FREDERICK DOUGLASS

In this snippet from an 1857 speech, Douglass argued that people entrenched in positions of power will concede nothing without a struggle. He added, "Those who profess to favor freedom and yet deprecate agitation, are men who want crops without plowing the ground, they want rain without thunder and lightning."

If we did all the things we are capable of doing,
we would literally astound ourselves.

THOMAS A. EDISON

If my theory of relativity is proven successful,
Germany will claim me as a German
and France will declare that I am a citizen of the world.

ALBERT EINSTEIN

This came in a 1922 address to the French Philosophical Society. It had been only six years since Einstein's *Relativity* was published, and the jury was still out on the potentially groundbreaking theory. Einstein was engaging in a little "what if" thinking about what would happen if his ideas turned out to be correct. He also imagined the consequences if he were wrong: "Should my theory prove untrue, France will say that I am a German and Germany will declare that I am a Jew."

If you put a chain around the neck of a slave,
the other end fastens itself around your own.

RALPH WALDO EMERSON

If you would rule the world quietly, you must keep it amused.

RALPH WALDO EMERSON

In this observation, Emerson was paraphrasing the maxim of a tyrant. Emerson was clearly familiar with the first-century Roman poet Juvenal, who had written: "Two things only the people anxiously desire—bread and circuses." Juvenal was writing about how Roman leaders distracted the citizens from other important issues by offering free food and staging spectacles in the Colosseum.

If you would keep your secret from an enemy, tell it not to a friend.

BENJAMIN FRANKLIN, *from*
Poor Richard's Almanack *(1741)*

As a young man, Franklin confided in several close friends only to discover later that his private plans were leaked to his adversaries. A strikingly similar sentiment had been advanced seven hundred years earlier by the eleventh-century philosopher Solomon Ibn Gabriol, a man who is often called "the Jewish Plato." In his 1050 book, *The Choice of Pearls*, he wrote: "If you want to keep something concealed from your enemy, do not disclose it to your friend."

If men are so wicked with religion, what would they be without it?

BENJAMIN FRANKLIN

If an exchange between two parties is voluntary,
it will not take place unless both believe they will benefit from it.

MILTON AND ROSE FRIEDMAN

This appeared in *Free to Choose*, a 1980 book by the Nobel Prize–winning economist and his wife. Hailing it as "the key insight" from Adam Smith's 1776 classic *The Wealth of Nations*, they added: "Most economic fallacies derive from the neglect of this simple insight, from the tendency to assume that there is a fixed pie, that one party can only gain at the expense of another."

If Christians would really live according to the teachings of Christ, as found in the Bible, all of India would be Christian today.

MOHANDAS GANDHI

Thomas Carlyle offered a related thought: "If Jesus were to come today, people would not even crucify him. They would ask him to dinner, and hear what he had to say, and make fun of him." And in his *Notebook* Mark Twain expressed the sentiment this way: "If Christ were here there is one thing he would not be—a Christian."

If a man is to achieve all that is asked of him,
he must take himself for more than he is,
and as long as he does not carry it to an absurd length,
we willingly put up with it.

JOHANN WOLFGANG VON GOETHE

It is commonly believed that people who have an inflated view of themselves are engaging in self-deception, but Goethe suggests in this observation that a modest amount of immodesty is a good thing.

If the world were good for nothing else, it is a fine subject for speculation.

WILLIAM HAZLITT

If pleasures are greatest in anticipation,
just remember that this is also true of trouble.

ELBERT HUBBARD

If you want that good feeling that comes from doing things for other folks then you have to pay for it in abuse and misunderstanding.

ZORA NEALE HURSTON

This passage from *Moses, Man of the Mountain* (1939) is a reminder that doing good deeds can be a complex and perplexing affair, sometimes leading not to gratitude but to resentment and hard feelings. Hurston's thought may be seen as an early variation on the theme of "No good deed goes unpunished."

If I repeat "My will be done"
with the necessary degree of faith and persistency,
the chances are that, sooner or later and somehow or other,
I shall get what I want.

ALDOUS HUXLEY

This observation from *The Perennial Philosophy* (1945) emphasizes the importance of a determined will—as opposed to divine involvement—in human affairs.

If you have been put in your place long enough,
you begin to act like the place.

RANDALL JARRELL

If a man talks of his misfortunes,
there is something in them that is not disagreeable to him.

DR. SAMUEL JOHNSON

If people can be educated to see the lowly side of their own natures,
it may be hoped that they will also learn to understand
and to love their fellow men better.

CARL JUNG

Getting in touch with the lowly side of our nature seems counterintuitive, but Jung explained it this way: "A little less hypocrisy and a little more tolerance towards oneself can only have good results in respect for our neighbor."

If man no longer had enemies, he would have to invent them, for his strength only grows through struggle.

LOUIS L'AMOUR

If we resist our passions, it is more from their weakness than from our strength.

FRANÇOIS DE LA ROCHEFOUCAULD

If only we could have two lives: the first in which to make one's mistakes, which seem as if they have to be made; and the second in which to profit by them.

D. H. LAWRENCE

If we could read the secret history of our enemies, we should find in each man's life sorrow and suffering enough to disarm all hostility.

HENRY WADSWORTH LONGFELLOW

This observation from *Table-Talk*, an 1857 collection of Longfellow's thoughts, is very similar to a well-known Italian proverb, and it is possible he was influenced by it: "If the secret sorrows of everyone could be read on their foreheads, how many who now cause envy would suddenly become the objects of pity."

If you're half evil, nothing soothes you more than to think the person you are opposed to is totally evil.

NORMAN MAILER

If you ever forget you're a Jew, a Gentile will remind you.

BERNARD MALAMUD

In 1989, London's *The Sun* quoted Jesse Jackson as making a similar, and even more sobering, remark: "If you wake up in the morning and think you're white, you're bound to meet someone before five o'clock who will let you know you are just another nigger."

If you are possessed by an idea,
you find it expressed everywhere, you even smell it.

THOMAS MANN

If you make people think they're thinking, they'll love you;
but if you really make them think, they'll hate you.

DON MARQUIS

If nobody spoke unless he had something to say . . .
the human race would very soon lose the use of speech.

W. SOMERSET MAUGHAM,
in The Painted Veil *(1925)*

If slaughterhouses had glass walls, everyone would be vegetarian.

PAUL MCCARTNEY

In a 1990 "Meat Stinks" advertising campaign for PETA, the singer k. d. lang said similarly, "If you knew how meat was made, you'd lose your lunch."

If someone tells you he is going to make "a realistic decision,"
you immediately understand that he has resolved to do something bad.

MARY MCCARTHY

The first person to express this sentiment may have been Eliza Leslie, a nineteenth-century etiquette expert who wrote in *Miss Leslie's Behavior Book* (1859): "If a person begins by telling you, 'Do not be offended at what I am going to say,' prepare yourself for something that she knows will certainly offend you."

If you can tell anyone about it, it's not the worst thing you ever did.

MIGNON MCLAUGHLIN

McLaughlin's point is that people rarely confess their worst offenses to anyone, choosing instead to carry their unspeakable offenses with them to the grave.

If a scientist were to cut his ear off,
no one would take it as evidence of a heightened sensibility.

PETER B. MEDAWAR,
in an allusion to Vincent van Gogh

If it was the fashion to go naked, the face would hardly be observed.

MARY WORTLEY MONTAGU

If one only wished to be happy, this could be easily accomplished;
but we wish to be happier than other people,
and this is always difficult, for we believe others to be happier than they are.

CHARLES DE MONTESQUIEU

If you gaze long into an abyss, the abyss will also gaze into you.

FRIEDRICH NIETZSCHE

This famous line from Nietzsche's classic *Beyond Good and Evil* (1886) was preceded by an equally famous line: "He who fights with monsters should be careful lest he thereby become a monster."

If we're looking for the sources of our troubles,
we shouldn't test people for drugs,
we should test them for stupidity, ignorance, greed, and love of power.

P. J. O'ROURKE

If you are planning for a year, sow rice;
if you are planning for a decade, plant trees;
if you are planning for a lifetime, educate people.

CHINESE PROVERB

If you want to change the way people think,
you can educate them, brainwash them, bribe them, drug them.
Or you can teach them a few carefully chosen new words.

HOWARD RHEINGOLD

If wicked actions are atoned for only in the next world,
stupid ones are only atoned for in this.

ARTHUR SCHOPENHAUER

If all the year were playing holidays,
To sport would be as tedious as to work . . .

WILLIAM SHAKESPEARE,
in Henry IV, Part 1

In these famous words delivered by the character Prince Hal, Shakespeare reminds us that every human activity, even those that are enjoyable, can become tedious unless there is an occasional break from the routine.

If there was nothing wrong in the world
there wouldn't be anything left for us to do, would there?

GEORGE BERNARD SHAW, *the character*
Hannah in The Devil's Disciple *(1911)*

**If you take a passionate interest in a subject,
it is hard not to believe yourself specially equipped for it.**

ETHEL SMYTH

**If a man loves the labor of his trade,
apart from any question of success or fame, the gods have called him.**

ROBERT LOUIS STEVENSON

So few people love their work that those who do are fortunate indeed. Kahlil Gibran expressed the idea even more forcefully: "If you cannot work with love but only with distaste, it is better that you should leave your work."

**If a man would register all his opinions upon love, politics, religion, learning, etc.,
beginning from his youth and so on to old age,
what a bundle of inconsistencies and contradictions would appear at last!**

JONATHAN SWIFT

**If you pick up a starving dog and make him prosperous, he will not bite you.
This is the principal difference between a dog and a man.**

MARK TWAIN

If man had created man he would be ashamed of his performance.

MARK TWAIN

**If the world should blow itself up,
the last audible voice would be that of an expert saying it can't be done.**

PETER USTINOV

**If there were only one religion in England, there would be danger of despotism,
if there were two, they would cut each other's throats.
but there are thirty, and they live in peace and happiness.**

VOLTAIRE *(François Marie Arouet)*

Voltaire, the freethinking Frenchman, came from a country with only one major religion—Catholicism—and he was very familiar with ecclesiastical tyranny. Even though Voltaire was antireligious, he believed that the more religions, the better. In his view, a multireligious society was a tolerant society.

If there were only two men in the world, how would they get on?

VOLTAIRE *(François Marie Arouet)*

Voltaire posed this hypothetical question in his *Philosophical Dictionary* (1764). And then he answered it: "They would help one another, harm one another, flatter one another, slander one another, fight one another, make it up; they could neither live together nor do without one another."

If you walk down a well-trodden path long enough,
you will eventually end up alone.

MARIE VON EBNER-ESCHENBACH

If you stop to be kind, you must swerve often from your path.

MARY WEBB

Mother Teresa wrote similarly: "If you really love one another, you will not be able to avoid making sacrifices." The implication of both observations is clear: People focused solely on themselves and their goals have little time for others.

If the whole human race lay in one grave,
the epitaph on its headstone might well be:
"It seemed a good idea at the time."

REBECCA WEST

West also offered another intriguing thought: "If I wanted life to be easy, I should have gotten born in a different universe."

**If the world were merely seductive, that would be easy.
If it were merely challenging, that would be no problem.
But I rise in the morning torn between a desire to improve (or save) the world and a desire to enjoy (or savor) the world.
This makes it hard to plan the day.**

E. B. WHITE

If there were a verb meaning "to believe falsely," it would not have any significant first person, present indicative.

LUDWIG WITTGENSTEIN

This is one of my all-time favorite quotations (although, to be honest, I have failed to persuade some close friends of its brilliance). Wittgenstein is suggesting that we only use the past tense when admitting to false beliefs. If we summarized the thought in other words, it might go this way: In the middle of falsely believing something, we are incapable of saying "I am wrong in my belief." Only later, after we realize we were wrong, can we say, "I once falsely believed something."

If people are highly successful in their professions they lose their senses.

VIRGINIA WOOLF

When highly successful people have no time to listen to music or engage in conversation with others, Woolf argued that they often develop a distorted sense of proportion and lose their humanity. She added: "What then remains of a human being who has lost sight, sound, and a sense of proportion? Only a cripple in a cave."

5

If You Can't Be Kind, At Least Be Vague

NOT-SO-IFFY ADVICE

On July 4, 1918, identical twin girls were born to Abraham and Rebecca Friedman, Russian Jewish immigrants who ten years earlier had fled from the czarist pogroms and settled in Sioux City, Iowa. In a fascinating naming reversal, the girls were formally named Esther Pauline and Pauline Esther, but from the very beginning they were called *Eppie* and *Popo*. Growing up Jewish in an overwhelmingly Christian community was not without its challenges, and the two girls, usually dressed in matching outfits, were inseparable as they grew up.

After graduating from high school, the Friedman twins attended Morningside College, a local liberal arts institution. Throughout college, they retained their close bond, sitting alongside each other in courses, partying with the same friends, and even cowriting a gossip column for the college newspaper. In 1939, at age twenty-one, the twins announced that they were dropping out of school to get married. Nobody was surprised when the brides-to-be said they had decided to wear identical gowns in a double-wedding ceremony.

Eppie and new husband Julius Lederer, a talented young salesman, bounced around a bit before settling in Eau Claire, Wisconsin. When Julius left to serve in the war effort, Eppie and her daughter Margo moved back to Sioux City to live with her parents. Except for that brief period, the Lederers lived in Eau Claire until 1955, where he was a founder of Budget Rent-a-Car and she, the wife of a prosperous businessman, a devoted mother, and a tireless community volunteer.

In 1955, the Lederers moved to Chicago to further Julius's business career. It was the beginning of a new chapter for the family, and Eppie was also thinking about new possibilities for herself. She had become a regular reader of a *Chicago Sun-Times* advice column titled "Ask Ann Landers." The column, written by a Chicago nurse named Ruth Crowley, had appeared in the paper since 1942 and enjoyed a modest syndication. One day, Eppie called the newspaper to see if she might volunteer to help Crowley sort through her mail and possibly even help with research. In a coincidence of cosmic proportions, Eppie was told that Crowley had died a week earlier.

In a contest to select a replacement, the newspaper provided all contestants with a series of letters and asked for sample replies. Instead of simply providing her own opinions, Eppie interviewed experts such as Supreme Court justice William O. Brennan and Notre Dame president Theodore Hesburgh and incorporated their views into her sample columns. In October 1955, Eppie Lederer became the new Ann Landers and she soon transformed the daily advice column into the most successful syndicated column in history (at the height of its popularity, it appeared in 1,200 newspapers and had a readership of ninety million people). Eppie eventually acquired legal rights to the Ann Landers name, and the use of the name died along with her when she passed away in 2002.

In 1956, several months into Eppie's new career, twin sister Popo was living in San Francisco with her husband Mort Phillips. Inspired by her sister's new job in Chicago, she approached the editor of the *San Francisco Chronicle* and persuaded him to let her write a daily advice column for his paper. She titled the column "Dear Abby" and adopted the pen name Abigail Van Buren. Within a few years, her column began to rival the popularity of Eppie's column. The competition between the sisters put a great strain on their relationship and, in a great irony, the two famous advice givers became so estranged they refused to talk to one another for nearly a decade. While they publicly reconciled in 1964, the once-inseparable twins continued their fierce professional competition and would never regain the closeness they once enjoyed.

In their half-century of providing advice, Landers and Van Buren wrote millions of words that were discussed at coffee klatches and hair salons, posted on refrigerators and bulletin boards, and even debated in professional journals. And some of their best lines were expressed ifferistically. One day, Landers received a letter from a woman who was about to wed a man with whom she had been having an extramarital affair. Landers didn't mince her words:

**If you marry a man who cheats on his wife,
you'll be married to a man who cheats on his wife.**

Another time, to a woman who requested an etiquette ruling, she simply wrote:

If nobody minds, it doesn't matter.

Van Buren also commonly expressed herself in the conditional format. In two of her best-remembered lines, she wrote:

**If we could sell our experiences for what they cost us,
we'd all be millionaires.**

**If you want a place in the sun,
you've got to put up with a few blisters.**

These offerings may all qualify as ifferisms, but there are some who would say they are simply observations, or perhaps opinions, and not advice. To rise to the level of advice, according to this point of view, they must suggest that people do something or act in a certain way. According to language maven William Safire, "The essence of advice is a verb—do this or do that, or never do either." *The American Heritage Dictionary* defines *advice* this way: "Opinion about what could or should be done about a situation or problem." Notice how the following Van Buren ifferisms clearly rise to the status of advice:

**If you want your children to turn out well,
spend twice as much time with them, and half as much money.**

**If you want your children to keep their feet on the ground,
put some responsibility on their shoulders.**

The same can be said about these offerings from Ann Landers:

If you want to have the last word in any argument, be classy. Apologize.

If you want your children to listen, try talking softly—to someone else.

Ann Landers and Abigail Van Buren were the most famous advice columnists of the twentieth century, but they were simply carrying on a centuries-old tradition of providing guidance to the perplexed and the confused. In the last years of the first century, a former Greek slave named Epictetus became the advice guru of his era. Unlike so many of his contemporaries, who often seemed to have their heads in the clouds, Epictetus was a down-to-earth guy who translated many philosophical concepts into practical terms. In a famous observation, he said:

If you hear that someone is speaking ill of you,
instead of trying to defend yourself you should say:
"He obviously does not know me very well,
since there are so many other faults he could have mentioned."

This is clever as well as practical advice, and has for centuries been followed by people in the public arena. Frederick the Great greatly admired the writings of Epictetus, and was fond of quoting him. In a 1775 letter to Voltaire, he said that another piece of advice from the ancient Greek philosopher had helped him:

I think of satire like Epictetus:
"If people speak ill of you, and it is true, amend yourself;
if lies, laugh at them."

Mark Twain began a private journal in 1855 at age twenty, and kept at it until shortly before he died in 1910. In an 1894 entry, he wrote:

If you tell the truth you don't have to remember anything.

I'm not sure if Twain was writing this as a reminder to himself or as a piece of advice he intended to deliver in the future. No matter what his plan, it's a helpful warning about the dangers of deception and a reminder about one major benefit of truth telling. As the years passed, other writers weighed in on the subject, and they also chose to express themselves conditionally:

If you tell a lie, always rehearse it.
If it don't sound good to you, it won't sound good to anybody.

LEROY "SATCHEL" PAIGE

If you want to be thought a liar, always tell the truth.

LOGAN PEARSALL SMITH

If one cannot invent a really convincing lie,
it is often better to stick to the truth.

ANGELA THIRKELL

When people talk about an *iffy* proposition, they are generally describing something doubtful or uncertain, or something that cannot be relied on. The opinions and advice to be found in the rest of this chapter are the farthest thing from *iffy* one could find, even though they all begin with the word *if*.

If you don't like something, change it.
If you can't change it, change your attitude.
Don't complain.

MAYA ANGELOU

If it is not right, don't do it;
if it is not true, don't say it.

MARCUS AURELIUS

Aurelius, the most philosophical of all Roman emperors, wrote this in a private journal nearly 2,000 years ago. More recently, the science fiction writer Ray Bradbury echoed the sentiment: "If you don't like what you're doing, then don't do it." A similar recommendation also appears in an ancient Chinese proverb: "If you don't want anyone to know it, don't do it."

If you want to say something radical, you should dress conservative.

STEVE BIKO

If I had to give anyone advice, it would be
to live at least one year of your life completely alone—whoever you are.
If you can't do it, you are in trouble.

RITA MAE BROWN

The "trouble" is now well known; many people are so afraid to be alone they jump into questionable, unhealthy, or even toxic relationships.

If you wish to be loved, show more of your faults than your virtues.

EDWARD GEORGE BULWER-LYTTON

If you want to conquer fear, do not sit at home and think about it. Go out and get busy.

DALE CARNEGIE

Carnegie was famous for advising people to *do something*. In a related opinion, he wrote, "If you can't sleep, then get up and do something instead of lying there and worrying. It's the worry that gets you, not the loss of sleep."

If you have a garden and a library, you have everything you need.

CICERO *(1st century B.C.)*

If you can find a path with no obstacles, it probably doesn't lead anywhere.

FRANK A. CLARK

If a man, notoriously and designedly, insults and affronts you, knock him down . . .

LORD CHESTERFIELD *(Philip Dormer Stanhope), in a 1752 letter to his son*

When you are viciously attacked, Chesterfield advised, you should strike back forcefully. Regarding lesser affronts, he recommended a very different strategy: "If he only injures you, your best revenge is to be extremely civil to him in your outward behavior, though at the same time you counterwork him, and return him the compliment, perhaps with interest."

If you have an important point to make, don't try to be subtle or clever.

WINSTON CHURCHILL

Churchill added: "Use a pile-driver. Hit the point once. Then come back and hit it again. Then hit it a third time—a tremendous whack!"

If you're going through hell, keep going.

WINSTON CHURCHILL

If you can, help others. If you can't, at least don't hurt others.

THE DALAI LAMA

If you can dream it, you can do it.

WALT DISNEY

If you wish to win a man's heart, allow him to confute you.

BENJAMIN DISRAELI

Confute is a word that was once popular, but is no longer in favor. It means "to prove or show to be false." In the context of this observation, it means to allow someone to prove you wrong; or, in other words, to have a victory over you.

If *A* is success in life, then *A* equals *x* plus *y* plus *z*.
Work is *x*; *y* is play; and *z* is keeping your mouth shut.

ALBERT EINSTEIN

This remark has not been verified, but its authenticity has never been seriously challenged. It even appears in *The New Quotable Einstein* (2005), where editor Alice Calaprice wrote: "Einstein often spoke about keeping one's mouth shut."

If you haven't the strength to impose your own terms upon life, you must accept what it offers you.

T. S. ELIOT, *from* The Confidential Clerk *(1953)*

If you cannot be free, be as free as you can.

RALPH WALDO EMERSON

If you make money your god, it will plague you like the devil.

HENRY FIELDING

If you have a talent, use it in every way possible.

BRENDAN FRANCIS

Francis finished off this observation by adding, "Don't hoard it. Don't dole it out like a miser. Spend it lavishly like a millionaire intent on going broke."

If you would persuade, think of interest, not of reason.

BENJAMIN FRANKLIN

Franklin suggests here that when trying to convince people to do something, an appeal to their self-interest is more effective than a recitation of rational arguments.

If you desire a wise answer, you must ask a reasonable question.

JOHANN WOLFGANG VON GOETHE

If you accept a limiting belief, then it will become a truth for you.

LOUISE L. HAY

If you always do what interests you, at least one person is pleased.

KATHARINE HEPBURN

If what you did yesterday seems big, you haven't done anything today.

LOU HOLTZ

Coach Holtz also once said: "If you're bored with life—you don't get up every morning with a burning desire to do things—you don't have enough goals."

If you are ever at a loss to support a flagging conversation, introduce the subject of eating.

LEIGH HUNT

If you want a quality, act as if you already had it.

WILLIAM JAMES

If there's nobody in your way, it's because you're not going anywhere.

ROBERT F. KENNEDY

If you don't stand for something, you will fall for anything.

MARTIN LUTHER KING, JR.

Peter Marshall, the United States Senate chaplain, offered an early version of this sentiment when he said in a 1947 prayer: "Give us clear vision, that we may know where to stand and what to stand for—because unless we stand for something, we shall fall for anything."

If you wish to grow thinner, diminish your dinner.

HENRY S. LEIGH

This is the well-known first line of an 1880 poem (titled "On Corpulence") from a not-so-well-known English poet. The rest of the quatrain goes this way:

And take to light claret instead of pale ale;
Look down with an utter contempt upon butter,
And never touch bread till it's toasted—or stale.

If you ever need a helping hand, you'll find one at the end of your arm.

SAM LEVENSON

In his 1973 bestseller *In One Era and Out the Other*, Levenson said he was celebrating his fifth birthday when his father offered him these words of advice. After the book's publication, the saying began to enjoy widespread popularity. Many celebrities, including Audrey Hepburn, adopted it as a personal motto, and the saying is commonly misattributed to her.

If you falter, and give up, you will lose the power
of keeping any resolution, and will regret it all your life.

ABRAHAM LINCOLN,
in an 1862 letter

If you get gloomy, just take an hour off
and sit and think how much better this world is than hell.
Of course, it won't cheer you up if you expect to go there.

DON MARQUIS

If you can't be kind, at least be vague.

JUDITH MARTIN *("Miss Manners")*

If you are rude to your ex-husband's new wife at your daughter's wedding,
you will make her feel smug. Comfortable.
If you are charming and polite, you will make her feel uncomfortable.
Which do you want to do?

JUDITH MARTIN *("Miss Manners")*

Martin gave this advice to a woman who had asked for help on how to behave toward her former husband's new wife at their daughter's upcoming wedding.

If you reject the food, ignore the customs, fear the religion, and avoid the people, you might better stay home.

JAMES A. MICHENER

If you want a golden rule that will fit everything, this is it: Have nothing in your houses that you do not know to be useful or believe to be beautiful.

WILLIAM MORRIS

On the same subject, Frank Lloyd Wright wrote: "If you foolishly ignore beauty, you'll soon find yourself without it. Your life will be impoverished. But if you wisely invest in beauty, it will remain with you all the days of your life."

If ambition doesn't hurt you, you haven't got it.

KATHLEEN NORRIS

This comes from Norris's 1931 book *Hands Full of Living*, where she makes an important point: "If you have a genuine desire to do anything in this world, then *not* doing it will be a source of great discomfort."

If you put off everything till you're sure of it, you'll get nothing done.

NORMAN VINCENT PEALE

If you're not feeling good about you, what you're wearing outside doesn't mean a thing.

LEONTYNE PRICE

If you have much, give of your wealth; if you have little, give of your heart.

ARAB PROVERB

**If you are patient in one moment of anger,
you will avoid one hundred days of sorrow.**

CHINESE PROVERB

If you bow at all, bow low.

CHINESE PROVERB

If you can alter things, alter them. If you cannot, put up with them.

ENGLISH PROVERB

If you kick a stone in anger, you'll hurt your own foot.

KOREAN PROVERB

If there is no wind, row.

POLISH PROVERB

**If thou wouldst preserve a sound body, use fasting and walking;
if a healthful soul, fasting and praying.**

FRANCIS QUARLES

Quarles concluded: "Walking exercises the body, praying exercises the soul, fasting cleanses both." Quarles is remembered chiefly for his 1635 book *Emblems*, the most popular of the "emblem books" that first appeared in the Renaissance.

If you wish to avoid seeing a fool, you must first break your mirror.

FRANÇOIS RABELAIS

If any part of your uncertainty . . .
is a conflict between your heart and your mind, follow your mind.

AYN RAND

The words come from John Galt, the protagonist of *Atlas Shrugged* (1957), but they reflect the views of Rand. Marilyn vos Savant wrote similarly: "If your head tells you one thing, and your heart tells you another, before you do anything, you should first decide whether you have a better head or a better heart."

If you want to succeed, you should strike out on new paths
rather than travel the worn paths of accepted success.

JOHN D. ROCKEFELLER

If you can't afford the expensive one, don't buy it.

ANDY ROONEY

If you can't be funny, be interesting.

HAROLD ROSS

If you're going to do something wrong, at least enjoy it.

LEO ROSTEN

If you want to "get in touch with your feelings," fine—
talk to yourself, we all do.
But if you want to communicate with another thinking human being,
get in touch with your thoughts.

WILLIAM SAFIRE

If we suspect that a man is lying, we should pretend to believe him.

ARTHUR SCHOPENHAUER

This pretense strategy, from an 1851 essay, works for a very simple reason: "For then he becomes bold and assured, lies more vigorously, and is unmasked."

If you are losing your leisure, look out! You may be losing your soul.

LOGAN PEARSALL SMITH

If you pursue happiness you'll never find it.

C. P. SNOW

Snow expresses an ancient theme in this observation. In the sixth century B.C., the Chinese sage Chuang-tzu observed: "Perfect happiness is the absence of striving for happiness." Edith Wharton also expressed the thought ifferistically: "If only we'd stop trying to be happy, we'd have a pretty good time."

If you hear a voice within you say "you cannot paint," then by all means paint, and that voice will be silenced.

VINCENT VAN GOGH

This is similar to a piece of advice that John Cage said he got from his father: "If someone says *can't*, that shows you what to do."

If your employer criticizes your report, don't take it personally. Instead, find out what's needed and fix it. If your girlfriend laughs at your tie, don't take it personally. Find another tie or find another girlfriend.

MARILYN VOS SAVANT

Vos Savant prefaced this observation by writing: "I believe that one becomes stronger emotionally by taking life less personally."

If you're losing the battle against a persistent bad habit, an addiction, or a temptation, and you're stuck in a repeating cycle of good intention-failure-guilt, you will not get better on your own! You need the help of other people.

RICK WARREN, *from*
The Purpose-Driven Life *(2002)*

If you want to achieve excellence, you can get there today. As of this second, quit doing less-than-excellent work.

THOMAS J. WATSON, SR.

If you don't know what your passion is, realize that one reason for your existence on earth is to find it.

OPRAH WINFREY

If you want to reach a goal, you must *see the reaching* in your own mind before you actually arrive at your goal.

ZIG ZIGLAR, *on the importance of visualization*

6

If You Rest, You Rust

AGES & STAGES OF LIFE

On February 7, 1883, Eubie Blake was born to former slaves living in Baltimore, Maryland. The couple's previous ten children had all died at birth, and it is said that they were devoted to their only child. When Eubie was six years old, he astonished his mother by climbing onto an organ stool at a local department store and picking out a melody. According to researchers at *The Eubie Blake National Museum and Cultural Center* in Baltimore, Mrs. Blake almost immediately bought a seventy-five dollar organ for her young prodigy, paying it off in twenty-five cent installments. Soon, young Eubie was taking lessons from a neighbor, and within a few years was sneaking out of his bedroom window at nights to play at local bars and brothels.

Blake went on to become one of America's most respected musicians. He was one of the first African American performers to appear on the professional stage without minstrel makeup, and his "Charleston Rag" helped establish ragtime as a unique American art form. Although he had smoked since childhood and—strangely—refused to drink water, he lived to be ninety-six years old (Blake claimed to be one hundred, but that is now known to have been an exaggeration). On his ninetieth birthday, he was asked by a reporter, "How do you feel, Mr. Blake?" The great showman replied:

**If I'd known I was going to live this long,
I'd have taken better care of myself!**

Observations about the aging process are among the most interesting things ever said or written. Helen Hayes, who was often called "The First Lady of the American Theater," had a career that lasted a full eighty years. She made her first stage appearance in 1905, at age five, and her last in 1985, when she played Miss Marple in a made-for-TV adaptation of an Agatha Christie novel. Hayes lived such a long and productive life that she wrote two autobiographies: *On Reflection* in 1968 and *My Life in Three Acts* in 1990. In the latter book, she wrote:

If you rest, you rust.

It's a lovely line, and one that has enjoyed great popularity with seniors in recent years. The basic idea is centuries old, however, originally authored by the seventeenth-century English theologian Richard Cumberland: "It is better to wear out than to rust out. There will be time enough for repose in the grave."

As people age, many begin to hypothetically think, "if only I could live a little longer." In a 1902 interview, eighty-two-year-old Susan B. Anthony said:

**If I could but live another century
and see the fruition of all the work for women!
There is so much yet to be done.**

Anthony lived four more years, not long enough to see the cause of her lifework, women's suffrage, come into existence. (That happened in 1920, with the ratification of the Nineteenth Amendment, often called the *Anthony Amendment*.)

Even more common than thinking about living longer is thinking about what life would be like if we could live it over again. Over the centuries, countless numbers of people have entertained this hypothetical thought. You'll find more examples later in the chapter, but here are several to whet your appetite:

If I had to live my life again, I'd make the same mistakes, only sooner.

TALLULAH BANKHEAD

If I had my life to live over again, I'd live over a saloon.

W. C. FIELDS

If I had my life to live over, I would do it all again,
but this time I would be nastier.

JEANNETTE RANKIN

The subject of age and aging almost always leads to the discussion of death and dying, another topic that has stimulated some memorable observations. In September 2007, Randy Pausch, a professor of computer science at Carnegie-Mellon University gave his legendary "last lecture." After showing CAT scans of his pancreatic cancer to students and announcing the grim verdict that he would die in less than a year, Pausch said, "That is what it is; we can't change it and we just have to decide how we are going to respond to it. We cannot change the cards we are dealt, just how we play the hand." And then, to a hearty laugh from the students, he said:

If I don't seem as depressed or morose as I should be,
sorry to disappoint you.

In the remainder of the chapter, I'll provide many more observations about the ages and stages of life. I'm hoping they will help you look at your life—and the lives of those around you—in a richer, fuller, and more appreciative way.

If you feel that you're not ready to die, never fear,
nature will give you complete and adequate assistance when the time comes.

EDWARD ABBEY

Abbey, a former park ranger, helped found the environmental movement. This comes from *A Voice in the Wilderness*, a 1990 book that also contained this intriguing thought: "If my decomposing carcass helps nourish the roots of a juniper tree or the wings of a vulture—that is immortality enough for me."

If you want to be adored by your peers
and have standing ovations wherever you go—live to be over ninety.

GEORGE ABBOTT,
who died at age 107 in 1995

A few years before her death at age ninety-six in 2003, the legendary actress Katharine Hepburn expressed a similar sentiment: "If you survive long enough, you're revered—rather like an old building." The iconoclastic American journalist I. F. Stone—who died at age eighty-one in 1989—offered a related observation: "If you live long enough, the venerability factor creeps in; you get accused of things you never did and praised for virtues you never had."

If you can't recall it, forget it.

GOODMAN ACE, *describing this as*
"The secret formula for a carefree Old Age"

If I could write my epitaph, it would read:
Here lies Margaret Walker, Poet and Dreamer
She tried to make her life a Poem.

MARGARET WALKER ALEXANDER,
written when she was nineteen years old

If I were younger, I'd know more.

JAMES M. BARRIE

This line on the arrogance of youth is widely attributed to Barrie—the author of *Peter Pan*—but I've yet to find it in his works. In *The Admirable Crichton* (1918), Barrie has a character express the thought this way: "I'm not young enough to know everything."

If I had my life to live over again,
I would have talked less and listened more.

ERMA BOMBECK

These words appear in *Eat Less Cottage Cheese and More Ice Cream* (1979). In 1978, Bombeck was asked if she would change anything if she could live her life over again. She answered, "No." As she reflected on her answer, she changed her mind and included her new thinking in this delightful little book.

If in the last few years you haven't discarded a major opinion
or acquired a new one, check your pulse. You may be dead.

GELETT BURGESS

If you live to be one hundred, you've got it made.
Very few people die past that age.

GEORGE BURNS

If you continue to work and to absorb the beauty in the world around you, you will find that age does not necessarily mean getting old.

PABLO CASALS, *at age ninety-three*

If you're not a liberal when you're twenty-five, you have no heart. If you're not a conservative by the time you're thirty-five, you have no brain.

WINSTON CHURCHILL,
in a common misattribution

There is no evidence that Churchill ever said this, much less believed it. In fact, Churchill was a Conservative as a young man, a Liberal at age thirty-five, and a Conservative again in his later years. Very similar observations have been attributed to other luminaries, but none have ever been documented and verified. The original author of the sentiment appears to be the nineteenth-century French historian and statesman François Guizot, who said, "Not to be a republican at twenty is proof of want of heart; to be one at thirty is proof of want of head." In a 1933 address to students at the University of Hong Kong, George Bernard Shaw offered a related thought: "If you don't begin to be a revolutionist at the age of twenty, then at fifty you will be a most impossible old fossil."

If the soul has food for study and learning, nothing is more delightful than an old age of leisure.

CICERO *(1st century B.C.)*

If you want to stay young-looking, pick your parents very carefully.

DICK CLARK

Clark's youthful appearance in middle age—and later, in old age—along with his "hip" demeanor earned him the title of "America's oldest living teenager." Even though Clark was undoubtedly aided by surgical procedures, in this observation he humorously emphasizes the genetic component.

**If growing up is the process
of creating ideas and dreams about what life should be,
then maturity is letting them go again.**

MARY BETH DANIELSON

**If I had to live my life again, I would have made a rule
to read some poetry and listen to some music at least once every week;
for perhaps the parts of my brain now atrophied
would thus have been kept active through use.**

CHARLES DARWIN

After this sober hypothetical reflection Darwin added, "The loss of these tastes is a loss of happiness, and may possibly be injurious to the intellect, and more probably to the moral character, by enfeebling the emotional part of our nature." This remarkable passage comes from Darwin's autobiography, written in 1876, when he was seventy-seven years old. After writing, "My mind seems to have become a kind of machine for grinding general laws out of a large collection of facts," he confessed that his memory was so poor that he had never been able to remember a single date or line of poetry for more than a few days.

If you live long enough, you'll see that every victory turns into a defeat.

SIMONE DE BEAUVOIR,
in All Men Are Mortal *(1946)*

De Beauvoir had a half-century romantic and intellectual relationship with Jean-Paul Sartre. Over the years, the two thinkers heavily influenced each other, and this observation from de Beauvoir is very similar to a line that appeared a few years later in Sartre's 1949 play *The Devil and the Good Lord*: "If a victory is told in detail, one can no longer distinguish it from a defeat."

If you haven't been happy very young,
you can still be happy later on, but it's much harder.
You need more luck.

SIMONE DE BEAUVOIR

If God had to give a woman wrinkles,
he might at least have put them on the soles of her feet.

NINON DE LENCLOS, *said in 1665*

If I had my life story offered to me to film, I'd turn it down.

KIRK DOUGLAS

Douglas began this observation by saying, "Life is like a B-picture script." His point was that there is a big difference between what actually happens in life and what people look for in films. When we examine a person's life, there are clearly moments of great drama and excitement, but they are usually separated by lengthy—sometimes very lengthy—periods of dullness and lack of action. Alfred Hitchcock nicely communicated this idea when he once said, "Drama is life with the dull bits cut out."

If you live enough before thirty, you won't care to live at all after fifty.

FINLEY PETER DUNNE,
in a 1901 opinion from Mr. Dooley

If in youth we fell in love with beauty,
in maturity we can make friends with genius.

WILL DURANT

Durant offered this observation in his 1953 book *The Pleasures of Philosophy*. He introduced the subject by writing: "Each age, like every individual, has its own characteristic intoxication." And then he added, "If play is the effervescence of childhood, and love is the wine of youth, the solace of age is understanding."

If you want to look young and thin, hang around old fat people.

JIM EASON

If you don't want to get old, don't mellow.

LINDA ELLERBEE,
from her memoir Move On *(1991)*

**If we could be twice young and twice old,
we could correct all our mistakes.**

EURIPIDES *(5th century B.C.)*

If I were reincarnated, I'd want to come back a buzzard.

WILLIAM FAULKNER,
in a 1958 interview

Faulkner added: "Nothing hates him or envies him or wants him or needs him. He is never bothered or in danger, and he can eat anything." On the same subject, rock and roll legend Freddy Fender said, "I'm so damned unlucky, if I died and got reincarnated, I'd probably come back as myself."

If thou wouldst live long, live well; for folly and wickedness shorten life.

BENJAMIN FRANKLIN, *from*
Poor Richard's Almanack *(1739)*

**If you resolve to give up smoking, drinking, and loving,
you don't actually live longer; it just seems longer.**

CLEMENT FREUD

If wrinkles must be written upon our brows,
let them not be written upon the heart.
The spirit should not grow old.

JAMES A. GARFIELD

If the very old will remember, the very young will listen.

CHIEF DAN GEORGE

If one could recover the uncompromising spirit of one's youth,
one's greatest indignation would be for what one has become.

ANDRÉ GIDE

The gap between the dreams of youth and the realities of old age is generally an index of the joy or sorrow one feels in later years. Gide suggests here that a recollection of one's youthful spirit may spur an adult to indignation—and maybe even to some long-overdue changes. In his 1891 novel *The Little Minister*, James M. Barrie described it this way: "The life of every man is a diary in which he means to write one story, and writes another, and his humblest hour is when he compares the volume as it is with what he vowed to make it."

If youth is a fault, it is one which is soon corrected.

JOHANN WOLFGANG VON GOETHE,
from Proverbs in Prose *(1819)*

This is an early appearance of an idea that has enjoyed great popularity over the years. In an 1886 address at Harvard University, James Russell Lowell put it this way: "If youth be a defect, it is one that we outgrow only too soon."

If you're given a choice between money and sex appeal, take the money.
As you get older, the money will become your sex appeal.

KATHARINE HEPBURN

If I had my life to live over, I would try to make more mistakes. I would relax. I would be sillier than I have on this trip.

DON HEROLD

This appeared in "I'd Pick More Daisies," an article in an October 1953 issue of *Reader's Digest.* Herold, a sixty-four-year-old humorist, was reflecting on his life and offering thoughts "that may be of benefit to a coming generation." The essay included some succinct ifferisms:

If I had my life to live over, I'd pick more daisies.

And some more expansive ones:

If I had my life to live over, I would start barefooted
a little earlier in the spring and stay that way
a little later in the fall.
I would play hooky more. I would shoot more
paper wads at my teachers.
I would have more dogs. I would keep later hours.
I'd have more sweethearts.
I would fish more. I would go to more circuses.
I would go to more dances.
I would ride on more merry-go-rounds.
I would be carefree as long as I could,
or at least until I got some care—
instead of having my cares in advance.

Over the years, many of Herold's best lines were blatantly plagiarized. The essay also inspired many other writers; the title of Erma Bombeck's book, mentioned earlier, was likely inspired by Herold's resolve to "eat more ice cream and less spinach." I have an original copy of Herold's essay in my possession. If you would like to see it, go to the Ifferisms page on my Web site: www.DrMardy.com.

If you want to know how old a woman is, ask her sister-in-law.

EDGAR WATSON HOWE

Howe first achieved fame with his 1883 novel, *The Story of a Country Town*, often described as the first realistic portrayal of life in the recently settled Midwest. In the late 1800s and early 1900s, he was editor of the *Atchison Globe*, a small Kansas newspaper, and publisher of *E. W. Howe's Monthly*, a magazine with a tiny circulation. However, when his pithy observations and plain-spoken advice were reprinted in newspapers across America, he became something of a national celebrity. In two other memorable ifferisms, Howe wrote:

If a man dies and leaves his estate in an uncertain condition,
the lawyers become his heirs.

If you don't learn to laugh at trouble,
you won't have anything to laugh at when you're old.

If being a kid is about learning how to live,
then being a grown-up is about learning how to die.

STEPHEN KING

If you have achieved something in life, age doesn't scare you.

SOPHIA LOREN

If you associate enough with older people who do enjoy their lives,
who are not stored away in any golden ghettos,
you will gain a sense of continuity and of the possibility for a full life.

MARGARET MEAD

If, after I depart this vale, you ever remember me
and have thought to please my ghost,
forgive some sinner and wink your eye at some homely girl.

H. L. MENCKEN

Mencken called this his "Epitaph," but it was first printed in a 1921 issue of *The Smart Set*, when Mencken was forty-one. He lived for another thirty-five years.

If you want to go on working after you're sixty,
some degree of asceticism is inevitable.

MALCOLM MUGGERIDGE

If we want to be productive in our senior years, according to Muggeridge, we cannot live a life of excess, especially when it comes to eating and drinking. He also wrote, "When you reach your sixties, you have to decide whether you're going to be a sot or an ascetic." Asceticism is an ancient philosophical doctrine that advocates a life of austerity and self-denial. In its extreme forms, it involves the complete renunciation of worldly pleasures.

If you are young and you drink a great deal it will spoil your health,
slow your mind, make you fat—in other words, turn you into an adult.

P. J. O'ROURKE

This comes from *Modern Manners: An Etiquette Book for Rude People*, O'Rourke's 1994 spoof of etiquette guides. In a piece on "Alcohol and Young People," he continued with his tongue-in-cheek advice: "If you want to get one of those great red beefy, impressive-looking faces that politicians and corporation presidents have, you had better start drinking early and stick with it. Drinking will also give you a mature and authoritative-sounding voice, especially when combined over a long period of time with lots of cigarettes."

**If the young knew and the old could,
there is nothing that couldn't be done.**

ITALIAN PROVERB

It has long been observed that the old have the knowledge to make things happen, but not the energy; and the young the energy, but not the knowledge. This proverb imagines what would happen if the two groups had both. In a 1594 book, the French writer Henri Éstienne expressed the thought more succinctly: "If youth but knew; if old age could." An old French proverb put it this way: "If youth but had the knowledge and old age the strength."

If you wish to die young, make your physician your heir.

ROMANIAN PROVERB

**If I were to begin life again, I should want it as it was.
I would only open my eyes a little bit more.**

JULES RENARD

**If every day is an awakening, you will never grow old.
You will just keep growing.**

GAIL SHEEHY

If you're old, don't try to change yourself, change your environment.

B. F. SKINNER

If you carry your childhood with you, you never become older.

ABRAHAM SUTZKEVER

Sutzkever, a Polish poet who published his first poem in 1934, fought with the Polish partisans against the Nazis. After the war, he settled in Israel, where he became a popular Yiddish poet.

If I could be reincarnated as a fabric,
I would like to come back as a 38DD bra.

JESSE VENTURA,
in a 1999 Playboy *interview*

If we are the younger, we may envy the older.
If we are the older, we may feel that the younger is always being indulged.

JUDITH VIORST

This observation from Viorst's 1986 bestseller *Necessary Losses* is followed by the logical conclusion: "In other words, no matter what position we hold in family order of birth, we can prove beyond a doubt that we're being gypped."

7

If His IQ Slips Any Lower, We'll Have to Water Him Twice a Day

CRITICAL & INSULTING IFFERISMS

In 1970, twenty-six-year-old Molly Ivins began working as a political reporter for the *Texas Observer*, an alternative publication with a meager budget and a limited circulation. With a bachelor's degree from Smith College and a master's degree from the Columbia School of Journalism, she had hoped for a slightly better-paying job, but a reporter's position was a big step up from her recent stint at the *Houston Chronicle*, where she worked in such a low-level position that she often described herself as the paper's sewer editor. The new job was also compatible with her left-leaning political orientation—no small thing in conservative Texas.

At six feet tall and graced with striking red hair, Ivins cut quite a figure in and around the Texas state house. Within a short time, the feisty feminist and card-carrying member of the ACLU won over many of the good ol' boys in the legislature, became friends with future governor Ann Richards, and began to develop a reputation as a new and special kind of political journalist. After reading her columns (which included such lines as "Texas is a fine place for men and dogs, but hell on women and horses"), many Texans said her style was unlike anything they had ever seen. Ivins didn't merely "tell it like it is," she told it like it had never been told before.

In 1976, *The New York Times* offered Ivins a five-fold increase in salary and an opportunity to be a political reporter for the self-proclaimed "world's greatest newspaper." From the beginning, it was not a good fit. If the newspaper was the journalistic equivalent of a gray flannel suit, Ivins was a red satin dress with a feather boa. To further complicate matters, Ivins was no longer in her element—that soap-opera drama known as Texas politics. The irrepressible writer continued to write in her uniquely colorful way, only to be brutally edited again and again. In the first-draft of a column, she once described a man as having "a beer gut that belongs in the Smithsonian." Her staid editors at the paper changed it to "a man with a protuberant abdomen."

After struggling for a year in New York, Ivins asked for a transfer and soon found herself in Denver, where she worked for another three years as chief of the newspaper's Rocky Mountain bureau. In 1979, her tenure at the newspaper came to an end when she was abruptly terminated for writing a column in which she described a chicken-killing event as "a gang pluck."

In 1982, the managing editor of the now-defunct *Dallas Times Herald* made Ivins an offer she could not refuse. He suggested that she write a regular political column, work out of the capital city of Austin—home of the Texas legislature—and most important of all, he said she could write whatever she wanted. That pledge would be tested again and again in the next few years, as irate Dallas residents cancelled their subscriptions and local businesses refused to buy advertising space, all citing an Ivins column for their decision. It all came to a head when Ivins wrote a column in which she said about a Texas congressman:

If his IQ slips any lower, we'll have to water him twice a day.

It was a remarkable *conditional insult* and a wickedly witty suggestion that, at best, the congressman's intelligence was only a little higher than that of a plant. Even by Texas standards, which are notoriously low, it was a devastating characterization. There were howls of protest from the man's supporters, and even a few complaints from nonpartisans who felt it was a below-the-belt attack. How would the paper's bosses respond? Amazingly, they stood by their original promise to Ivins. They quickly launched an advertising campaign and, within weeks, commuters all around Dallas were driving by huge billboards that proclaimed, "Molly Ivins Can't Say That, Can She?" It turned out to be one of the most successful advertising slogans in journalism history. In 1992, Ivins borrowed the slogan and made it the title of her first book, which was on the *New York Times* best seller list for a full twelve months.

Conditional insults have become some of the most popular insults of modern times. Many point out a victim's lack of intelligence:

If brains were dynamite, he couldn't blow his nose.

If she had a brain, she'd be dangerous.

If he had another brain cell, it'd be lonely.

If brains were taxed, she'd get a rebate.

If he were any smarter, you could teach him to fetch.

Others have to do with an abundance of stupidity:

If stupidity were a crime, he'd be on the Ten Most Wanted list.

If stupidity were beauty, her face could launch a million ships.

If stupidity were painful, he'd be in agony.

If stupidity was an Olympic event, she'd win the Gold Medal.

If stupidity was a currency, he'd be the world's richest man.

Observers of pop culture have also slung their share of profane insults. In the 1970s, a music critic said of a popular singer from Down Under:

If white bread could sing, it would sound like Olivia Newton-John.

And in 1946, critic Robert Garland remarked about a production of a Chekhov play:

If you were to ask me what *Uncle Vanya* is about,
I would say about as much as I can take.

Sometimes, it's hard to know whether a conditional remark is a veiled insult or a spectacular compliment. In 1962, the little-known actor Peter O'Toole starred as T. E. Lawrence in the film *Lawrence of Arabia*. Director David Lean had offered the role to Albert Finney and Marlon Brando, but both turned him down. The two box office stars would later regret the decision, for it turned out to be the movie of the year, nominated for ten Academy Awards and winning seven, including Best Picture. O'Toole, who was nominated for Best Actor but didn't win, was visually stunning on the screen, especially when framed against the desert sand in his golden blond hair, his flowing white robe, and as one critic put it, "his staggeringly blue eyes." On screen, the young O'Toole was quite a sight. Handsome, yes, but in an androgynous way that made him look—if the word can be applied to a man—almost beautiful. But it took the witty Noël Coward to put it all into perspective when he remarked to O'Toole:

If you'd been any prettier, it would have been *Florence of Arabia*.

Some ifferistic insults have the good-humored quality that men use when, in their own perverse way, they express affection for one another. These forms of banter are especially common in sports, as when Los Angeles Dodgers manager Tommy Lasorda remarked on the foot speed of catcher Mike Scioscia:

If he raced his pregnant wife, he'd finish third.

Or when Oakland A's pitcher Dennis Lamp commented on the defensive skills of teammate Luis Polonia:

If you hit Polonia 100 fly balls,
you could make a movie out of it: *Catch–22*.

It's almost impossible to talk about insults without talking about retorts, and you may recall that one of history's best known *conditional insults* was also followed by one of history's most famous *conditional comebacks*. The story is well known, but it deserves retelling here. At a 1912 dinner party, the American-born English socialite Nancy Astor grew frustrated with a young and arrogant Winston Churchill. In a fit of anger, Lady Astor exclaimed to Churchill:

If you were my husband, I'd put poison in your coffee.

Churchill calmly replied:

If you were my wife, Nancy, I would drink it.

Churchill's clever quip, which is now enshrined in the Repartee Hall of Fame, also brings to mind one of the best things ever said about insults and how to deal with them. Writing in the mid-1900s, Russell Lynes, a popular columnist and the managing editor of *Harper's Magazine* wrote:

If you can't ignore an insult, top it; if you can't top it, laugh it off; and if you can't laugh it off, it's probably deserved.

I've been collecting cleverly phrased insults for many years, and have been delighted to discover that some of the best have been expressed ifferistically. Let's continue our look at them.

If Attila the Hun were alive today, he'd be a drama critic.

EDWARD ALBEE

If the soup had been as hot as the claret,
if the claret had been as old as the bird,
and if the bird's breasts had been as full as the waitress's,
it would have been a very good meal.

ANONYMOUS

This classic culinary critique, which goes back to the English taverns of a few centuries ago, strings together three *ifs* in a most interesting way.

If anything happens to Nixon,
the Secret Service have orders to shoot Agnew.

ANONYMOUS JOKE *during the Nixon administration about Vice President Spiro Agnew*

If not a great man, he is at least a great poster.

MARGOT ASQUITH,
on Lord Horatio Kitchener

Lady Asquith, wife of British prime minister H. H. Asquith, was noted for her barbed wit, and here she directs it at one of England's most recognizable figures. In 1914, England was plastered with what are now called the *Lord Kitchener Wants You* posters. The posters, part of a massive British

Army recruitment campaign, featured an image of the secretary of state for war, with his trademark moustache and piercing eyes, pointing his finger straight ahead. Just under Kitchener's image were the words *Wants You* (a later version had the words *Your Country Needs You*). The poster was so effective in England that it inspired a later American poster with an image of Uncle Sam and featuring the words *I Want You*.

If ever get my hands on that hag, I'll tear every hair out of her moustache!

TALLULAH BANKHEAD, *on Bette Davis*

If Ed Sullivan can be a TV legend, it tells you something about TV.

PETER BOYLE

If you can imagine a man having a vasectomy without anesthetic to the sound of frantic sitar-playing, you will have some idea of what popular Turkish music is like.

BILL BRYSON

If you stay in California, you lose one point of IQ every year.

TRUMAN CAPOTE

If Hitler invaded hell, I would make at least a favorable reference to the devil in the House of Commons.

WINSTON CHURCHILL

Churchill, who made this remark in 1941, was justifying his willingness to cooperate with a sworn enemy, the Soviet Union, if it would help him achieve a more important goal, defeating Hitler and the Nazi menace.

If life were fair, Dan Quayle would be making a living asking, "Do you want fries with that?"

JOHN CLEESE

J. Danforth Quayle was a little-known senator from Indiana when George H. W. Bush selected him as his vice presidential running mate in 1988. During his single term, Quayle was one of the most ridiculed politicians of all time, routinely described as an "empty suit" or a vacuous airhead. Much of the criticism seemed warranted, as Quayle routinely made verbal gaffes and offered up such head-scratching pronouncements as "If we don't succeed, we run the risk of failure." *Washington Post* critic Tom Shales also offered a stinging comment: "If a tree fell in the forest, and no one was there to hear it, it might sound like Dan Quayle looks."

If a literary man puts together two words about music, one of them will be wrong.

AARON COPLAND

If Democrats Had Any Brains, They'd Be Republicans.

ANN COULTER, *title of 2007 book*

Coulter's provocatively titled book was soon followed by a "response" book from Jon L. Fisher: *If Republicans Had Any Hearts, They'd Be Democrats.*

If I had a third hand, I wouldn't need you at all.

MICHAEL DEBAKEY,
to surgical assistants who failed to perform to his exacting standards

If it must be Thomas, let it be Mann,
and if it must be Wolfe, let it be Nero,
but never let it be Thomas Wolfe.

PETER DE VRIES

**If it were thought that anything I wrote was influenced by Robert Frost,
I would take that particular work of mine, shred it,
and flush it down the toilet, hoping not to clog the pipes.**

JAMES DICKEY

After an early career as an advertising copywriter, Dickey turned to his early love, poetry. He went on to author more than twenty volumes of poetry and received numerous awards, including the National Book Award in 1966. Despite his reputation as a poet, he is remembered primarily for the best-selling novel *Deliverance* (1970), which was adapted into one of the most popular films of 1972.

**If a traveler were informed that such a man
was Leader of the House of Commons, he may well begin
to comprehend how the Egyptians came to worship an insect.**

BENJAMIN DISRAELI, *on Lord John Russell*

**If Mr. Gladstone fell into the Thames, that would be a misfortune;
if anyone pulled him out, that would be a calamity.**

BENJAMIN DISRAELI

Disraeli offered this remark when asked to describe the difference between a misfortune and a calamity. For several decades in the nineteenth century, English politics was dominated by political clashes between Disraeli and his chief adversary, William E. Gladstone. In his private life, Gladstone was emotionally distant, leading his wife Catherine to famously say to him, "If you weren't such a great man, you'd be a terrible bore."

If brains was lard, that boy wouldn't have enough to grease a skillet.

BUDDY EBSEN, *as Jed Clampett, describing
Jethro in a 1962 episode of* The Beverly Hillbillies

If that's the world's smartest man, God help us.

LUCILLE FEYNMAN, *on her son Richard*

Mrs. Feynman offered this affectionate insult shortly after *Omni* magazine described her son, the 1965 Nobel laureate in physics, as "the world's smartest man." Feynman, one of America's most influential physicists, was also a free-spirited eccentric who juggled, played the bongos, experimented with mind-altering drugs, and enjoyed playing pranks on people. When a reporter once asked Feynman for a simple explanation of his work, the physicist replied, "If I could explain it in three minutes, it wouldn't be worth the Nobel Prize."

**If you're going to have a plane crash in Cleveland,
it's better to have one on the way in than on the way out.**

PETER GAMMONS

If you say "Hiya Clark, how are you?" he's stuck for an answer.

AVA GARDNER, *on Clark Gable*

Gardner's comment speaks to a lack of intelligence, but it's not the worst thing ever said about the iconic star of the 1939 film classic *Gone With the Wind*. According to legend, Gable wasn't exactly well-endowed, leading Carole Lombard (his third wife) to make a devastating observation on the subject: "If Clark had one inch less, he'd be the Queen—not the King—of Hollywood."

If he were any dumber, he'd be a tree.

BARRY GOLDWATER,
on Senator William Scott

If they made a movie of President Bush's administration, it would be called *Honey, I Shrunk the Economy.*

AL GORE

Vice presidential candidate Gore said this about President George H. W. Bush during the 1992 presidential election. He added: "Or considering what he's done to the economy, we would call it *The Terminator.*"

If we are going to teach "creation science" as an alternative to evolution, then we should also teach the stork theory as an alternative to biological reproduction.

JUDITH HAYES

If ignorance ever goes to $40 a barrel, I want drilling rights on George Bush's head.

JIM HIGHTOWER,
on George H. W. Bush, in 1988, when oil was less than twenty dollars a barrel

If we practiced medicine like we practice education, we'd look for the liver on the right side and left side in alternate years.

ALFRED KAZIN,
on cyclical trends in education

If the NBA were on Channel Five and a bunch of frogs making love was on Channel Four, I'd watch the frogs even if they were coming in fuzzy.

BOBBY KNIGHT

If you cut a thing up, of course it will smell. Hence, nothing raises such an infernal stink, at last, as human psychology.

D. H. LAWRENCE

This comes from Lawrence's 1925 novella, *St. Mawr*. It was the concluding line to a passage about the stench that ultimately comes from taking a morbid interest in other people.

If poetry is like an orgasm, an academic can be likened to someone who studies the passion-stains on the bedsheets.

IRVING LAYTON

If McClellan is not using the army, I should like to borrow it for a while.

ABRAHAM LINCOLN

Lincoln made this remark in 1862 after growing frustrated over General George McClellan's failure to aggressively prosecute the war against Confederate troops. Two years after Lincoln removed McClellan as commander of the Army of the Potomac, the two men faced each other in the 1864 presidential election. McClellan lost the election, but ultimately went on to become governor of New Jersey in 1878.

If I ever write a part for a cigar store Indian, she'll get it.

ANITA LOOS, *on actress Louise Brooks*

If a man is not talented enough to be a novelist,
not smart enough to be a lawyer,
and his hands are too shaky to perform operations,
he becomes a journalist.

NORMAN MAILER

If you're in the peanut business, you learn to think small.

EUGENE MCCARTHY, *on Jimmy Carter,*
a peanut farmer before becoming president

**If he had been sent to check out Bluebeard's castle,
he would have come back with a glowing report
about the admirable condition of the cutlery.**

MARY MCGRORY, *on Attorney General Ed Meese's investigation of the "Iran–Contra" affair in 1987*

**If he became convinced tomorrow that coming out for cannibalism
would get him the votes he so sorely needs,
he would begin fattening a missionary
in the White House backyard come Wednesday.**

H. L. MENCKEN, *on Franklin D. Roosevelt*

**If Los Angeles is not the one authentic rectum of civilization,
then I am no anatomist.**

H. L. MENCKEN, *in a 1927 remark to F. Scott Fitzgerald and wife Zelda*

The American daredevil motorcyclist Evel Knievel used a similar anatomical reference in a remark about residents of another famous American city: "If God ever gives this world an enema, he'll stick the tube in the Lincoln Tunnel and he'll flush everybody in New York City clear across the Atlantic."

**If I saw Mr. Haughey buried at midnight at a crossroads,
with a stake driven through his heart—politically speaking—
I should continue to wear a clove of garlic round my neck, just in case.**

CONOR CRUISE O'BRIEN, *on Charles J. Haughey, an Irish politician known for his treachery.*

If George Bush reminds many women of their first husbands,
Pat Buchanan reminds women
why an increasing number of them are staying single.

JUDY PEARSON

Pearson piggybacks here on a popular line that surfaced in the 1988 presidential campaign: "George Bush reminds every woman of her first husband."

If a swamp alligator could talk, it would sound like Tennessee Williams.

REX REED

If there's one thing I admire about you more than any other,
it's your original discovery of the Ten Commandments.

THOMAS REED, *to Theodore Roosevelt*

If he'd been making shell cases during the war
it might have been better for music.

CHARLES-CAMILLE SAINT-SAËNS,
on Maurice Ravel

If there was one thing worse
than being married to a ruthless, unsuccessful poet,
it was being married to a ruthless, successful poet.

CHRISTOPHER RICKS, *on Robert Frost*

If the English can survive their food, they can survive anything.

GEORGE BERNARD SHAW

If you will only take the precaution to go in long enough after it commences and to come out long enough before it is over, you will not find it wearisome.

GEORGE BERNARD SHAW, *in an 1891*
review of Charles Gounod's Redemption

If I had my choice, I would kill every reporter in the world, but I am sure we would be getting reports from Hell before breakfast.

WILLIAM TECUMSEH SHERMAN

If Heaven had looked upon riches to be a valuable thing, it would not have given them to such a scoundrel.

JONATHAN SWIFT, *on John Barber*

Swift wrote this about his publisher in a 1720 letter. It was the first appearance of a sentiment that was picked up by Alexander Pope, who wrote in a 1727 book: "We may see the small value God has for riches, by the people he gives them to." Both observations morphed into a popular modern quotation that is often attributed to Dorothy Parker but was actually authored by the English journalist Maurice Baring: "If you would know what the Lord God thinks of money, you have only to look at those to whom he gives it." Parker herself attributed the observation to Baring in a 1958 *Paris Review* interview.

If a lump of soot falls into the soup, and you cannot conveniently get it out, stir it well in, and it will give the soup a French taste.

JONATHAN SWIFT

If Bret Harte ever repaid a loan, the incident failed to pass into history.

MARK TWAIN

If God were a writer and wrote a book that Randall did not think was good, Randall would not have hesitated to give it a bad review. And if God complained, Randall would then set about showing God what was wrong with his sentences.

ROBERT WATSON,
on English critic Randall Jarrell

If builders built buildings the way programmers wrote programs, then the first woodpecker that came along would destroy civilization.

HARRY WEINBERGER

If your job is to leaven ordinary lives with elevating spectacle, be elevating or be gone.

GEORGE F. WILL,
on the British royal family, in 1992

8

If the World Were a Logical Place, Men Would Ride Side-Saddle

GENDER DYNAMICS

In 1990, a Georgetown University linguistics professor named Deborah Tannen moved from relative obscurity to national celebrity when her book on male-female communication shot to the top of the *New York Times* best seller list (it remained on the list for the next four years, eight months in the number one position). Titled *You Just Don't Understand*, the book examined the critical role that gender plays in communication. In one oft-quoted passage, Tannen wrote:

**If women are often frustrated because
men do not respond to their troubles by offering matching troubles,
men are often frustrated because women do.**

When I first came upon this observation, it struck me as just another example of a familiar theme in the gender wars—women becoming frustrated with men who don't talk, and men getting frustrated with women who do.

And while that may be true, Tannen went on to offer a fuller and richer explanation.

In Tannen's view, men and women approach communication in different ways. Women, she says, are more likely to view conversation as a way to establish a connection (she calls it *rapport-talk*). Consequently, when a woman reveals a problem to a man, she likes it if he says, "You know, a similar thing happened to me." According to Tannen, a woman will view such problem sharing as an attempt to show empathy and make a parallel connection. If the man just listens—respectfully, from his point of view—and says nothing at all in response, the woman may find it frustrating and annoying.

Men, in Tannen's view, are more likely to view conversation as a way to impart knowledge or convey information (she calls it *report-talk*). When a man reveals a problem to a woman and she says, "You know, a similar thing happened to me," he may regard it as an attempt to shift the focus from him to her, and possibly even view it as an attempt to compete with him in some way.

Men and women not only approach the same conversation with different motives, according to Tannen, they often walk away from those conversations with different interpretations about what happened. Tannen's book captures some of these gender differences in a series of intriguing ifferisms:

If women and men talk equally in a group,
people think the women talked more.

If men see life in terms of contest,
a struggle against nature and other men,
for women life is a struggle against
the danger of being cut off from their community.

If women resent men's tendency to offer solutions to problems,
men complain about women's refusal to take action
to solve the problems they complain about.

The notion that men and women are different—and that these differences are the source of important problems—has been much discussed over the centuries. A little over three centuries ago, English writer Mary Astell was creating quite a stir in London for arguing that it was morally wrong and socially unproductive to funnel all women into the narrow life options of wife and mother. In 1694, she outlined her ideas for the education of women in a pamphlet titled *A Serious Proposal to the Ladies for the Advancement of Their True and Greatest Interest*. For her pioneering efforts, she is often described as "the first English feminist."

In *Reflections on Marriage*, published in 1700, Astell offered a number of other provocative thoughts, including the notions that men choose women for their superficial beauty and that women too easily submit to arbitrary authority on the part of men. The book also contained Astell's most famous observation:

If all men are born free, how is it that all women are born slaves?

While the topic of gender dynamics has been explored in serious ways by thoughtful people, it has also been explored in humorous ways by witty people whose names we'll never know. Some have been offered by women:

If you catch a man, throw him back.

If it has tires or testicles, you're going to have trouble with it.

If they can put one man on the moon, why can't they put them all there?

And some by men:

**If a man says something in a forest,
and there's no woman around to hear him, is he still wrong?**

This last observation reflects the common male belief that women—especially wives—tend to be hypercritical of men. It is based on a famous sentiment attributed to the eighteenth-century English theologian Bishop George Berkeley: "If a tree falls in a forest and no one is there to hear it, does it make a sound?" Even though Berkeley never expressed the thought in exactly this way, he did believe that things had to be perceived by someone in order to exist.

In the remainder of the chapter, I will present more conditional, counterfactual, and hypothetical quotations on the theme of gender dynamics. You'll find a wide-ranging series of remarks that men and women have made about each other, some intriguing contributions from members of the gay community, and a host of other observations about the age-old battle of the sexes.

If a stranger taps you on the ass and says,
"How's the little lady today!" you will probably cringe.
But if he's an American, he's only being friendly.

MARGARET ATWOOD, *Canadian writer, on American men, in a 1977 interview*

If you go out with a girl and they say she has a great personality, she's ugly.
If they tell you a guy works hard, he's got no skills.

CHARLES BARKLEY

If a woman has to choose between catching a fly ball
and saving an infant's life, she will choose to save the infant's life
without even considering if there are men on base.

DAVE BARRY

If all women's faces were cast in the same mold,
that mold would be the grave of love.

MARIE FRANÇOIS XAVIER BICHAT

Bichat is a man, by the way, and the point of his observation is that if women all looked alike, men would not desire them. Bichat, a eighteenth-century French anatomist and physiologist, is regarded as the father of modern pathology.

If a woman gets nervous, she'll eat or go shopping.
A man will attack a country—it's a whole other way of thinking.

ELAYNE BOOSLER

This is a humorous adaptation of an old theme—that men are warlike, and women are not. The notion shows up in a popular saying ("If women ruled the world, there'd be no more wars") that has been much-parodied over the years:

If women ruled the world . . .

. . . PMS would be a legitimate defense in court.

. . . shopping would be considered an aerobic activity.

. . . men would bring drinks, chips, and dip to women watching soap operas.

. . . men would pay as much attention to their women as to their cars.

. . . men would not eat gas-producing foods within two hours of bedtime.

. . . singles bars would have metal detectors to detect hidden wedding rings.

If the world were a logical place, men would ride side-saddle.

RITA MAE BROWN

**If Michelangelo had been a heterosexual,
the Sistine Chapel would have been painted basic white and with a roller.**

RITA MAE BROWN

Was Michelangelo gay? Many people think so, and it is true that he was accused of sodomy in his lifetime, a charge he denied. He also wrote some passionate and suggestive letters to men, notably to Tommaso de Cavalieri, who was at the artist's bedside when he died. The great Renaissance artist was also the subject of an intriguing hypothetical question from Cher: "If Michelangelo painted in Caesar's Palace, would that make it any less art?"

**If you want to say it with flowers,
remember that a single rose screams in your face, "I'm cheap!"**

DELTA BURKE

**If you fall asleep on the couch in a house where a woman is present,
there will be a blanket or a coat covering you when you awaken.**

GEORGE CARLIN

If you wish women to love you, be original.

ANTON CHEKHOV

This insight into male-female relationships comes from Chekhov's private *Note-Book*, first published in America in 1921. Chekhov added: "I know a man who used to wear felt boots in summer and winter, and women fell in love with him."

**If men were as unselfish as women,
women would very soon become more selfish than men.**

J. CHURTON COLLINS

Collins, an English critic in the late 1800s, lived in an era when women subjugated their lives to men, appearing on the surface to be selfless or unselfish. If the roles of men and women were reversed, he is suggesting that women would become even more selfish than men are under the current arrangement.

**If a man is vain, flatter. If timid, flatter. If boastful, flatter.
In all history, too much flattery never lost a gentleman.**

KATHRYN CRAVENS

If I were asked to describe the difference between the sexes in the gay world, I would say that the men wanted to be amused; the girls sought vindication.

QUENTIN CRISP

Crisp was one of the most flamboyant members of London's gay community. He once piggybacked on the famous line about "the stately homes of England" to observe, "I am one of the stately homos of England."

**If people are worried about unfair advancement,
they should look at the sons-in-law of the world running companies.
They've truly slept their way to the top.**

MARY E. CUNNINGHAM

If God is male, then male is God.

MARY DALY, *American feminist theologian,*
in Beyond God the Father *(1973)*

**If men can run the world, why can't they stop wearing neckties?
How intelligent is it to start the day by tying a little noose around the neck?**

LINDA ELLERBEE

**If men and women are to understand each other,
to enter into each other's nature with mutual sympathy,**

and to become capable of genuine comradeship,
the foundation must be laid in youth.

HAVELOCK ELLIS

If talking were aerobic, I'd be the thinnest person in the world.

CARRIE FISHER

Many women bristle when they hear the observation that "woman talk more than men." But not Fisher, who doesn't merely accept the generalization, she embraces it.

If women were in charge,
all men's underwear would come with an expiration date.

DIANE FORD

If the heart of a man is depressed with cares,
The mist is dispelled when a woman appears.

JOHN GAY, *in* The Beggar's Opera *(1728)*

If high heels were so wonderful, men would be wearing them.

SUE GRAFTON

The words come from Kinsey Millhone, the protagonist in *"I" Is for Innocent*, the ninth novel in Grafton's "alphabet series" of mysteries. In the fictional world created by Grafton, Kinsey was forced to live with a maternal aunt at age five, after both parents died in a car accident. Growing up, she hung out with the boys in high school and learned from her aunt how to shoot a gun. She became a police officer after high school, and then a private investigator.

If they ever invent a vibrator that can open pickle jars, we've had it.

JEFF GREEN

The underlying notion—that men are becoming increasingly unnecessary to women—emerged in a saying from the early years of the women's movement: "If somebody invents a vibrator that can mow the lawn, men will be history."

If any human being is to reach full maturity, both the masculine and feminine sides of the personality must be brought up into consciousness.

M. ESTHER HARDING

If a man hears much that a woman says, then she is not beautiful.

HENRY S. HASKINS

That is, if a woman is beautiful, a man will be so focused on her looks that he will not hear anything she says. The English writer Peter York put it this way: "If beauty isn't genius it usually signals at least a high level of animal cunning."

If I had learned to type, I never would have made brigadier general.

ELIZABETH HOISINGTON,
in 1970, after being promoted to rank of U.S. Army brigadier general

If she is homely, the doors of opportunity are firmly closed against her.

MARTHA EVERTS HOLDEN

This remarkable line about the role of beauty in a woman's career was written in 1894, in response to a small-town girl who had asked for advice about moving to the city. Holden, who believed that "a great city is a cruel place for young lives," said she wanted to cry out, "Stay where you are," but instead wrote a bleak reply discouraging such a decision. The prospects for an attractive girl were not much better, according to Holden, who added: "And if she is pretty she will have to carry herself like snow on high hills to avoid contamination."

If men knew all that women think,
they would be twenty times more daring.

ALPHONSE KARR

The suggestion here is that men mistakenly think women are more innocent and diffident than they really are. Karr, by the way, is the author of one of history's most famous sayings: "The more things change, the more they remain the same."

If men could get pregnant, abortion would be a sacrament.

FLORYNCE KENNEDY

While this quotation is almost always attributed to Kennedy, a colorful and outspoken attorney in the early years of the feminist movement, she said she heard it from an elderly female cabdriver in Boston in the 1960s. Anna Quindlen, in *Living Out Loud* (1988), offered a related thought: "If men got pregnant, there would be safe, reliable methods of birth control. They'd be inexpensive, too."

If I had to wear high heels and a dress, I would be a mental case.

K.D. LANG

If a woman hasn't got a tiny streak of harlot in her, she's a dry stick as a rule.

D. H. LAWRENCE, *from the 1929 essay "Pornography and Obscenity"*

If you removed all of the homosexuals and homosexual influence from what is generally regarded as American culture, you would pretty much be left with "Let's Make a Deal."

FRAN LEBOWITZ, *on the importance of a "gay sensibility" in American culture*

If man is only a little lower than the angels, the angels should reform.

MARY WILSON LITTLE

In this observation, Little uses the biblical passage that God made man "a little lower than the angels" (Psalms 8:5) as a springboard to suggest that men, in general, are not even close to being angelic.

If it can't be fixed by duct tape or WD-40, it's a female problem.

JASON LOVE

If I fail, no one will say, "She doesn't have what it takes." They will say, "Women don't have what it takes."

CLARE BOOTHE LUCE

Luce began this observation by saying, "Because I am a woman, I must make unusual efforts to succeed." After she was elected to Congress, Luce responded to the sexist view that women should stay home and raise children by saying, "If God wanted us to think with our wombs, why did He give us a brain?"

If you were on a sinking ship and yelled, "Women and children first!" how much feminist opposition do you think you'd get?

BILL MAHER

In a rant on "convenient feminism," Maher went on to say, "Women want to fight men for equal pay, but how often do they fight a man for the check?" And then he added, "Any man who questions a woman's physical capabilities gets branded a sexist; but who do they call when there's a spider to be killed?"

If American men are obsessed with money,
American women are obsessed with weight.

MARYA MANNES

This appeared in *More in Anger* (1958), where Mannes added: "The men talk of gain, the women talk of loss, and I do not know which talk is the more boring."

If women dressed for men,
the stores wouldn't sell much—just an occasional sun visor.

GROUCHO MARX

Here Marx puts a new spin on an old saying. If women truly did dress for men, he suggests, they'd wear no clothing at all.

If a woman chooses to look sexy, that is her right.
If a man chooses to misinterpret her signal, that's his problem.

SUZY MENKES

Biologically speaking,
if something bites you it is more likely to be female.

DESMOND MORRIS

If a man and woman, entering a room together, close the door behind them,
the man will come out sadder and the woman wiser.

H. L. MENCKEN

For most of his life, Mencken was a major league misogamist (marriage hater) and a minor league misogynist (woman hater). Nowadays, people might be inclined to say just the reverse—that men will come out wiser and women sadder.

If men liked shopping, they'd call it research.

CYNTHIA NELMS

If a woman does possess masculine virtues, we want to run away from her; and if she does not possess masculine virtues, then she runs away.

FRIEDRICH NIETZSCHE

If women didn't exist, all the money in the world would have no meaning.

ARISTOTLE ONASSIS

If I hadn't been a woman, I'd have been a drag queen.

DOLLY PARTON

If every woman in the world was weeping her heart out, men would be found dining, feeding, feasting.

ARTHUR WING PINERO

The suggestion here is that men want nothing to do with women who are going through difficult times. It's a commentary on the shallowness of men, and their tendency to flee from unhappy women for more pleasurable activities.

If women are expected to do the same work as men, we must teach them the same things.

PLATO

If a woman has any malicious mischief to do, her memory is immortal.

TITUS MACCIUS PLAUTUS

If a man mulls over a decision, they say, "He's weighing the options."
If a woman does it, they say, "She can't make up her mind."

BARBARA PROCTOR

If I ever claim sexual harassment,
I will be confronted with every bozo I once dated,
every woman I once impressed as snotty and superior,
and together they will provide a convenient excuse to disbelieve me.

ANNA QUINDLEN, *written in 1991, during the Clarence Thomas–Anita Hill controversy*

If women must insist on having men's privileges,
they have to take men's chances.

WILL ROGERS, *said in 1925*

If you never want to see a man again, just tell him,
"I love you. I want to marry you. I want to have your children."
They leave skid marks.

RITA RUDNER

There are two separate meanings of the term *skid marks*, and both of them apply. If you don't know what they mean, ask a friend who is familiar with American idioms. If you don't have such a friend, do a Google search.

If a woman drinks the last glass of apple juice in the refrigerator,
she'll make more apple juice.
If a man drinks the last glass of apple juice,
he'll just put back the empty container.

RITA RUDNER

If you quit, you'll never get a phone call from a beautiful woman again. The secret of your attraction is your proximity to power.

WILLIAM SAFIRE, *to Henry Kissinger*

Safire said this to Kissinger after he had threatened to resign as President Nixon's national security advisor in 1971. Kissinger fancied himself as a ladies' man and was often seen with a beautiful woman on his arm. (It was also about this time that he made his famous observation: "Power is the ultimate aphrodisiac.") Safire made the remark in jest, but it seemed to get Kissinger's attention. He thought for a moment before replying, "That would be quite a sacrifice."

If a woman has her Ph.D. in physics, has mastered in quantum theory, plays flawless Chopin, was once a cheerleader, and is now married to a man who plays baseball, she will forever be "Former Cheerleader married to Star Athlete."

MARYANNE ELLSON SIMMONS, *wife of major league baseball player Ted Simmons*

If a man lies to you, don't get mad, get even.

LIVIA SQUIRES

Squires, an American stand-up comic, concluded her observation by adding: "I once dated a guy who waited three months into our relationship before he told me he was married. I said, 'Hey, don't worry about it; I used to be a man.' "

If they're attractive, they're presumed to have slept their way to the top. If they're unattractive, they are presumed to have chosen a profession because they could not get a man.

GLORIA STEINEM,
on women's "double whammy," first reported in Ms. *magazine, 1979*

If men had more up top, we'd need less up front.

JACI STEPHEN

In this quip, the popular British television critic cleverly suggests that if men were more intelligent, they'd be less focused on women's breasts.

If you talk about yourself, he'll think you're boring. If you talk about others, he'll think you're a gossip. If you talk about him, he'll think you're a brilliant conversationalist.

LINDA SUNSHINE

If you want something said, ask a man. If you want something done, ask a woman.

MARGARET THATCHER, *in a 1965 speech*

Bette Davis offered an earlier version of this sentiment when she famously observed: "If you want a thing done well, get a couple of old broads to do it."

If I were a woman, I would never trust men who say they are feminists.

DAVID THOMAS

Thomas, a contemporary British journalist, added: "Either they are acting out of guilt, trying to establish credentials, or they think they might be able to pick up more girls. If I were a woman, I would say, go away and have your first period. Then come back and tell me you are a feminist."

If you put a woman in a man's position, she will be more efficient, but no more kind.

FAY WELDON, *challenging a common stereotype*

If there hadn't been women we'd still be squatting in a cave eating raw meat, because we made civilization in order to impress our girl friends.

ORSON WELLES, *in a 1970 interview with David Frost*

The civilizing influence of women on men is a common theme. In a 1983 speech, Ronald Reagan said, "If it wasn't for women, us men would still be walking around in skin suits carrying clubs." More recently, the comedian Sinbad observed, "If there were no women in the world, men would be naked, driving in trucks, living in dirt. Women came along and gave us a reason to comb our hair." These observations, however, all come from men. In *Sexual Personae* (1990), the provocative Camille Paglia offered her perspective: "If civilization had been left in female hands, we would still be living in grass huts."

If I were shabby, no one would have me; a woman is asked out as much for her clothes as for herself.

EDITH WHARTON

If you can make a woman laugh, you can do anything with her.

NICOL WILLIAMSON

Williamson, the popular Scottish actor, here puts a new twist on an old saying (Arthur Bullard's 1913 novel *The Barbary Coast* contains this passage: "An old proverb says that if you can make a woman laugh, your point is won"). More recently, Bette Milder corroborated the validity of the notion: "If somebody makes me laugh, I'm his slave for life."

9

If You Want to Have a Friend, Be a Friend

HUMAN RELATIONSHIPS

On June 19, 1623, Blaise Pascal was born in a small French village about 260 miles south of Paris. His mother died when he was three years old and his father, a local judge and counselor to Louis XIII, took on the job of caring for and educating his son and two daughters. While all of the children showed early intellectual promise, young Blaise was so precocious that it quickly became apparent that he needed more help than his father could provide.

In 1631, when Pascal was eight years old, the family moved to Paris to find a more fertile educational environment for the young prodigy. In the next few years, the boy flourished. As a young teen, he wrote a treatise on geometry that was so original it aroused the interest of the philosopher and mathematical genius, René Descartes. As Pascal matured, he went on to make fundamental contributions in mathematics, physics, religion, and philosophy. He was a penetrating observer of the human condition as well as a master of French prose. He also penned some of history's most famous ifferisms:

**If you want people to think well of you,
do not speak well of yourself.**

**If a laborer were to dream
for twelve hours every night that he was a king,
I believe he would be almost as happy as
a king who should dream for twelve hours every night
that he was a laborer.**

**If all men knew what others say of them,
there would not be four friends in the world.**

The point of this last observation is that people say things *about* us that they would never dream of saying directly *to* us. Almost three centuries later, Bertrand Russell extended the notion to the things people *think* about us:

**If we were all given by magic the power to read each other's thoughts,
I suppose the first effect would be to dissolve all friendships.**

And more recently, the comedian George Carlin updated the sentiment:

**If everybody knew the truth about everybody else's thoughts,
there'd be way more murders.**

All these observations are based on an important dynamic in human relationships—we believe our friends are honest with us, and our friends believe that we are honest with them. But it is also true that people often harbor unflattering thoughts about their friends, thoughts they prefer to keep to themselves but that they divulge to other people. If we knew what our friends were thinking and sometimes saying about us, would we still consider them friends? It's a hypothetical idea worth thinking about.

Human relationships are so deeply fascinating that observations about them have been offered by all great thinkers and writers. Agatha Christie is best known for her legendary detective stories, such as *Murder on the Orient Express*, and the unforgettable characters Hercule Poirot and Miss Marple. She also wrote seventeen plays, including *The Mousetrap* (1952), which holds the distinction of being the longest-running play in theatrical history. In her 1957 play *Towards Zero*, a character says:

If one sticks too rigidly to one's principles, one would hardly see anybody.

If you are perceived as rigid and inflexible, according to this observation, your relationships will suffer and you will see the number of your friendships dwindle. It's an age-old theme. In the nineteenth century, the French writer Jules Renard offered a related version:

If you are afraid of being lonely, don't try to be right.

Also writing in the nineteenth century, the humorist Josh Billings (the pen name of American writer Henry Wheeler Shaw) continued the theme:

If a man was completely virtuous,
I doubt whether he would be happy, he would be so lonesome.

The point of this observation is that in a world of flawed people, completely virtuous individuals would be bizarre oddities who would likely be shunned by their fellow human beings. Mark Twain was making the same point when he once wrote, "Be good and you will be lonesome."

So far, we've looked at observations that explore a common theme in human interaction—*connecting with* as opposed to being *alienated from* others. Another powerful theme has to do with the challenge of understanding people who are different from us. The psychoanalyst Carl Jung expressed the problem well:

If one does not understand a person, one tends to regard him as a fool.

And when it comes to understanding people, it helps if we understand ourselves, as Nikki Giovanni said in a 1971 conversation with James Baldwin:

If you don't understand yourself, you don't understand anybody else.

The concept of understanding other people is a powerful idea when it comes to forging strong relationships with friends, and an absolute necessity if we are to deal effectively with enemies. Over the centuries, the idea has been expressed in many different ways, but the underlying principle is always the same: If you fail to understand your enemies, you will likely fail in a war against them.

Failure to understand the enemy was a critical blunder made by George III in England's eighteenth-century struggle with American colonists, a crucial factor in America's costly struggle in Vietnam, and a serious question to ponder in the contemporary struggle that is known as the *War on Terror*. The Chinese sage Sun Tzu was the first to fully explore the idea, and he did it masterfully in his sixth-century B.C. classic, *The Art of War*:

If you know the enemy and know yourself,
you need not fear the result of a hundred battles.
If you know yourself but not the enemy,
for every victory gained you will also suffer a defeat.
If you know neither the enemy nor yourself,
you will succumb in every battle.

In his 1908 book of essays *All Things Considered*, G. K. Chesterton weighed in on the subject in a most interesting way:

If you do not understand a man you cannot crush him.
And if you do understand him, very probably you will not.

In the first part of the observation, Chesterton makes the familiar argument that we need to understand our enemies in order to defeat them. But then he surprises us by saying that the same capacity for understanding an enemy also allows us to become merciful toward them. He explained himself this way: "For the power which makes a man able to entertain a good impulse is the same as that which enables him to make a good gun; it is imagination. It is imagination that makes a man outwit his enemy, and it is imagination that makes him spare his enemy."

For many centuries, people have been reflecting on the ways in which human beings interact, and much of the speculation has been expressed conditionally. In the remainder of the chapter, let's take a look at some of the best examples of this kind of thinking.

If you cannot make yourself be as you would like to be,
how can you expect another person to be entirely to your liking?

THOMAS À KEMPIS, *in his classic*
The Imitation of Christ *(c. 1418)*

If you are committed to a relationship,
you must stick with it through thick and thin.

WALLY AMOS, *aka "Famous Amos"*

Amos, a former William Morris talent agent who formed the Famous Amos Chocolate Chip Cookie Company, said this in his 1996 book, *Watermelon Magic*. He added, "Instead of looking for ways to get out, look for ways to work it out."

If I am not good to myself, how can I expect anyone else to be good to me?

MAYA ANGELOU

If you're treated a certain way you become a certain kind of person.

JAMES BALDWIN

Baldwin said this to Nikki Giovanni in a 1971 conversation. He added: "If certain things are described to you as being real, they're real for you whether they're real or not."

If you want to get to know someone better,
you shouldn't take them out for a candlelit dinner,
you should watch them at work.
When they're full of concentration, only not concentrating on you.

JULIAN BARNES

If you have it, you don't need to have anything else;
and if you don't have it, it doesn't much matter what else you have.

J. M. BARRIE, *on charm,*
in his 1908 play What Every Woman Knows

If you have done a little wrong to your neighbor, let it seem to you large;
if you have done him a big kindness, let it seem to you small.

JUDAH BEN TEMA

Ben Tema was a second-century rabbi and Talmud contributor. He followed up with this additional thought: "If he has done you a big evil, let it seem to you small; if he has done to you a small kindness, let it seem to you large."

If you would make yourself agreeable wherever you go,
listen to the grievances of others but never relate your own.

JOSH BILLINGS *(Henry Wheeler Shaw)*

If you would be accounted great by your contemporaries,
be not too much greater than they.

AMBROSE BIERCE

This appeared in a collection of "Epigrams" in Bierce's *Collected Works*, first published in 1911. It's an intriguing suggestion that, in order to stand out, we must fit in—at least a little. In his 1720 *Lacon*, English writer Charles Caleb Colton offered a related thought: "If you want enemies, excel others; if you want friends, let others excel you."

If we would build on a sure foundation in friendship,
we must love friends for their sake rather than for our own.

CHARLOTTE BRONTË

If we treated everyone we meet with the same affection
we bestow upon our favorite cat, they, too, would purr.

MARTIN BUXBAUM

As director of communications for the Marriott Corporation for many years, Buxbaum edited *Table Talk*, a monthly compilation of quotes and anecdotes that, at one point in the 1960s, had a circulation of more than 400,000.

If I have to lead another life in any of the planets,
I shall take precious good care
not to hang myself around any man's neck, either as a locket or a millstone.

JANE CARLYLE

Here Mrs. Carlyle, the wife of English writer Thomas Carlyle, makes it clear that she didn't want to be seen as either a trophy wife or as a burdensome shrew.

If you want to win friends, make it a point to remember them.

DALE CARNEGIE

Carnegie's *How to Win Friends and Influence People*, first published in 1937, soon became a best seller and ultimately one of history's best-selling books. He followed up this observation by adding: "If you remember my name, you pay me a subtle compliment; you indicate that I have made an impression on you."

If you want to change people without giving offense or arousing resentment, use encouragement.

DALE CARNEGIE

If you can once engage people's pride, love, pity, ambition (or whatever is their prevailing passion) on your side, you need not fear what their reason can do against you.

LORD CHESTERFIELD, *in a 1746 letter to his son, on winning people's hearts, if not their minds*

If a relationship is based on "what am I getting?" all is lost.

OSSIE DAVIS

If you want to be respected by others, the great thing is to respect yourself.

FYODOR DOSTOYEVSKY, *from a character in the 1861 novel,* The Insulted and Injured

If you visit your friend, why need you apologize for not having visited him, and waste his time and deface your own act?

RALPH WALDO EMERSON

If your boyfriend or girlfriend wants to leave you,
they should give you two weeks' notice.
There should be severance pay, and before they leave you,
they should have to find you a temp.

BOB ETTINGER

Ettinger, an American stand-up comic, began by saying, "Relationships are hard. It's like a full-time job, and we should treat it like one."

If you want to make a friend, let someone do you a favor.

BENJAMIN FRANKLIN

I have not been able to find this oft-quoted observation in Franklin's writings, and consider it apocryphal. The basic idea challenges the thinking of those who believe just the opposite—that the way to make friends is to do favors for them. While doing favors can pay dividends, it can also backfire if people feel in our debt or obligated to return the favor. When we ask people to do us a favor, or let them do something nice for us, they often feel valued or empowered. In a related Franklin observation, also of doubtful authenticity, he said: "If you want to make a friend, ask him for his advice or borrow a book from him."

If a friend tell thee a fault,
imagine always that he telleth thee not the whole.

THOMAS FULLER, M.D.

This insight into human relationships—that friends never lay out the complete and unvarnished truth when providing feedback—comes from Dr. Fuller's 1731 *Introductio ad Prudentiam*, a collection of sayings about leading a prudent life.

If we meet someone who owes us thanks, we immediately think of it.

JOHANN WOLFGANG VON GOETHE

This comes from a character in Goethe's 1809 novella, *Elective Affinities*. It is immediately followed by this reflection: "But how often do we meet someone to whom we owe thanks without remembering that?"

If you're not comfortable within yourself,
you can't be comfortable with others.

SYDNEY J. HARRIS

If you hate a person, you hate something in him that is part of yourself.
What isn't part of ourselves doesn't disturb us.

HERMANN HESSE

If you are foolish enough to be contented,
don't show it, but grumble with the rest.

JEROME K. JEROME,
in Idle Thoughts of an Idle Fellow *(1886)*

If a man does not make new acquaintance as he advances through life,
he will soon find himself left alone.
A man, Sir, should keep his friendship in *constant repair.*

DR. SAMUEL JOHNSON

Johnson said this to Sir Joshua Reynolds in 1755. Many quotation books and Web sites say *acquaintances* and *friendships*, but this is exactly the way Thomas Boswell recorded it in his *Life of Johnson*, first published in 1791. He also put the two final words in italics, suggesting that Johnson stressed that portion of the remark.

If two men quarrel in print,
they do not speak to each other, they speak at each other.

CHARLES KINGSLEY, *in an 1846 letter*

Kingsley, an English theologian, was referring to famous literary feuds, but the quality of *speaking at* as opposed to *speaking to* probably applies to all quarrels.

If you don't have the facts and knowledge required, simply listen.
When word gets out that you can listen when others tend to talk,
you will be treated as a sage.

EDWARD KOCH

If you wish to form a clear judgment on your friends, consult your dreams.

KARL KRAUS

If we had no faults,
we should not take so much pleasure in noticing them in others.

FRANÇOIS DE LA ROCHEFOUCAULD

In a 1914 issue of the *Edinburgh Review*, the English critic J. Churton Collins offered a related idea: "If we knew each other's secrets, what comforts we should find!"

If we did not flatter ourselves, the flattery of others could never harm us.

FRANÇOIS DE LA ROCHEFOUCAULD

The point is that flattery works best when the person being flattered is already engaging in a fair amount of self-deception. The corollary is equally fascinating. If you see yourself accurately, you will be less likely to swallow flattering lies.

**If you wish to appear agreeable in society,
you must consent to be taught many things which you know already.**

JOHANN KASPAR LAVATER

Lavater, an eighteenth-century Swiss theologian, suggests here that it is wise to occasionally hide the extent of our knowledge. Today we'd say, "If you want to get along with people, you must be willing to play dumb from time to time."

**If you talk to a man in a language he understands, that goes to his head.
If you talk to a man in his language, that goes to his heart.**

NELSON MANDELA

**If it's painful for you to criticize your friends, you're safe in doing it;
if you take the slightest pleasure in it, that's the time to hold your tongue.**

ALICE DUER MILLER

And if you are going to criticize your friends, it is helpful to recall the advice of Kahlil Gibran: "If indeed you must be candid, be candid beautifully."

**If one were given five minutes' warning before sudden death,
five minutes to say what it had all meant to us,
every telephone-booth would be occupied
by people trying to call up other people to stammer that they loved them.**

ROBERT MORLEY

**If we have injured someone, giving him the opportunity
to make a joke about us is often enough
to provide him personal satisfaction, or even to win his good will.**

FRIEDRICH NIETZSCHE,
from Human, All Too Human *(1878)*

If you do good, good will be done to you;
but if you do evil, the same will be measured back to you again.

THE PANCHATANTRA

If you sacrifice a friend in a difficult hour,
you never make another friend again.

SHIMON PERES

If you want to have a friend, be a friend.

AMERICAN PROVERB

Many people have cited this as one of the most important lessons they learned while growing up. At a 2004 meeting in New York City, the Iraq War was on everyone's mind when a member of the audience asked Bill Clinton, "In light of current events, how can the U.S. regain favor in the eyes of the world?" The former president put the audience at ease and paved the way for his subsequent remarks by saying, "Like my mama always said, 'If you want to *have* a friend, you have to *be* a friend.' "

If men could see the epitaphs their friends write,
they would believe they had gotten into the wrong grave.

AMERICAN PROVERB

This proverb suggests that the positive things said about recently deceased people often bear little resemblance to the reality of their actual lives.

If one person calls you a jackass, ignore it.
If two people call you a jackass, ignore it.
If three people call you a jackass, buy a bridle.

SPANISH PROVERB

If you treat people right they will treat you right—ninety percent of the time.

FRANKLIN DELANO ROOSEVELT

If you want to know yourself,
Just look how others do it;
If you want to understand others,
Look into your own heart.

JOHANN FRIEDRICH VON SCHILLER

In this quatrain from *Tabulae Votivae* (1797), Schiller expresses an important truth about the human condition—people are able to learn a lot about themselves by observing others, and a lot about others by examining themselves.

If you want to discover your true opinion of anybody, observe the impression made on you by the first sight of a letter from him.

ARTHUR SCHOPENHAUER

If you value a man's regard, strive with him.

GEORGE BERNARD SHAW,
in an 1896 letter to Ellen Terry

If I could live my life over again, I would change a lot of things, but the one thing I would work on most is controlling what I say to others.

GARY SMALLEY

If we shake hands with icy fingers, it is because we've burnt them so hatefully before.

LOGAN PEARSALL SMITH

If you judge people, you have no time to love them.

MOTHER TERESA

**If you just set out to be liked,
you would be prepared to compromise on anything at any time,
and you would achieve nothing.**

MARGARET THATCHER

**If you don't have an understanding of your opponent,
things aren't going to work out very well for you.**

DONALD TRUMP

**If you call your bosom friend a fool, and *intend* it for an insult, it *is* an insult;
but if you do it playfully, and meaning no insult, it is *not* an insult.**

MARK TWAIN

Good-natured teasing of an insulting nature is a staple of human relationships, especially among men. The phenomenon goes by many names: *banter*, *ribbing*, and *busting each other's chops*. A formal name for these kinds of playful insults is *badinage* (BAD-uh-nazh), a word we borrowed from the French and that the *Oxford English Dictionary* defines as "light trifling raillery or humorous banter."

**If the first law of friendship is that it has to be cultivated,
then the second law is to be indulgent when the first law has been neglected.**

VOLTAIRE *(François Marie Arouet),*
from a 1740 letter

**If you have once thoroughly bored somebody
it is next to impossible to unbore him.**

ELIZABETH VON ARNIM,
in The Enchanted April *(1922)*

**If a person tells me he has been to the worst places,
I have no reason to judge him;**

but if he tells me it was his superior wisdom that enabled him to go there, then I know he is a fraud.

LUDWIG WITTGENSTEIN

If you go looking for a friend, you're going to find they're very scarce. If you go out to be a friend, you'll find them everywhere.

ZIG ZIGLAR

If I Don't Do It Every Day, I Get a Headache

SEX, LOVE & ROMANCE

In 1959, a struggling twenty-six-year-old Texas songwriter named Willie Nelson was elated when he sold the rights to one of his songs for $150. The song, titled "Night Life," went on to become one of the most frequently performed country songs of all time. Nelson—who never made any additional money from the song—bought a used Buick with the cash and set out to Nashville to chase his dream.

By most standards, Nelson's career during the 1960s was a great success. He wrote some of the decade's best country songs, including Patsy Cline's "Crazy" and Faron Young's "Hello Walls." He also had several minor hits of his own and for a time was a regular on the Grand Ole Opry. With his distinctive look and gravelly voice, though, he didn't fit into the Nashville music scene and never achieved the fame he sought. By the end of the decade, he considered his career a failure, packed up his belongings, and headed back to Texas. Many years later, he recalled those days this way: "I always thought I could sing pretty good and I guess it kind of bothered me that nobody else thought so."

Back in the Lone Star state, Nelson settled in Austin, which had a bustling and very eclectic music scene. Soon he was performing again, this time to an enthusiastic audience who appreciated the way he creatively blended such diverse musical influences as country, rhythm and blues, jazz, and rock and roll. Buoyed by the reception of his Austin fans, Nelson decided to start recording his own songs instead of writing them for other artists. In 1973, he came out with *Shotgun Willie*, an album that received excellent reviews, but was not a commercial success. Slowly, Nelson began to develop a loyal fan base, and in the next few years his career began to soar. In 1975, "Blue Eyes Crying in the Rain". gave Nelson his first number one hit as a singer. It appeared on the album *Red Headed Stranger*, which Country Music Television hailed in 2006 as the best country album of all time.

In the early 1970s, Nelson began teaming up with fellow Texan Waylon Jennings and the two men set fire to a burgeoning "country outlaw" movement (so called because the music refused to conform to Nashville standards of country music). Their first album, *Wanted! The Outlaws*, released in 1976, became the first country music album to sell a million copies. And the success of that first effort paled by comparison to their next album, the monumentally successful *Waylon and Willie*, a 1978 effort that included the smash hit, "Mammas, Don't Let Your Babies Grow Up to Be Cowboys." Also in 1978, Willie demonstrated his versatility, and his willingness to take musical risks, when he released *Stardust*, an album of pop standards sung by Nelson and accompanied by a full string orchestra. Many predicted the experiment would flop, but the album went platinum and only increased the singer's popularity. By the end of the 1970s, the Texas singer was an international celebrity and, with his signature look, a cultural icon.

Over the next few decades, Nelson had some ups and downs (notably a sixteen-million-dollar debt to the IRS and a few arrests for marijuana possession), but he continued to perform and he cemented his reputation as a music legend. He also took his career to the big screen, with respectable performances in a number of films, including *The Electric Horseman* (1979) and *Honeysuckle Rose* (1980).

In 1988, Nelson came out with *Willie: An Autobiography*, a book that contained a frank revelation: "I've been married nearly my whole life, and I've been a road musician nearly my whole life, and I know those two are incompatible." Nelson cheated on every wife he had, and one can't read about his life on the road without concluding that he comes very close to fitting the profile of a sex addict. At one point, he offers this intriguing disclosure:

If I don't do it every day, I get a headache.

Another time, he admits that he was incapable of resisting a sexual overture:

**If a girl baited her trap with sex, she'd catch me every time—
and it's unlikely this will ever cease to work.**

The memoir also contains sections in which people from Nelson's past, including some ex-wives, provide their version of Nelson's life story. My favorite observation comes from a man whose wife ran away with Nelson and went on to become the music legend's second wife. Instead of feeling bitter, the former husband, a musician named Bif Collie, remarks philosophically:

**If there's any man I'd like to have run off with my wife,
it would be Willie Nelson.**

Men have been writing about the beauty and allure of women for centuries. In 1786, while serving as American minister to France, the forty-three-year-old Thomas Jefferson was attending a party in Paris when he met the twenty-seven-year-old Maria (pronounced like "Mariah") Cosway, the beautiful daughter of a well-to-do English father and an Italian mother. Jefferson had been a widower for four years and, according to some accounts, was instantly smitten. For a time the couple clearly flirted with a romantic relationship, despite many difficulties standing in their way. In a 1786 letter to Cosway, Jefferson wrote:

If your letters are as long as the Bible, they will appear short to me. Only let them be brim full of affection.

By today's standards, Jefferson's words sound a little sappy, but that is what happens when people are caught up in the throes of love. And speaking of sappy, readers of a certain age will recall a saying that became very popular in that "you do your thing—I'll do my thing" era known as the 1970s:

If you love someone, set them free.
If they come back, they're yours.
If they don't, they never were.

Many people have been credited with authorship of this saying, including Frederick "Fritz" Perls, the colorful leader of the gestalt psychology movement in America, and Richard Bach, author of *Jonathan Livingston Seagull* and a host of other popular New Age books.

The sentiment was immensely popular for more than a decade before its usage began to decline. The last great moment for the saying may have been in 1985, when "If You Love Somebody Set Them Free" was the first single released from Sting's solo debut album *The Dream of the Blue Turtles*. The song was a big hit in America and England at about the same time the saying was beginning to be viewed as a cliché, and parodied in some clever ways:

If you love someone, set them free.
If they come back, they're probably broke.

If you love someone, set him free.
He'll probably just get fat and bald anyhow.

Throughout history, memorable observations about sex, love, and romance have been offered by the famous and the unknown, the cultured and the common, and the cynical as well as the idealistic. And happily for our purposes, many of the best have been expressed ifferistically. Let's continue our look at them.

If you smoke after sex, you're doing it too fast.

WOODY ALLEN

This line was almost certainly inspired by the old joke in which one bedmate looks over at the other and asks, "Do you smoke after sex?" The sexual partner replies, "I don't know; I never looked."

If I could come back in another life, I want to be Warren Beatty's fingertips.

WOODY ALLEN

Beatty, a long-time Hollywood bachelor, dated some of the world's sexiest and most beautiful women. Here, Allen imagines where those fingertips have been.

If you go through life trading on your good looks,
there'll come a time when no one wants to trade.

LYNNE ALPERN *and*
ESTHER BLUMENFELD, *from* Oh Lord,
I Sound Just Like Momma *(1986)*

If you swing both ways, you really swing.
I just figure, you know, double your pleasure.

JOAN BAEZ, *on bisexuality*

If the right man does not come along, there are many fates far worse. One is to have the wrong man come along.

LETITIA BALDRIGE

If you live with a man you must conquer him every day. Otherwise he will go to another.

BRIGITTE BARDOT

If it is your time, love will track you down like a cruise missile.

LYNDA BARRY

"If I Said You Had a Beautiful Body, Would You Hold It Against Me?"

THE BELLAMY BROTHERS,
title of 1979 song

This is one of music history's most creative song titles, cleverly playing on the literal as well as the figurative meaning of the phrase *would you hold it against me*. With music and lyrics by David Bellamy, it topped the country charts in 1979, and went on to become one of the most popular pick-up lines in the 1980s.

If God had meant us to have group sex, he'd have given us more organs.

MALCOLM BRADBURY

If we listened to our intellect, we'd never have a love affair. We'd never have a friendship. We'd never go into business because we'd be cynical.

RAY BRADBURY

Bradbury added: "Well, that's nonsense. You're going to miss life. You've got to jump off the cliff all the time and build your wings on the way down."

If homosexuality were the normal way,
God would have made Adam and Bruce.

ANITA BRYANT

Bryant made this and a number of similar comments during a bitter 1977 election battle to repeal a Florida law that prohibited discrimination on the basis of sexual orientation. At the time, Bryant was a former Miss Oklahoma, a respected pop vocalist, and a popular television pitchwoman for Coca-Cola, Kraft Foods, Holiday Inn, and the Florida Citrus Commission. Bryant was successful in helping to repeal the law, but the victory marked the beginning of the end of her career. After gay rights supporters announced a nationwide boycott of Florida orange juice, Bryant was quickly dropped from the Citrus Commission job, and shortly thereafter from her other assignments. Within a few years, her career was in shambles, her marriage ended in divorce, and in a cruel irony, many fundamentalist Christians who once supported Bryant began to shun her.

If I had to write a book on morality,
it would have a hundred pages and ninety-nine would be blank.
On the last page I would write:
"I recognize only one duty, and that is to love."

ALBERT CAMUS

If half the engineering effort and public interest
that go into the research on the American bosom
had gone into our guided-missile program,
we would now be running hot-dog stands on the moon.

AL CAPP

If you are ever in doubt as to whether or not you should kiss a pretty girl,
always give her the benefit of the doubt.

THOMAS CARLYLE

If love be good, from whence cometh my woe?

GEOFFREY CHAUCER

This plaintiff cry from "The Song of Troilus," which Chaucer translated from a sonnet by Petrarch, is a reminder that people long for love and then, when it finally comes, are shocked to discover that the pains of love can be very deep.

If grass can grow through cement,
love can find you at every time of your life.

CHER, *quoted in* The New York Times
in 1998, when she was fifty-two

If you cannot inspire a woman with love of you,
fill her above the brim with love of herself;
all that runs over will be yours.

CHARLES CALEB COLTON

If love lives on hope, it dies with the death of hope.
It is a fire that goes out when there is nothing left to feed it.

PIERRE CORNEILLE, *in* El Cid *(1636)*

If you betray me, can I take a better revenge
than to love the person you hate?

PIERRE CORNEILLE, *in* Titus and Berenice *(1670)*

If it weren't for pickpockets, I'd have no sex life at all.

RODNEY DANGERFIELD

If we seek the pleasures of love,
passion should be occasional, and common sense continual.

ROBERTSON DAVIES

Here Davies suggests that for most people in love, the exact opposite is true—passion is continual and common sense only occasional.

If you really worship women they'll forgive you everything, even if your balls are dropping off.

LAWRENCE DURRELL

If I could be "the condom queen" and get every young person who engaged in sex to use a condom . . . I would wear a crown on my head with a condom on it!

JOYCELYN ELDERS

This was Dr. Elders's reply after she had been denigrated as "the condom queen" by a conservative lobbying group. Elders, appointed surgeon general of the United States by President Clinton, became a lightning rod in the 1990s when she became an outspoken advocate of providing contraceptives to teenagers.

If Jack's in love, he's no judge of Jill's beauty.

BENJAMIN FRANKLIN

This observation, from a 1748 edition of *Poor Richard's Almanack*, was a clear extension of the proverbial saying "Love is blind." And speaking of that famous saying, in 1988 a Texas woman by the name of Margarita Farias wrote a letter to *Parade* magazine in which she offered some of the cleverest words ever written on the subject: "If love is blind, sex is the blindfold."

If you would be loved, love and be lovable.

BENJAMIN FRANKLIN

If a few lustful and erotic reveries
make the housework go by "as if in a dream," why not?

NANCY FRIDAY

This is from Friday's 1975 *Forbidden Flowers*, a sequel to *My Secret Garden*, a 1973 best seller that explored sexual fantasies and their role in the lives of women.

If a person loves only one other person
and is indifferent to the rest of his fellow men,
his love is not love but a symbiotic attachment, or an enlarged egotism.

ERICH FROMM

This is from *The Art of Loving* (1956), in which Fromm argued that love is not an emotion attached to a specific person but an orientation to the world. He added, "If I truly love one person, I love all persons, I love the world, I love life."

If love does not know how to give and take without restrictions, it is not love,
but a transaction that never fails to lay stress on a plus and a minus.

EMMA GOLDMAN

If you have loved, then
You have cried.

JOHN GORKA, *from the song "Riverside,"*
in the 2003 album Old Futures Gone

If I were a girl, I'd despair; the supply of good women
far exceeds that of the men who deserve them.

ROBERT GRAVES

If you are trying to run a whorehouse in the sky, then get a license.

MARTHA GRIFFITHS

Griffiths, a Democratic congresswoman from Michigan, made this remark to airline industry executives in the late 1960s. The airlines were attempting to force flight attendants—or stewardesses, as they were then called—to retire when they reached their thirties, a move vigorously opposed by Griffiths. At the time, flight attendants were hired for their physical attractiveness, and it was called, with some accuracy, the *coffee, tea, or me?* era.

If I were asked for a one-line answer to the question,
"What makes a woman good in bed?"
I would say, "A man who is good in bed."

BOB GUCCIONE, *founder of* Penthouse

If there was going to be a sexual revolution, I would be its pamphleteer.

HUGH HEFNER, *on his vision for* Playboy *magazine*

If you don't swing, don't ring.

HUGH HEFNER, *in words he had inscribed on the front door of the Playboy mansion*

If two people love each other there can be no happy end to it.

ERNEST HEMINGWAY

This comes from *Death in the Afternoon*, Hemingway's 1932 homage to the sport of bullfighting. The book also contains reflections on many other topics, from fear and bravery to life and love. This observation appears at the end of a passage that begins: "All stories, if continued far enough, end in death." His point is that love affairs will always end unhappily because one partner will ultimately die and the other person will be left alone.

If two people are in love, they can sleep on the blade of a knife.

EDWARD HOAGLAND

If my business was legitimate,
I would deduct a substantial percentage for depreciation of my body.

XAVIERA HOLLANDER

In 1972, Hollander burst on the scene with *The Happy Hooker*, a bestselling memoir about her life as a "high-class New York madam." The book inspired a 1975 film starring Lynn Redgrave and made Hollander an international celebrity.

If a woman doesn't chase a man a little, she doesn't love him.

EDGAR WATSON HOWE

If we spend our lives in loving,
we have no leisure to complain or to feel unhappiness.

JOSEPH JOUBERT

If you have love in your life,
it can make up for a great many things you lack.
If you don't have it, no matter what else there is, it's not enough.

ANN LANDERS

If we judge love by the majority of its results,
it rather resembles hatred than friendship.

FRANÇOIS DE LA ROCHEFOUCAULD,
on the tragic fate of most love affairs

If you think you love your mistress for her own sake, you are quite mistaken.

FRANÇOIS DE LA ROCHEFOUCAULD,
on the egocentric nature of love

If you can stay in love for more than two years, you're *on* something.

FRAN LEBOWITZ, *on the fleeting nature of love*

**If your sexual fantasies were truly of interest to others,
they would no longer be fantasies.**

FRAN LEBOWITZ

If someone has to study a textbook on sexual behavior in order to learn how to make love to his wife or his girl, something is wrong with him.

HERBERT MARCUSE

Marcuse said this in a 1971 *Psychology Today* article. He began by saying, "I may be wrong but I feel that a human being has to learn some things by himself." More recently Bette Midler offered a similar thought: "If sex is such a natural phenomenon, how come there are so many books on how to do it?"

**If you're a gifted flirt
talking about the price of eggs will do as well as any other subject.**

MIGNON MCLAUGHLIN

**If intelligence were taken out of my life,
it would only be more or less reduced.
If I had no one to love, it would be ruined.**

HENRY DE MONTHERLANT

If there were no husbands, who would look after our mistresses?

GEORGE MOORE, *from the 1886 book,* Confessions of a Young Man

If you aren't going all the way, why go at all?

JOE NAMATH

When Namath made this observation in the 1960s, many wondered if the superstar quarterback of the New York Jets was talking about sports or about sex. People who knew the playboy athlete well believed he was talking about both.

If I hadn't had them, I would have had some made.

DOLLY PARTON, *on her ample bosom*

In a 2003 appearance on *The Larry King Show*, Parton offered yet another observation on the subject of plastic surgery: "If I see something sagging, dragging, or bagging, I'm going to have the stuff tucked or plucked."

If you love him, don't lend him.

POLISH PROVERB

If a woman thinks she's sexy, she is.

BURT REYNOLDS

If a man prepares dinner for you,
and the salad contains three or more types of lettuce, he is serious.

RITA RUDNER

If you would not step into the harlot's house, do not go by the harlot's door.

THOMAS SECKER

Secker was trained as a physician, but decided to become an Anglican priest after getting his medical degree. He was Archbishop of Canterbury from 1758 to 1768.

If you hear bells, get your ears checked.

ERICH SEGAL, *on love*

Segal prefaced this observation by writing, "True love comes quietly, without banners or flashing lights."

If you're a guy and you ask for a doggie bag on a date,
you might as well have them wrap up your genitals, too.
You're not going to be needing those for a while, either.

JERRY SEINFELD

If I had as many affairs as you fellows claim,
I'd be speaking to you today from a jar in the Harvard Medical School.

FRANK SINATRA

Sinatra said this to reporters in 1965, downplaying his reputation as a ladies' man. It is believed, however, that Sinatra was one of the great womanizers of his time, with a string of affairs that included countless groupies and such stars as Lauren Bacall, Angie Dickinson, Judy Garland, Gina Lollobrigida, Marilyn Monroe, and Natalie Wood. Sinatra was married four times, most famously to Ava Gardner and Mia Farrow (he was fifty when they wed in 1966; she was twenty-one). During his short-lived marriage (a little over a year) to Farrow, he continued his womanizing ways and more than once joked on stage, "I finally found a broad I can cheat on."

If I could find a way to have sex with myself
that was as exciting as it is with a lady,
I'd live in a white tower and never come out.

ROD STEIGER

If a man doesn't look at me when I walk into a room, he's gay.

KATHLEEN TURNER

If you get on well out of bed, half the problems of bed are solved.

PETER USTINOV

If most men and women
were forced to rely upon physical charm to attract lovers,
their sexual lives would be not only meager
but in a youth-worshiping country like America painfully brief.

GORE VIDAL

If somebody says, "I love you" to me,
I feel as though I had a pistol pointed at my head.

KURT VONNEGUT, JR.

Vonnegut said this in a 1973 speech. He added: "What can anybody reply under such conditions but that which the pistol-holder requires? 'I love you, too.'"

If there was a good deal or a woman—I would probably go after the woman.

DAVID WICKINS

Wickins, one of England's most successful entrepreneurs, was also a colorful character and an unabashed ladies' man, famous for hiring beautiful women to chauffeur his limousines and pilot his planes and helicopters.

11

If You Marry for Money, You Will Earn Every Penny

MARRIAGE, HOME & FAMILY LIFE

In early 1901, the forty-one-year-old Anton Chekhov announced his intention to marry Olga Knipper, a Russian actress who had appeared in one of his plays three years earlier. Close friends were surprised at the news, for Chekhov's views on the subject of matrimony were well known. As a young man, he said, "Alas, I am not capable of such a complex, involved business as marriage." And when he was thirty-five, he responded in a most unusual way to his editor's suggestion that he should consider the idea of matrimony:

> Very well then, I shall marry if you so desire. But under the following conditions: everything must continue as it was before, in other words, she must live in Moscow and I in the country, and I'll go visit her. . . . I promise to be a splendid husband, but give me a wife who, like the moon, does not always appear in my sky every day.

In marrying Olga, Chekhov couldn't have picked a wife better suited to his preferences. After their marriage in May 1901, Olga's busy career as an actress resulted in frequent absences from the home, just as her husband desired. She also accepted—without complaint—her husband's busy professional schedule as well as his many visits to mountain spas to attend to his shaky health.

Despite Chekhov's fear that marriage might have a deleterious effect on his writing, he produced two of his best plays shortly after the nuptials: *The Three Sisters* and *The Cherry Orchard*. Sadly, though, the marriage lasted only a little more than three years. On July 2, 1904, Chekhov died alone in a hotel room at age forty-four. He had been suffering from tuberculosis for a number of years and his health had been steadily deteriorating. In his weakened condition, he finally succumbed to two heart attacks in the days just before he died.

After Chekhov's death, his widow found a large collection of personal papers that he had titled "Themes, Thoughts, Notes, and Fragments." The playwright had kept the notebook for the previous twelve years, periodically jotting down ideas he planned to explore in his writings. Chekhov's widow was the first person to read the papers in their entirety, and she must have been a little unsettled when she read some of the entries:

A man and woman marry because both of them
don't know what to do with themselves.

When I married I became an old woman.

Going to Paris with one's wife is like going to Tula with one's samovar.

Tula was a Russian city where samovars (a small metal urn used for boiling water) were manufactured. The meaning had to be clear to Mrs. Chekhov: Why take a wife to Paris when there are so many other women already there? The notebooks also contained one of Chekhov's most famous observations:

If you are afraid of loneliness, do not marry.

In this somewhat dismal reflection, Chekhov reveals his awareness of one of history's great ironies: People often marry to escape the pain of being single, but after marrying fail to experience the companionship they hoped for. Many, in fact, discover that the worst kind of loneliness comes to people who are not alone, but who are in an unsatisfying relationship with another person.

Was Chekhov thinking about his own life in these entries? We cannot be sure, but after reading such lines, Olga Kipper had to wonder, at least a bit. To her credit, though, she didn't excise such passages and deprive future generations from some of her husband's innermost thoughts and ideas. The papers were passed on to Chekhov's editor, who organized and edited them. They were eventually translated into English and first published in America in 1921 under the title *The Note-Book of Anton Chekhov*.

Thoughts about marriage, home, and family life are some of history's most interesting quotations, and some of the best have been expressed conditionally. Let's explore them in the rest of the chapter.

If it were not for the presents, an elopement would be preferable.

GEORGE ADE, *on weddings*

If a man works like a horse for his money,
there are a lot of girls anxious to take him down the bridal path.

MARTY ALLEN

If you have only one smile in you, give it to the people you love.
Don't be surly at home, then go out in the street
and start grinning "Good morning" at total strangers.

MAYA ANGELOU, *quoting her mother*

**If it weren't for marriage,
men would spend their lives thinking they had no faults at all.**

ANONYMOUS

**If a wife can induce herself to submit patiently to her husband's mode of life,
she will have no difficulty managing him.**

ARISTOTLE

**If you were to open up a baby's head—
and I am not for a moment suggesting that you should—
you would find nothing but an enormous drool gland.**

DAVE BARRY

**If the husband wants to drive a fancy sports car,
let him drive a fancy sports car.
If he wants to wear gold jewelry, let him wear gold jewelry.
If he wants to see other women, shoot him in the head.**

DAVE BARRY, *advice to wives with husbands in midlife crisis*

If you can give your son or daughter only one gift, let it be enthusiasm.

BRUCE BARTON

**If you think marriage is going to be perfect,
you're probably still at your reception.**

MARTHA BOLTON

If your kid isn't you, don't blame the kid.

CHASTITY BONO, *who added that this was something "parents have to understand"*

If we fail to teach our children the skills they need to think clearly, they will march behind whatever guru wears the shiniest cloak.

PAUL BOYER, *1997 Nobel laureate*

If, in instructing a child, you are vexed with it for want of adroitness, try, if you have never tried before, to write with your left hand, and then remember that a child is all left hand.

J. F. BOYSE

If we had paid no more attention to our plants than we have to our children, we would now be living in a jungle of weed.

LUTHER BURBANK

If variety is the spice of life, marriage is the big can of leftover Spam.

JOHNNY CARSON

If a child is to keep alive his inborn sense of wonder, he needs the companionship of at least one adult who can share it, rediscovering with him the joy, excitement, and mystery of the world.

RACHEL CARSON

Carson, best known for her 1962 classic *Silent Spring*, often spoke about the need to kindle a sense of wonder in children. She also wrote: "If I had influence with the good fairy who is supposed to preside over the christening of all children, I should ask that her gift to each child in the world be a sense of wonder so indestructible that it would last throughout life."

If you haven't time to help youngsters find the right way in life, somebody with more time will help them find the wrong way.

FRANK A. CLARK

If the new American father feels bewildered and even defeated, let him take comfort from the fact that whatever he does in any fathering situation has a fifty percent chance of being right.

BILL COSBY

If you have been married more than ten years, being good in bed means you don't steal the covers.

BRENDA DAVIDSON

If you've never been hated by your child, you've never been a parent.

BETTE DAVIS

Davis said this in 1985, just after the publication of a scathing "tell-all" book by her daughter B. D. (for Barbara Davis) Hyman, *My Mother's Keeper: A Daughter's Candid Portrait of Her Famous Mother*. After reading the book, Davis threw it in the trash and never spoke to her daughter again. Davis may have been a less-than-ideal mother, but even her critics believed the seventy-seven-year-old actress, a recent breast cancer and stroke victim, did not deserve the harsh treatment by her daughter.

If your house is really a mess and a stranger comes to the door, greet him with, "Who could have done this? We have no enemies!"

PHYLLIS DILLER

If you want to see what children can do, you must stop giving them things.

NORMAN DOUGLAS

If you as parents cut corners, your children will too. If you lie, they will too.

MARIAN WRIGHT EDELMAN

This is from *The Measure of Our Success: A Letter to My Children and Yours* (1992). She added: "If you spend all your money on yourselves and tithe no portion of it for charity, colleges, churches, synagogues, and civic causes, your children won't either. And if parents snicker at racial and gender jokes, another generation will pass on the poison adults still have not had the courage to snuff out."

If pregnancy were a book, they would cut the last two chapters.

NORA EPHRON

If a guy says my wife and I are going through a trial separation, this inevitably refers to a separation that will end in a trial.

BRUCE FEIRSTEIN

If you can't remember the last time you had sex with a woman, then you're either gay, or married.

JEFF FOXWORTHY

If you would have a good wife, marry one who has been a good daughter.

THOMAS FULLER, M.D.

If you want your children to improve, let them overhear the nice things you say about them to others.

HAIM GINOTT

If children grew up according to early indications, we should have nothing but geniuses.

JOHANN WOLFGANG VON GOETHE

If you are willing to inconvenience yourself in the name of discipline, the battle is half over.

FRED G. GOSMAN

This advice comes from *How to Be a Happy Parent . . . In Spite of Your Children* (1995). Gosman explained himself this way: "Leave Grandma's early if the children are acting impossible. Depart the ballpark in the sixth inning if you've warned the kids and their behavior is still poor. If we do something like this once, our kids will remember it for a long time."

If you feel like getting a divorce,
you are no exception to the general rule.

ELIZABETH HAWES

If you ever marry, I would wish you to marry the woman you like.
Do not be guided by the recommendation of friends.

WILLIAM HAZLITT

If men knew how women pass the time when they're alone,
they'd never marry.

O. HENRY

If you want to sacrifice the admiration of many men
for the criticism of one, go ahead, get married.

KATHARINE HEPBURN

Hepburn said she got this advice from her mother, who was likely inspired by an observation from Helen Rowland, who in the early nineteenth century wrote *Reflections of a Bachelor Girl* and *A Guide to Men*. Rowland famously wrote: "When a girl marries, she exchanges the attentions of all the other men of her acquaintance for the inattention of just one."

If a wife does not cause all your troubles,
she at least conveniently symbolizes them at times.

DON HEROLD

**If nature had arranged that husbands and wives
should have children alternately,
there would never be more than three in a family.**

LAURENCE HOUSMAN

It took a moment before the meaning of this observation became clear, but I have come to regard it as very clever and very true: If men were able to give birth, they would be so traumatized by the process they would never have more than one child. Princess Diana said it this way: "If men had to have babies, they would only ever have one each."

**If there were no schools to take the children away from home part of the time,
the insane asylum would be filled with mothers.**

EDGAR WATSON HOWE

**If you desire to drain to the dregs the fullest cup of scorn and hatred
that a human fellow creature can pour out for you,
let a young mother hear you call her baby "it."**

JEROME K. JEROME

**If there is anything that we wish to change in the child,
we should first examine it and see whether
it is not something that could better be changed in ourselves.**

CARL JUNG

**If you bungle raising your children,
I don't think whatever else you do well matters very much.**

JACQUELINE KENNEDY,
*said in a 1960 television interview as wife of
presidential candidate John F. Kennedy*

If you want to read about love and marriage,
you've got to buy two separate books.

ALAN KING

If you look back on high school as the happiest days of your life,
you got a big fucking problem.

STEPHEN KING

This comes from a 1998 *New Yorker* profile in which King told writer Mark Singer that he often said this to his children when they were adolescents.

If you are truly serious about preparing your child for the future,
don't teach him to subtract—teach him to deduct.

FRAN LEBOWITZ

If you are a parent, it helps if you are a grown-up.

EDA LE SHAN

If grandparents want to have a meaningful and constructive role,
the first lesson they must learn is that
becoming a grandparent is not having a second chance at parenthood!

EDA LE SHAN

If you educate a man you educate a person,
but if you educate a woman you educate a family.

RUBY MANIKAN

If people waited to know one another before they married,
the world wouldn't be so grossly over-populated as it is now.

W. SOMERSET MAUGHAM,
in Mrs. Dot *(1910)*

If you focus your attention on housework and meal preparation and diapers, raising children does start to look like drudgery pretty quickly.

JOYCE MAYNARD

Writing in *Parenting* magazine in 1995, Maynard added: "On the other hand, if you see yourself as nothing less than your child's nurturer, role model, teacher, spiritual guide, and mentor, your days take on a very different cast."

If you marry for money, you will earn every penny.

DR. PHIL MCGRAW

The American humorist Frank McKinney "Kin" Hubbard earlier observed: "Nobody works as hard for his money as the man who marries it."

If you made a list of the reasons why any couple got married, and another list of the reasons for their divorce, you'd have a hell of a lot of overlapping.

MIGNON MCLAUGHLIN

If women believed in their husbands, they would be a good deal happier—and also a good deal more foolish.

H. L. MENCKEN

Mencken's point is that wives—often quite wisely—don't believe in the foolish schemes of their husbands. If they did, they might be happier in the short run. But in the long run, it is unwise to support activities that might jeopardize family security, and possibly even bring ruin.

If I ever marry, it will be on a sudden impulse—as a man shoots himself.

H. L. MENCKEN

Mencken railed against marriage most of his adult life, and once even wrote that marriage was "the end of hope." In 1930, at age forty-nine, he married Sara Haardt, a Goucher College professor eighteen years his junior. Given his well-known views, the marriage made national headlines. Always ready with a quip, Mencken responded by writing: "Getting married, like getting hanged, is a great deal less dreadful than it has been made out." Mencken finally found love, but it was short-lived. His wife died of meningitis five years later.

If there is such a thing as a good marriage,
it is because it resembles friendship rather than love.

MICHEL DE MONTAIGNE

If you are really Master of your Fate,
It shouldn't make any difference to you whether Cleopatra
Or the Bearded Lady is your mate.

OGDEN NASH

If you want to be criticized, marry.

IRISH PROVERB

If the wife sins, the husband is not innocent.

ITALIAN PROVERB

For centuries, people have believed that husbands stray because there is something in the nature of men that propels them to do so. But when wives stray, many believe that husbands are partially responsible—probably because they've been neglecting or even abusing their wives in some way.

If men acted after marriage as they do during courtship,
there would be fewer divorces—and more bankruptcies.

FRANCIS RODMAN

If spanking worked, we'd only have to do it once.

NANCY SAMALIN

**If your kids are giving you a headache,
follow the directions on the aspirin bottle,
especially the part that says "Keep away from children."**

SUSAN SAVANNAH

**If we try to control and hold onto our children, we lose them.
When we let them go,
they have the option of returning to us more fully.**

ANNE WILSON SCHAEF

Malcolm Forbes put it simply: "Let your children go if you want to keep them."

**If you cannot get rid of the family skeleton,
you may as well make it dance.**

GEORGE BERNARD SHAW

**If you must hold yourself up to your children as an object lesson
(which is not at all necessary),
hold yourself up as a warning and not as an example.**

GEORGE BERNARD SHAW

This appears in a preface that Shaw wrote for his 1914 play *Misalliance*. Shaw's observation almost certainly inspired a popular spin-off from the contemporary writer and editor Catherine Aird: "If you can't be a good example, then you'll just have to be a horrible warning." Shaw believed children should be allowed to go their own way, without parental interference, and that parents erred by trying to shape and mold their children. He wrote: "If you once allow yourself to regard a child as so much material for you to manufacture into any shape that happens to suit your fancy you are defeating the experiment of the Life Force. You are assuming the child does not know its own business, and that you do."

If you can tell me of any trustworthy method of selecting a wife,
I shall be happy to make use of it.

GEORGE BERNARD SHAW

The words, also from Shaw's 1914 play *Misalliance*, are delivered by the character Joey Percival. This was the conclusion to a line that began in this provocative hypothetical way: "If marriages were made by putting all the men's names into one sack and the women's names into another, and having them taken out by a blindfolded child like lottery numbers, there would be just as high a percentage of happy marriages as we have here in England."

If mothers are to their children the domestic world,
the humdrum, the predictable, the familiar and routine,
fathers are the other—periodic, bigger, stronger, strange, different.

VICTORIA SECUNDA

This is from *Women and Their Fathers* (1992). Secunda added: "Mothers represent the day, fathers the night—and the weekend, the holiday, the special dinner out."

If marriages are made in heaven, they should be happier.

THOMAS SOUTHERNE, *in a 1694 poem*

If women have young children, they are one man away from welfare.

GLORIA STEINEM

If we take matrimony at its lowest . . .
we regard it as no more than a sort of friendship recognized by the police.

ROBERT LOUIS STEVENSON

If you don't understand how a woman could both love her sister dearly
and want to wring her neck at the same time,
then you were probably an only child.

LINDA SUNSHINE

If a man's character is to be abused, say what you will,
there's nobody like a relation to do the business.

WILLIAM MAKEPEACE THACKERAY

This classic observation on a darker aspect of family relationships comes from *Vanity Fair*, which was first published in twenty serial installments in 1847 and 1848. Earlier in the novel, Thackeray offered a similar but less well-known thought: "If a man has committed wrong in life, I don't know any moralist more anxious to point his errors out to the world than his own relations."

If common sense had been consulted,
how many marriages would never have taken place?

HENRY DAVID THOREAU

If your mother tells you to do a thing, it is wrong to reply that you won't.

MARK TWAIN

This is from "Advice for Good Little Girls," published in the *California Youth's Companion* in 1865. It was followed by this devilish recommendation: "It is better and more becoming to intimate that you will do as she bids you, and then afterwards act quietly in the matter according to the dictates of your better judgment."

**If you raise your children to feel
that they can accomplish any goal or task they decide upon,
you will have succeeded as a parent
and you will have given your children the greatest of all blessings.**

BRIAN TRACY

**If men do not keep on speaking terms with children, they cease to be men,
and become merely machines for eating and earning money.**

JOHN UPDIKE

If you want a baby, have a new one. Don't baby the old one.

JESSAMYN WEST

**If I had known how wonderful it would be to have grandchildren,
I'd have had them first.**

LOIS WYSE

**If you treat your wife like a thoroughbred,
you'll never end up with a nag.**

ZIG ZIGLAR

12

If Winning Isn't Important, Why Do They Keep Score?

SPORTS IFFERISMS

In 1993, New England Patriots owner Bob Kraft convinced Bill Parcells to come out of retirement and return to the role of an NFL head coach. Parcells had retired in 1990 after taking the New York Giants to three division titles and two Super Bowl victories. Long-suffering fans in New England quickly warmed to the coach, who soon became well-known as *The Big Tuna*.

From the very beginning, there were rumors of tension between the owner and his new coach, but the success of the team seemed to put those questions to bed. In his second year at the helm, Parcells took the team to its first playoff game in eight years. In the 1996 season, his third year, Parcells took the team to Super Bowl XXXI, which the Patriots lost to the Green Bay Packers 35–21.

In the months prior to the Super Bowl, there was rampant speculation about a serious rift between Kraft and Parcells. Even though Kraft denied the reports, Parcells fueled the fires when he said, "On a scale of one to ten, I'd say we have a relationship of about a five." One of the most contentious issues had been the selection of players in the NFL draft. Parcells believed that head coaches should have control over which players to select, but Kraft had given player personnel director Bobby Grier the ultimate authority to make final draft picks. The issue came to a head when the coach's desire to draft a top defensive player was trumped by Grier's decision to draft Ohio State wide receiver Terry Glenn.

A week before the Super Bowl in January 1997, the Boston Globe shocked the sports world when it reported that Parcells would be resigning from the Patriots after the game. It was a huge sports story and a major distraction for the team. While Parcells neither confirmed nor denied the reports in the days before the big game, he was more than willing to talk about the controversial issue of player selection. In one of the year's most famous sports quotes, he said:

**If you're going to cook the meal,
you ought to be able to shop for the groceries.**

Parcells did resign after the Super Bowl, and this comment went on to follow him for the rest of his career—first as head coach of the New York Jets, then as head coach of the Dallas Cowboys, and most recently as executive vice president of football operations for the Miami Dolphins. In his latest role, Parcells shops for the groceries, but is no longer responsible for cooking any of the meals.

Parcells had a deep need to be in control and a deep hatred of losing, two characteristics shared by many other NFL coaches, including George Allen, the legendary coach of the Washington Redskins and the Los Angeles Rams. During his twelve years as a coach, his teams never had a losing record, and among NFL coaches he has the third-highest career winning percentage (after Vince Lombardi and John Madden). On losing, Allen once said:

If you can accept defeat and open your pay envelope without feeling guilty, you're stealing.

While great coaches hate to lose, they almost always shoulder the responsibility when their teams are defeated. Victories, on the other hand, are generally credited to the team. Paul "Bear" Bryant was one of the winningest coaches in the history of college football. In his twenty-five-year coaching career at the University of Alabama, he took the Crimson Tide to twenty-four bowl games and six national championships. He once said about his coaching philosophy:

If anything goes bad, I did it.
If anything goes semi-good, then we did it.
If anything goes real good, then you did it.
That's all it takes to get people to win football games.

The goal of competitive athletics has always been the same: to win by defeating an opponent. From the earliest days of history, though, people in charge of sporting events have decried a winning-at-any-cost approach and promulgated rules of the game. Nowadays, rule books are extremely detailed documents, but in the early days of competitive sport, they were stated in simple and sensible ways. In the first century B.C., the Roman writer Marcus Tullius Cicero wrote:

If a man is running a race in the stadium, he ought to use every effort to win, but on no account must he cut in on a rival or push him with his hand.

While cheating has always been frowned upon, the idea of taking advantage of an opponent's weakness—even when that opponent is a friend—has always been celebrated. All great athletes have talked about it, but few have described it more memorably than Billie Jean King, who once said:

**If you're playing against a friend who has big boobs,
bring her to the net and make her hit backhand volleys.**

With buxom opponents, according to King, backhand volleys were especially effective. About them she said, "That's the hardest shot for the well-endowed."

In the remainder of the chapter, observations from every major sport will be represented, and a few minor ones as well. The observations come mainly from athletes and coaches, but you'll also find contributions from journalists, actors, and celebrities. And, of course, all are expressed ifferistically.

If you break 100, watch your golf. If you break 80, watch your business.

JOEY ADAMS

The point is that golf, when one has a talent for it, can be dangerously addictive. Most golf addicts, however, work at their game for years without ever becoming proficient. Bob Hope, one of the great celebrity golfers, put it this way: "If you watch a game, it's fun. If you play it, it's recreation. If you work at it, it's golf."

**If you really want to advise me,
do it on Saturday afternoon between one and four o'clock.
And you've got twenty-five seconds to do it, between plays.
Not on Monday. I know the right thing to do on Monday.**

ALEX AGASE, *college football coach,*
on Monday-morning quarterbacks

If you don't practice, you don't deserve to dream.

ANDRE AGASSI

If a horse can't eat it, I don't want to play on it.

DICK ALLEN, *on artificial turf*

Look around the table.
If you don't see a sucker, get up, because *you're* the sucker.

AMARILLO SLIM, *poker name of Thomas Austin Preston, Jr.*

This is legendary poker advice from a life-long professional gambler. Slim, who became an overnight celebrity when he won the World Series of Poker in 1972, also once said, "If you're going to bluff, make it a big one."

If everything seems under control, you're not going fast enough.

MARIO ANDRETTI, *on car racing*

If you can't tie good knots, tie plenty of them.

ANONYMOUS, *aka "The Sailer's Credo"*

If I don't ask "Why me?" after my victories,
I cannot ask "Why me?" after my setbacks and disasters.

ARTHUR ASHE

If a man coaches himself,
then he has only himself to blame when he is beaten.

ROGER BANNISTER

If I weren't earning $3 million a year to dunk a basketball,
most people on the street
would run in the other direction if they saw me coming.

CHARLES BARKLEY

If people don't want to come out to the ballpark, nobody's going to stop them.

YOGI BERRA

In the 1950s, major league baseball attendance declined and many clubs began to experiment with special promotions to attract fans. After several players in the Yankee clubhouse voiced support for the idea, Berra offered his now-famous remark.

If you want to know the secret of my success with women,
then don't smoke, don't take drugs, and don't be too particular.

GEORGE BEST, *Irish soccer star*

If you are going to throw a club,
it is important to throw it ahead of you, down the fairway,
so you don't have to waste energy going back to pick it up.

TOMMY BOLT

If a tie is like kissing your sister,
losing is like kissing your grandmother with her teeth out.

GEORGE BRETT

Brett, a Hall of Fame third baseman for the Kansas City Royals, said this in 1968. He was piggybacking on a famous observation from the legendary Michigan State University football coach, Hugh "Duffy" Daugherty, who said in 1966: "A tie is like kissing your sister."

If fishing is a religion, fly fishing is high church.

TOM BROKAW

If you don't learn anything but self-discipline, then athletics is worthwhile.

PAUL "BEAR" BRYANT

If you have only one passion in life—football—and you pursue it
to the exclusion of everything else, it becomes very dangerous.
When you stop doing this activity it is as though you are dying.

ERIC CANTONA

Cantona is talking here about soccer, which is called *football* almost everywhere except in America and Canada. It's a warning to athletes about putting all their eggs in one basket—and failing to prepare for life after a short-lived career.

If women were umpiring, none of this would happen.

AMANDA CLEMENT, *on rowdyism in baseball*

There have been no female umpires in the history of major league baseball—and only a half-dozen in the minor leagues. Clement was the first female umpire in baseball history, working for a number of semi-pro teams in the early 1900s. She added: "Do you suppose any ball player in the country would step up to a good-looking girl and say to her, 'You color-blind, pickle-brained, cross-eyed idiot, if you don't stop throwing the soup into me I'll distribute your features all over your countenance!' Of course he wouldn't."

If a horse has four legs, and I'm riding it, I think I can win.

ANGEL CORDERO, JR.

Cordero was the first Puerto Rican to win racing's prestigious Triple Crown, and the first to be inducted into the National Thoroughbred Racing Hall of Fame.

If you don't take it seriously, it's no fun;
if you do take it seriously, it breaks your heart.

ARNOLD DALY, *on the game of golf*

If Satch and I were pitching on the same team,
we'd clinch the pennant by July Fourth
and go fishing until World Series time.

DIZZY DEAN, *on "Satchel" Paige*

While Dean was winning World Series titles for the St. Louis Cardinals, Paige was forced to pitch in the Negro Leagues. In 1948, a year after Jackie Robinson broke baseball's color barrier, the forty-two-year-old Paige became the oldest rookie in baseball history when he made his pitching debut with the Cleveland Indians. He had a respectable first season (6–1, with a 2.48 ERA), but was released by the Indians after a disappointing second season.

If it weren't for baseball,
many kids wouldn't know what a millionaire looked like.

PHYLLIS DILLER

If you keep thinking about what you want to do
or what you hope will happen, you don't do it, and it won't happen.

JOE DIMAGGIO

If I lose at play, I blaspheme, and if my fellow lose, he blasphemes,
so that God is always sure to be a loser.

JOHN DONNE

Swearing has long been an integral part of sport. This observation comes from a 1623 sermon that Donne, a preacher and a poet, gave at St. Paul's Cathedral.

If I were playing third base and my mother were rounding third
with the run that was going to beat us, I'd trip her.
Oh, I'd pick her up and brush her off and say, "Sorry, Mom,"
but nobody beats me.

LEO DUROCHER

Durocher, known as "Leo the Lip" for his fiery temperament and blunt manner, is best remembered as the colorful manager of the Brooklyn Dodgers and New York Giants. While managing the Giants in the 1950s, the expression "Nice guys finish last" began to be attributed to him. And while he never uttered those exact words, the saying will always be associated with him.

If you ain't first, you're last.

WILL FERRELL, *the motto of Ricky Bobby in the 2006 Nascar spoof* Talledega Nights

If the human body recognized agony and frustration, people would never run marathons, have babies, or play baseball.

CARLTON FISK

If I don't fight, I'll eat this planet.

GEORGE FOREMAN

During his boxing career, Foreman had a legendary appetite. He began this 1990 observation by saying, "I want to keep fighting because it is the only thing that keeps me out of hamburger joints." After his retirement, the former heavyweight boxing champ's love affair with food made him a natural pitchman for the popular grills that bear his name.

If there is any larceny in a man, golf will bring it out.

PAUL GALLICO

If it comes easy, it isn't worth a damn.

WOODY HAYES, *Ohio State football coach*

If my uniform doesn't get dirty, I haven't done anything in the baseball game.

RICKY HENDERSON

Henderson was one of the most aggressive players in baseball history, famous for his headfirst slides as a base runner and gravity-defying leaps as a center fielder for the Oakland A's, New York Yankees, and a few other teams. When he ended his seventeen-year career in 2003, he held a number of Major League Baseball records, including most steals in a single season (130). He was a first-ballot Hall of Fame selection in 2009.

If we could have screwed another head on his shoulders, he would have been the greatest golfer who ever lived.

BEN HOGAN, *on Tommy Bolt*

Bolt, who won the 1958 U.S. Open and fifteen other PGA tour titles, had a notorious temper that clearly hampered his career. Hogan offered another ifferistic observation about a golfer who didn't live up to his potential—but for a very different reason. About Jimmy Demaret, Hogan said: "If Jimmy had concentrated on golf as much as laughing and making people laugh, he might have won more tournaments. Of course, I wouldn't have liked him as much."

If he's got golf clubs in his trunk or a camper in his driveway, I don't hire him.

LOU HOLTZ, *Notre Dame head football coach, on his criteria for selecting assistant coaches*

If he keeps going like that, he'll be broke in 250 years.

H. L. HUNT

Hunt, an extremely wealthy Texas oilman, said this in 1981 after being told that his son Lamar Hunt was losing a million dollars a year as owner of the NFL's Kansas City Chiefs. The elder Hunt was a flamboyant figure and served as the inspiration for the J. R. Ewing character in the television series *Dallas*.

If profanity had an influence on the flight of the ball,
the game of golf would be played far better than it is.

HORACE G. HUTCHINSON

If ever I needed an eight-foot putt, and everything I owned depended on it,
I would want Arnold Palmer to putt for me.

BOBBY JONES

If you run into a wall, don't turn around and give up.
Figure out how to climb it, go through it, or work around it.

MICHAEL JORDAN, *on overcoming roadblocks*

If you play bridge badly you make your partner suffer,
but if you play poker badly you make everybody happy.

JOE LAURIE, JR.

If you think it's hard to meet new people,
try picking up the wrong golf ball.

JACK LEMMON

If it doesn't matter who wins or loses, then why do they keep score?

VINCE LOMBARDI

This sentiment has been offered in a number of different ways over the years. Adolph Rupp, the legendary basketball coach at the University of Kentucky, put it this way: "If winning isn't important, why do they keep score?"

If he gets you in trouble, and you see three bald heads, aim at the middle one.

ARCHIE MOORE

This was Moore's advice to James "Quick" Tillis just before Tillis's 1982 match against Earnie Shavers, a heavyweight boxer famous for his clean-shaven head. In the 1940s, the German heavyweight boxer Max Baer put it this way: "If you ever get belted and see three fighters through a haze, go after the one in the middle. That's what ruined me—I went after the two guys on the end."

If caring for a person is based on yelling and screaming,
then he loves us very much.

TERRY NELSON, *on coach Bob Huggins*

This was Nelson's tongue-in-cheek way of describing the fiery temperament of Huggins, the head coach at the University of Cincinnati from 1989 to 2005.

If you want to touch the other shore badly enough,
barring an impossible situation, you will.
If your desire is diluted for any reason, you'll never make it.

DIANA NYAD, *in her 1978 autobiography,* Other Shores

In 1979, Nyad completed history's longest swim—102.5 miles, from the island of Bimini to Florida. It took more than two days of constant swimming.

If I had to choose between my wife and my putter, well, I'd miss her.

GARY PLAYER

If you rush in and out of the clubhouse, you rush in and out of baseball.

PEE WEE REESE

Reese was a big believer in the mental aspect of the game, often arriving at Ebbets Field hours before a game began in order to get properly prepared, and staying long after a game ended to reflect on what had happened.

If God had an agent, the world wouldn't be built yet.
It'd only be about Thursday.

JERRY REYNOLDS

Reynolds, player personnel director for the Sacramento Kings in 1991, was alluding to how agents slow down negotiations between clubs and players.

If you make one mistake, it can result in a vasectomy.

MARK ROWLAND

Rowland was describing the perils of steeplechase racing, a track and field event in which, unlike the hurdles, the barriers do not fall over when a runner hits them. Because of this, most steeplechase racers actually choose to step on top of the barriers instead of leaping or hurdling over them.

If cocaine were helium, the NBA would float away.

ART RUST, JR., *on drug use in the 1970s*

Rust was a respected African American sportswriter and sportscaster. During his career, he was known for speaking frankly—and often controversially.

If it wasn't for baseball, I'd be in either the penitentiary or the cemetery.

BABE RUTH

If you want to know what you'll look like in ten years,
look in the mirror after you've run a marathon.

JACK SCAFF, *cardiologist and marathon runner, quoted in* Sports Illustrated *in 1978*

Dr. Scaff was a passionate advocate of long-distance running (he once said, "If you run marathons and don't smoke, it is absolutely impossible to have a heart attack"). He did concede, however, that there was a cost: "After a marathon we say everybody is automatically injured for six weeks, no matter what."

If professional wrestling did not exist, could you come up with this idea . . . huge men in tiny bathing suits, pretending to fight?

JERRY SEINFELD

If the players were armed with guns, there wouldn't be stadiums large enough to hold the crowds.

IRWIN SHAW

Sport is often described as a form of controlled violence. Here, Shaw suggests that it would be even more popular if the violence were uncontrolled.

If you make every game a life-and-death proposition, you're going to have problems. For one thing, you'll be dead a lot.

DEAN SMITH

If you don't get it by midnight, chances are you ain't gonna get it; and if you do, it ain't worth it.

CASEY STENGEL, *advice to players about chasing women*

If football taught me anything about business, it is that you win the game one play at a time.

FRAN TARKENTON

If you are caught up on a golf course during a storm and are afraid of lightning, hold up a 1-iron.

LEE TREVINO

Trevino famously added, "Not even God can hit a 1-iron." Bob Hope offered a related observation on lightning during a game of golf: "If I'm on the course and lightning strikes, I get inside fast. If God wants to play through, let him."

If I need a brain transplant, I'd choose a sportswriter because I'd want a brain that had never been used.

NORM VAN BROCKLIN

Writers usually deliver clever lines about players, so it's nice to see that pattern reversed from time to time. In 1980, after being diagnosed with a brain tumor, Van Brocklin offered this clever quip to a group of reporters. Van Brocklin was one of the best NFL quarterbacks in his era, named to the Pro Bowl nine times in a twelve-year career. After retiring as a player, he had a thirteen-year coaching career. As player and coach, he had a testy relationship with the press and a well-known animosity toward sports journalists. He died in 1983, a day after suffering a stroke.

Players like rules.
If they didn't have any rules, they'd have nothing to break.

LEE WALLS

If you want to surf, move to Hawaii.
If you like to shop, move to New York.
If you like acting and Hollywood, move to California.
But if you like college football, move to Texas.

RICKY WILLIAMS

If you see a tennis player who looks as if he's working hard, then that means he isn't very good.

HELEN WILLS

Wills, also known by her married name of Helen Wills Moody, was the most dominant female tennis player of her time, winning thirty-one Grand Slam titles in the 1920s and '30s, including eight Wimbledon championships (a record until 1990, when it was broken by Martina Navratilova). During her matches, she was focused and businesslike, rarely showing emotion and ignoring her opponent and the crowd; sportswriter Grantland Rice nicknamed her "Little Miss Poker Face." Here, she offers a sports truism—gifted athletes make it look effortless.

If you lose self-control everything will fall.

JOHN WOODEN

In *They Call Me Coach* (1972), Wooden added: "You cannot function physically or mentally or in any other way unless your emotions are under control."

If it moves, kick it. If it doesn't move, kick it until it does.

PHIL WOOSNAM, *describing the "simple" rules of soccer in 1974*

If you want to see a baseball game in the worst way—take your wife along.

HENNY YOUNGMAN

13

If You Want a Friend in Washington, D.C., Get a Dog

POLITICS & GOVERNMENT

In 1940, fifty-eight-year-old Sam Rayburn of Texas was elected Speaker of the House of Representatives. It was a great triumph for Rayburn, who had already served twenty-eight years in Congress. For twenty-one more years, until he died at age seventy-nine, he was reelected to Congress, serving as Speaker for seventeen of those years. He has the distinction of being the longest-tenured Speaker in history.

In his role as House leader, Rayburn met every two years with newly elected members of Congress. In his remarks to each freshmen class, he offered a host of recommendations: "Don't try to go too fast. Learn your job. Don't ever talk until you know what you're talking about." Also included in his advice was a saying that went on to achieve a legendary status in political history:

If you want to get along, go along.

As years passed, the saying began to be disparaged by those who viewed it as an admonition to unthinkingly toe the line and simply do what party bosses wanted. When "Tip" O'Neill wrote his 1987 memoir, *Man of the House*, he said of Rayburn's maxim: "This idea is no longer in fashion, as today's freshmen are more restless and independent. But when I first came to Congress, party discipline meant a great deal."

In the political arena, getting people to go along is sometimes a matter of gentle persuasion and sometimes a matter of forceful intimidation. And while all political leaders have occasionally had to use their own muscle to twist the arms of people, most have relied on others to do the bulk of their dirty work. During his years as prime minister of Great Britain, Clement Attlee had an especially effective enforcer, and he once described him in a memorable way:

"If you have a good dog, don't bark yourself" is a good proverb, and in Ernest Bevin I had an exceptionally good dog.

During Richard Nixon's presidency, Charles Colson's formal title was special counsel to the president, but his real job was to serve as a kind of presidential pit bull. Colson had a legendary reputation for ruthlessness and was once quoted as saying he'd run over his grandmother to reelect Nixon. He was responsible for many "dirty tricks," including the compilation of the president's infamous "Enemies List." Early in Nixon's first term, reporters discovered a plaque in Colson's White House office inscribed with a blunt saying:

**If you've got them by the balls,
their hearts and minds will follow.**

Colson denied authorship of the saying—he said a former Green Beret had given him the plaque as a gift—but it has always been associated with him. And almost everyone who knew Colson agreed that the saying perfectly captured his approach to solving political problems.

Colson was eventually brought down as a result of his involvement in the Watergate conspiracy as well as the 1971 burglary of the offices of the psychiatrist of Daniel Ellsberg, the man who leaked the Pentagon Papers. He was convicted of obstruction of justice in 1974, and ultimately disbarred. While serving time, he became an evangelical Christian and turned his life around. He also recanted the famous saying he once admired, but it lives on as a motto for people who favor aggressive and intimidating tactics.

While the manipulation of people is a fact of political life, the manipulation of ideas is an even more powerful reality. In the 1960s, Philip K. Dick was well known in the science fiction community but largely unknown in pop culture or the larger literary world. Things changed dramatically in 1982, however, when his 1968 novel *Do Androids Dream of Electric Sheep?* was made into the film *Blade Runner*, starring Harrison Ford. In the introduction to a 1985 collection of sci-fi stories titled *I Hope I Shall Arrive Soon*, Dick wrote, "The basic tool for the manipulation of reality is the manipulation of words." And then he added:

If you can control the meaning of words,
you can control the people who must use the words.

The manipulation of words and ideas shows up in every aspect of our lives, but nowhere is it more important than in the political world, where everyone from ancient rulers to modern "spin doctors" have tried to influence the debate, and the electorate, by the language they use.

When leaders spin the truth and deliberately slant the facts to achieve political ends, they run a risk that has been recognized for many centuries. The danger was first described more than twenty-five hundred years ago by the Chinese sage Confucius:

If terms be not correct,
language is not in accordance with the truth of things.
If language be not in accordance with the truth of things,
affairs cannot be carried on to success.

In the remainder of the chapter, you'll find many more observations about government, politics, and the lives of elected officials. The words come from a wide variety of commentators—and all are introduced by the word *if.*

If a poet meets an illiterate peasant,
they may not be able to say much to each other,
but if they both meet a public official,
they share the same feeling of suspicion;
neither will trust one further than he can throw a grand piano.

W. H. AUDEN, *in "The Poet and the City,"*
in The Dyer's Hand *(1962)*

If you have to eat crow, eat it while it's hot.

ALBEN W. BARKLEY

Eating crow is a popular American idiom meaning "to be forced to do something extremely disagreeable" (it's based on the notion that crows are not exactly a culinary delight). When politicians do or say something stupid, Barkley was advising them to quickly admit to the blunder and put it behind them. Henry Kissinger also believed in the hasty acknowledgment of mistakes, once saying, "If it's going to come out eventually, better have it come out immediately."

If you do not know how to lie, cheat, and steal,
turn your attention to politics and learn.

JOSH BILLINGS *(Henry Wheeler Shaw)*

In Joseph Heller's 1994 novel *Closing Time*, his sequel to *Catch-22*, the character G. Noodles Cook says similarly, "If I'm going to be trivial, inconsequential, and deceitful . . . then I might as well be in government."

If God had been a Liberal, we wouldn't have had the Ten Commandments; we'd have had the Ten Suggestions.

MALCOLM BRADBURY

This comes from *The After Dinner Game*, a 1982 collection of plays Bradbury wrote with Christopher Bigsby for British television. The underlying notion is that liberals are so inclined to positions of moral relativity that they offer tepid suggestions instead of firm commandments.

If the Government becomes a lawbreaker, it breeds contempt for law.

LOUIS D. BRANDEIS

If you turn on your set and see nothing is happening, do not call a serviceman: You have tuned in the U.S. Senate.

DAVID BRINKLEY

In 1985, Bob Dole made a similar point about the excitement level of the Senate: "If you're hanging around with nothing to do and the zoo is closed, come over to the Senate. You'll get the same kind of feeling and you won't have to pay."

If presidents don't do it to their wives, they do it to the country.

MEL BROOKS,
on sexually frustrated leaders

Brooks said this in his famous *2000 Year Old Man* routine. Bill Maher recently updated the idea and gave it a partisan twist: "What Democratic congressmen do to their women staffers, Republican congressmen do to the country."

If you want to get across an idea, wrap it up as a person.

RALPH J. BUNCHE

When politicians include stories about specific people in their speeches, they are following this advice from Bunche, a U.S. diplomat and 1950 Nobel Prize winner who believed the best way to communicate an abstract idea was to personalize it.

If you are to stand up for your Government you must be able to stand up *to* your Government.

HAROLD CACCIA

If you fear making anyone mad, then you ultimately probe for the lowest common denominator of human achievement.

JIMMY CARTER

Richard Nixon said something similar a few years earlier: "If an individual wants to be a leader and isn't controversial, that means he never stood for anything."

If we don't believe in freedom of expression for people we despise, we don't believe in it at all.

NOAM CHOMSKY, *in a 1992 interview*

If you have ten thousand regulations, you destroy all respect for the law.

WINSTON CHURCHILL

If our democracy is to flourish, it must have criticism; if our government is to function, it must have dissent.

HENRY STEELE COMMAGER

If you can't carry your own precinct, you're in trouble.

CALVIN COOLIDGE

This political axiom was often recalled in the 2000 presidential race, after Al Gore failed to carry his home state of Tennessee. Lyndon Johnson once offered a related thought: "If you can't raise money in your own state, you're in trouble."

If you don't say anything, you won't be called upon to repeat it.

CALVIN ("SILENT CAL") COOLIDGE

If every man was as true to his country as he was to his wife, we'd be in a lot of trouble.

RODNEY DANGERFIELD

If we were dog food, they would take us off the shelf.

TOM DAVIS, *on the Republican "brand"*

Davis, a Republican congressman from Virginia, said this after the GOP lost a 2008 special congressional election in Mississippi, their third consecutive special election defeat. "The Republican brand is in the trash can," Davis said in a twenty-page memo to party leaders.

If you want to make peace, you don't talk to your friends. You talk to your enemies.

MOSHE DAYAN

If a government commission had worked on the horse, you would have the first horse who could operate his knee joint in both directions. The only trouble would have been that he couldn't stand up.

PETER DRUCKER

If the government is big enough to give you everything you want, it is big enough to take away everything you have.

GERALD FORD

If a tax cut increases government revenues, you haven't cut taxes enough.

MILTON FRIEDMAN

Friedman, the 1976 Nobel laureate in economics and the philosophical voice of many conservatives and libertarians, also offered these ifferistic thoughts:

If you pay people not to work and tax them when they do, don't be surprised if you get unemployment.

If you look at the drug war from a purely economic point of view, the role of the government is to protect the drug cartel.

If you've got some news that you don't want to get noticed, put it out Friday afternoon at 4 P.M.

DAVID GERGEN

If you're going to plagiarize, go *way* back.

BARRY GOLDWATER

Goldwater made this remark in 1987, shortly after Senator Joe Biden of Delaware withdrew from the race for the Democratic Party's presidential nomination. Biden was a leading candidate when the Michael Dukakis campaign released an attack video charging (unfairly, according to most observers) that Biden had plagiarized remarks from the British politician Neal Kinnock. Goldwater's advice might have been based on an observation from the English writer Charles Caleb Colton, who wrote in *Lacon* (1820): "If we steal thoughts from the moderns, it will be cried down as plagiarism; if from the ancients, it will be cried up as erudition."

If the government was as afraid of disturbing the consumer as it is of disturbing business, this would be some democracy.

FRANK MCKINNEY "KIN" HUBBARD

If you're in politics and you can't tell when you walk into a room who's for you and who's against you, then you are in the wrong line of work.

LYNDON B. JOHNSON, *citing advice from his father*

If you have a mother-in-law with only one eye and she has it in the center of her forehead, you don't keep her in the living room.

LYNDON B. JOHNSON

This was Johnson's colorful way of talking about the importance of keeping embarrassing information from public view. LBJ was famous for his homely—and often coarse—reflections about life. In another example, he said, "If you let a bully come into your front yard, he'll be on your porch the next day, and the day after that he'll rape your wife in your own bed."

If you're going to play the game properly, you'd better know every rule.

BARBARA JORDAN, *on succeeding in politics*

**If we are to abolish the death penalty,
I should like to see the first step taken by my friends the murderers.**

ALPHONSE KARR

This is a favorite quotation of those who support capital punishment. In an opposing ifferism on the subject, Sister Helen Prejean wrote in *Dead Man Walking* (1993): "If I were to be murdered I would not want my murderer executed." She explained herself this way: "I would not want my death avenged. Especially by government—which can't be trusted to control its own bureaucrats or collect taxes equitably or fill a pothole, much less decide which of its citizens to kill."

If the ass is protecting the system, ass-kicking should be undertaken, regardless of the sex, ethnicity, or charm of the ass involved.

FLORYNCE KENNEDY

Kennedy, a leading 1970s feminist, decried sexism in society, no matter who was perpetrating it. Occasionally, she turned a critical eye on the women's movement as well. She once warned feminists about taking themselves too seriously, and even advised them to loosen up, saying, "If it's a movement, I sometimes think it needs a laxative."

**If we are strong, our strength will speak for itself.
If we are weak, words will be of no help.**

JOHN F. KENNEDY

**If you don't like the president,
it costs you 90 bucks to fly to Washington to picket.
If you don't like the governor,
it costs you 60 bucks to fly to Albany to picket.
If you don't like me, 90 cents.**

ED KOCH, *as New York City mayor in 1985, referring to the price of a subway token*

If Kuwait grew carrots, we wouldn't give a damn.

LAWRENCE KORB, *in 1990 on the U.S. motivation for "Operation Desert Storm"*

If we were to promise people nothing better than only revolution, they would scratch their heads and say, "Is it not better to have good goulash?"

NIKITA KHRUSHCHEV

Khrushchev was very popular with Western journalists, who could always count on him for colorful ifferistic idioms such as "If you live among wolves, you have to act like a wolf" and "If one cannot catch the bird of paradise, better take a wet hen."

If God wanted us to vote, he would have given us candidates.

JAY LENO

If slavery is not wrong, nothing is wrong.
I can not remember when I did not so think, and feel.

ABRAHAM LINCOLN, *in an 1864 letter*

If you want to succeed in politics,
you must keep your conscience well under control.

DAVID LLOYD GEORGE

If men were angels, no government would be necessary.

JAMES MADISON

If Tyranny and Oppression come to this land,
it will be in the guise of fighting a foreign enemy.

JAMES MADISON

If I knew of something that could serve my nation but would ruin another,
I would not propose it to my prince,
for I am first a man and only then a Frenchman.

CHARLES DE MONTESQUIEU

In *The Spirit of the Laws* (1748), Montesquieu also wisely observed: "If a republic is small, it is destroyed by a foreign force; if it is large, it is destroyed by an internal vice."

If you're going into politics, never let anyone take a picture of you
with a drink in your hand—whether it's a Coke or anything else—
because it projects the wrong image.

WALTER MONDALE

If Moses had gone to Harvard Law School
and spent three years working on the Hill, he would have
written The Ten Commandments with three exceptions and a saving clause.

CHARLES MORGAN

If the Third World War is fought with nuclear weapons,
the fourth will be fought with bows and arrows.

LORD LOUIS MOUNTBATTEN, *in 1975*

If one voice can change a room, then it can change a city.
And if it can change a city, then it can change a state.
And if it can change a state, then it can change a nation.
And if it can change a nation, then it can change the world.

BARACK OBAMA

This was one of President Obama's most effective oratorical riffs during the 2008 presidential campaign. He often began by saying, "One voice can change a room," and ended with, "Your voice can change the world."

If there is anyone out there who still doubts
that America is a place where all things are possible;
who still wonders if the dream of our founders is alive in our time;
who still questions the power of our democracy,
tonight is your answer.

BARACK OBAMA, *in his election night address, November 4, 2008*

If liberty means anything at all,
it means the right to tell people what they do not want to hear.

GEORGE ORWELL,
in the preface to Animal Farm *(1945)*

If I were an American, as I am an Englishman,
while a foreign troop was landed in my country,
I never would lay down my arms. Never! Never! Never!

WILLIAM PITT

Pitt was a former prime minister and an elder statesman when he said this in a 1777 debate in the House of Lords. During the Revolutionary War, most English citizens sided with their king. However, a number of prominent Englishmen such as Pitt and Edmund Burke, raised serious questions about their government's policies.

If a problem has no solution, it may not be a problem,
but a fact, not to be solved, but to be coped with over time.

SHIMON PERES

If we did not have such a thing as an airplane today,
we would probably create something the size of NASA to make one.

H. ROSS PEROT

If they can get you asking the wrong questions,
they don't have to worry about the answers.

THOMAS PYNCHON

This "Proverb for Paranoids" appeared in Pynchon's *Gravity's Rainbow* (1973). The implication is clear: To control the masses, leaders need only to distract people's attention from the real issues.

If you have a weak candidate and a weak platform,
wrap yourself up in the American flag and talk about the Constitution.

MATTHEW STANLEY QUAY

If government subsidized beaches, we would have a shortage of sand.

RONALD REAGAN

Reagan was fond of making lighthearted remarks that were critical of the government. In another popular example, he said: "Government's view of the economy could be summed up in a few short phrases: 'If it moves, tax it. If it keeps moving, regulate it. And if it stops moving, subsidize it.' "

If you ever injected truth into politics, you would have no politics.

WILL ROGERS

Rogers was famous for humorous quips, but he also offered one remarkably somber one. In 1931, after President Hoover suspended Germany's war reparations payments, a disappointed Rogers said: "If we ever pass out as a great nation, we ought to put on our tombstone, 'America died from a delusion that she had moral leadership.' "

If you're going to sin, sin against God, not the bureaucracy.
God will forgive you but the bureaucracy won't.

HYMAN RICKOVER

If it is committed in the name of God or country, there is no crime so heinous that the public will not forgive it.

TOM ROBBINS, *in* Skinny Legs and All *(1990)*

If the laws could speak for themselves, they would complain of the lawyers in the first place.

GEORGE SAVILE *(Lord Halifax)*

If nominated, I will not run; if elected, I will not serve.

WILLIAM TECUMSEH SHERMAN

This is how history books report Sherman's refusal to accept the Republican Party's presidential nomination in 1884. Ever since, refusing to become a candidate has been referred to as a *Shermanesque denial*, a *Sherman pledge*, or *pulling a Sherman*. As often happens, the familiar quotation is a mythologized version of his original denial (he actually wrote in a telegram: *I will not accept if nominated, and will not serve if elected*). Part of the reason for the confusion may be found in an earlier noncandidacy pledge from Sherman. In an 1871 *Harper's Weekly* article, he was quoted as saying, "If nominated by either party I should peremptorily decline; and even if unanimously elected I should decline to serve."

If I were married to her, I'd be sure to have dinner ready when she got home.

GEORGE SHULTZ, *on Margaret Thatcher*

Shultz said this while serving as secretary of state in the early 1980s. In 1979, Thatcher became the first female prime minister of England. A powerful and no-nonsense politician, she was soon dubbed "The Iron Lady" by the British press.

If the battle for civilization comes down to the wimps versus the barbarians, the barbarians are going to win.

THOMAS SOWELL

On the same subject, Sowell also once wrote, "If you are not prepared to use force to defend civilization, then be prepared to accept barbarism."

If they will stop telling lies about the Democrats, we will stop telling the truth about them.

ADLAI STEVENSON, *on the Republican Party*

This is a well-known line, but what is not so well known is that Stevenson stole the line from a Republican. A half-century earlier, Chauncey Depew said, "I will make a bargain with the Democrats. If they will stop telling lies about Republicans, we will stop telling the truth about them."

If he who breaks the law is not punished, he who obeys it is cheated.

THOMAS SZASZ, *in* The Second Sin *(1973)*

Szasz added: "This, and this alone, is why lawbreakers ought to be punished: to authenticate as good, and to encourage as useful, law-abiding behavior."

If you are guided by opinion polls, you are not practicing leadership—you are practicing followship.

MARGARET THATCHER

If you want a symbolic gesture, don't burn the flag; wash it.

NORMAN THOMAS

If I were consciously to join any party,
it would be that which is the most free to entertain thought.

HENRY DAVID THOREAU, *in an 1852 letter*

If law school is so hard to get through, how come there are so many lawyers?

CALVIN TRILLIN

If you can't convince 'em, confuse 'em.

HARRY S. TRUMAN

Almost all quotation collections present the remark in this way, suggesting that Truman was recommending political deception. Truman did say the words in a 1948 speech, but he was accusing Republicans of the practice: "It's an old political trick: *If you can't convince 'em, confuse 'em*. But this time it won't work."

If you want a friend in Washington, D.C., get a dog.

HARRY S. TRUMAN, *in a common misattribution*

If you believe political pundits, this observation captures one of America's starkest political realities and is one of President Truman's most famous remarks. The problem, however, is that Truman never said such a thing. The likely source of the erroneous attribution is a line attributed to Truman in Samuel Gallu's 1975 Broadway play *Give 'Em Hell, Harry*, starring James Whitmore. (The play was made into a movie a year later, with Whitmore's performance earning him a Best Actor Oscar nomination.) In the play, the words are, "You want a friend in life, get a dog." In 1981, the *Dictionary of Contemporary Quotations* by John Burke and Ned Kehde had Truman saying, "You want a friend in this life, get a dog." And in 1989, Maureen Dowd added to the confusion when she quoted Truman in a *New York Times* column as saying, "If you want a friend in Washington, buy a dog." Despite the lack of evidence, the line is now linked in the public mind to Truman, and countless people, including at least three U.S. presidents, have attributed the observation to the thirty-third president.

If you can find something everyone agrees on, it's wrong.

MORRIS K. "MO" UDALL

In 1976, Udall conceded the presidential nomination to Jimmy Carter after a series of second-place finishes in presidential primaries. When the 1984 election season rolled around, Udall had completely lost his presidential aspirations. When asked if he would once again be throwing his hat in the ring, the witty congressman from Utah offered his own version of a Sherman pledge: "If nominated, I shall run to Mexico. If elected, I shall fight extradition."

Years ago fairy tales all began with "Once upon a time . . ." Now we know they all begin with "If I am elected . . ."

CAROLYN WARNER

If you want to make enemies, try to change something.

WOODROW WILSON, *in a 1916 speech*

14

If You Can't Do Anything Else, There's Always Acting

STAGE & SCREEN

In 1939, fifty-one-year-old Raymond Chandler came out with *The Big Sleep*, a mystery novel that introduced one of history's best-known fictional characters, the hard-boiled private eye Philip Marlowe. The event was a personal triumph for Chandler, who seven years earlier had been fired from his job as an oil company executive because of a host of problems—heavy drinking, excessive absenteeism, and marital problems caused by his reckless womanizing.

Chandler was jolted by the termination and slowly began to turn his life around. He patched things up with his wife Cissy, stopped drinking, and embarked on a new career as a writer. He began to write short stories for pulp mystery magazines, modeling his style in part after Dashiell Hammett, the creator of the iconic private detective Sam Spade. His pulp writing career was never very successful (in 1938, his writing efforts earned him barely over a thousand dollars), but it did allow him to hone his craft and find his voice as a writer.

When *The Big Sleep* was published, Alfred A. Knopf announced the event with a full-page ad in *Variety* magazine. The book was very well received and went on to forever change the fortunes of Chandler and his wife. In the years to come, Chandler built a successful and highly lucrative Marlowe franchise with six more novels, including *Farewell, My Lovely*, *The Lady in the Lake*, and *The Long Goodbye*.

In 1943, executives at Paramount studios brought Chandler to Hollywood to help director Billy Wilder write the screenplay for *Double Indemnity*, an adaptation of a book by James M. Cain. It was an extremely unpleasant experience for Chandler, who constantly argued with Wilder during the making of the film. Even though the two men grew to detest each other, the film went on to become one of the most popular films of 1944, and ultimately a film noir classic. The film was also nominated for seven Oscars, including one for the feuding screenwriters.

Over the next few years, Chandler wrote many more screenplays, but he never enjoyed the experience. He especially disliked producers, saying they had "the morals of a goat, the artistic integrity of a slot machine, and the manners of a floorwalker with delusions of grandeur." In a 1945 letter to a friend, he confided:

If my books had been any worse,
I should not have been invited to Hollywood.
And if they had been any better, I should not have come.

Hollywood has always been regarded as a difficult place to work, but there are few who suffered more than employees at Columbia Pictures during Harry Cohn's despotic reign in the 1920s and '30s. Cohn ran his studio like a modern police state. His tyrannical rages were legendary, and he installed listening devices on sound stages in order to eavesdrop on employees. Like so many other studio heads at the time, he also demanded sexual favors from starlets in exchange for film roles. Long after Cohn's retirement, he was still despised by former employees and others in the film community.

When he died in 1958, a huge throng showed up for his funeral, leading comedian Red Skelton to remark, "If you give the people what they want, they'll show up."

Cohn was as arrogant as he was tyrannical. At a meeting with studio executives, he once launched into an attack on a film he'd seen the previous night in his private screening room. When someone suggested Cohn might have had a different reaction if he had viewed the film in a crowded theater, he scoffed at the idea, saying, "When I'm alone in a projection room, I have a foolproof device for judging whether a picture is good or bad." And then he added:

If my fanny squirms, it's bad. If my fanny doesn't squirm, it's good. It's as simple as that.

Attending the meeting that day was Herman J. Mankiewicz, an aspiring young filmmaker who would later go on to a distinguished career. At the time, though, he was simply a young gofer with an irreverent streak. The image of Cohn's squirming fanny was simply too much for Mankiewicz, who immediately lost his job when he quipped: "Imagine, the whole world wired to Harry Cohn's ass!"

Hollywood has been described in a wide variety of ways over the years, and some of the most memorable descriptions have been expressed conditionally:

If you say what you mean in this town, you're an outlaw.

KEVIN COSTNER

If you stay in Beverly Hills too long, you become a Mercedes.

DUSTIN HOFFMAN

If you don't have happiness, you send out for it.

REX REED, *on life in Hollywood*

If you have a vagina *and* an attitude in this town,
then that's a lethal combination.

SHARON STONE

Memorable ifferisms have also been used to hype Hollywood films. In 1981, Jack Nicholson and Jessica Lange starred in *The Postman Always Rings Twice*, a steamy remake of a 1946 film noir classic starring Lana Turner and John Garfield. Posters advertising the 1981 film declared:

If there was an 11th Commandment, they would have broken that too.

Classic ifferisms have also shown up in Hollywood films. In the 1978 film *Grease*, one of the very best sayings from the 1950s was delivered by Eve Arden in the role of the high school principal, Miss McGee:

If you can't be an athlete, be an athletic supporter.

Perhaps my favorite example, though, comes from the 1948 film *Mr. Blandings Builds His Dream House*. In the film, Cary Grant plays Jim Blandings, an adman who is in danger of losing his job because he can't come up with a client-pleasing advertising slogan for a baked ham account. One day, his cook and housekeeper Gussie (played by Louise Beavers) saves the day when she spontaneously utters the words:

If you ain't eatin' Wham, you ain't eatin' ham!

In the rest of the chapter, I'll present many more ifferisms from actors, directors, screenwriters, and others associated with the world of stage and screen.

If you look confident you can pull off anything—
even if you have no clue what you're doing.

JESSICA ALBA

If you're not careful, you may find that you're making one film and the leading man is making another.

ANN-MARGRET

If I'm going to be a success, I must be scandalous.

JOSEPHINE BAKER

Born in St. Louis, Baker was a teen dancer in New York City when she traveled to Paris in 1925 with an all-black troupe called *La Revue Nègre*. She quickly became the talk of the town, famous for her steamy sexuality and scandalous routines, which included a dance in which she wore only a string of bananas.

If you're an actor, it's always hard to be married.

LEX BARKER

This is one of the great understatements in Hollywood history. Barker, best known for his Tarzan roles, may not have matched the record of such serial spouses as Zsa Zsa Gabor (nine), Mickey Rooney (eight), or Liz Taylor (eight), but he contributed to the Hollywood stereotype by walking to the altar five times. He was the fourth husband of Lana Turner, who was married seven times.

If New York is the Big Apple, then Hollywood must be the Big Nipple.

BERNARDO BERTOLUCCI

Bertolucci made this remarkable observation at the 1988 Academy Awards ceremony. It was a huge night for the Italian filmmaker, whose film *The Last Emperor* won nine Oscars, including Best Picture and Best Director. The remark drew hearty laughter and a few shocked gasps. Bertolucci later explained: "I wanted to say that I was overwhelmed by the gratification, which poured forth like milk."

If you know you are going to fail, then fail gloriously!

CATE BLANCHETT

If you're successful,
acting is about as soft a job as anybody could ever wish for.
But if you're unsuccessful, it's worse than having a skin disease.

MARLON BRANDO

On the danger of typecasting, Brando said, "If you play a pig, they think you're a pig." And on another aspect of Hollywood life, he bluntly observed, "If there's anything unsettling to the stomach, it's watching actors on television talk about their personal lives."

If it's a good script, I'll do it.
And if it's a bad script, and they pay me enough, I'll do it.

GEORGE BURNS

If you're going to make rubbish, be the best rubbish in it.

RICHARD BURTON

Burton was the highest-paid actor in the 1960s. In the 1970s, with his career in decline, he was the best rubbish in such B-films as *Bluebeard* (1972) and *The Klansman* (1974).

If a movie is described as a romantic comedy
you can usually find me next door playing pinball.

GEORGE CARLIN

If I had the choice of having a woman in my arms
or shooting a bad guy on a horse, I'd take the horse. It's a lot more fun.

KEVIN COSTNER

If you're doing the devil, look for the angel in him.
If you're doing the angel, look for the devil in him.

HUME CRONYN, *on his acting method*

If you become a star, you don't change, everyone else does.

KIRK DOUGLAS

If Douglas did not change as a result of his star status, he would be an exception to the rule. Fame, like power, has a corrupting influence, unless people go to great lengths to guard against it. Robert Redford expressed it well in a 2007 interview on *60 Minutes*. Talking about his overnight success after he starred in the 1969 film *Butch Cassidy and the Sundance Kid*, he said, "Suddenly you realize that you're being treated like an object, and the danger to your psyche was that, if you didn't pay attention and you didn't stay clear, you'd begin to behave like one. And if you did that too long, you might end up becoming one."

If I'd known what a big shot Michael was going to be,
I would've been nicer to him as a kid.

KIRK DOUGLAS, *on son Michael*

The senior Douglas said this in a 1986 *Playboy* interview. In a 1990 interview, the mother of actor Albert Finney—Mrs. Alice Finney—offered a related thought: "If we'd known he was going to be an actor, we'd have given him a fancier name."

If a movie isn't a hit right out of the gate, they drop it.

ROGER EBERT, *on Hollywood executives*

The effect, according to Ebert, is that "the whole mainstream Hollywood product has been skewed toward violence and vulgar teen comedy."

If gentlemen prefer blondes, then I'm a blonde that prefers gentlemen.

BARBARA EDEN

If you're not part of the steamroller, you're part of the road.

RICHARD FRANK

When Frank became president of Disney Studios in 1985, the company was making ten films a year. In 1994, the company turned out sixty pictures.

If only those who dream about Hollywood knew how difficult it all is.

GRETA GARBO

If people making a movie didn't keep kissing, they'd be at each other's throats.

AVA GARDNER

If there wasn't something called acting,
they would probably hospitalize people like me.

WHOOPI GOLDBERG

Goldberg said this in a 1992 *Parade* magazine article. A generation earlier, actress Mia Farrow said, "If I weren't doing what I'm doing now . . . I'd be in an asylum. I'm sure of it." The action star Bruce Lee also echoed the theme: "If I hadn't become a star, I would probably have become a gangster."

If I can act, I want the world to know it; if I can't, I want to know it.

KATHARINE HEPBURN

The words undoubtedly capture what the real-life Hepburn believed, but she said them as an aspiring fictional actress in the 1937 film *Stage Door* (screenplay by Morrie Ryskind and Anthony Veiller). In the film, Hepburn plays a socialite who wants to become a Broadway actress without the help of her wealthy father. The film, based on a hit Broadway play by Edna Ferber and George S. Kaufman, received four Oscar nominations, including Best Picture and Best Screenplay. Kaufman was not impressed with the film, however, wryly observing that the screenwriters had so substantially changed the original script and storyline that the title of the film should have been changed to *Screen Door*.

If you give audiences a chance, they'll do half your acting for you.

KATHARINE HEPBURN

Jean Harlow concurred: "If audiences like you, you don't have to be an actress."

**If you need a ceiling painted, a chariot race run,
a city besieged, or the Red Sea parted—you think of me.**

CHARLTON HESTON, *in 1975*

Nobody starred in more epic films than Heston, and here he alludes to his roles as Michelangelo in *The Agony and the Ecstasy* (1965), as Judah Ben-Hur in *Ben-Hur* (1959), as the rugged construction engineer Stewart Graff in *Earthquake* (1974), and as Moses in *The Ten Commandments* (1956).

**If I make a film of *Cinderella*,
people will immediately start looking for the corpse.**

ALFRED HITCHCOCK

If I met Dorothy—me as a woman—at a party, I'd turn her down.

DUSTIN HOFFMANN, *on his role as Dorothy Michaels in* Tootsie *(1982)*

If I would be in this business for *business*, I wouldn't be in this business.

SOL HUROK, *on theatrical producing*

If you're afraid of movies that excite your senses, you're afraid of movies.

PAULINE KAEL

If you really want to see fireworks, it's better with the lights off.

GRACE KELLY, *to costar Cary Grant in the 1955 film* To Catch a Thief

After delivering the line, Kelly's character turns off the lights and says, "I have a feeling that tonight you're going to see one of the Riviera's most fascinating sights." Then she hastily adds, "I was talking about the fireworks."

If you haven't cried, your eyes can't be beautiful.

SOPHIA LOREN

If the boy and girl walk off into the sunset hand-in-hand in the last scene, it adds $10 million to the box office.

GEORGE LUCAS

If I had one percent of the millions *Dracula* has made, I wouldn't be sitting here now.

BELA LUGOSI

After starring in the 1931 film classic *Dracula*, Lugosi was typecast as a horror villain and was never able to successfully break out of the box. He was on the edge of poverty when he died at age seventy-three in 1956.

If you can't do anything else, there's always acting.

STEVE MCQUEEN, *to Chuck Norris*

According to Norris, McQueen used these exact words in 1974 when he urged him to take acting lessons at MGM Studios. McQueen was a skilled martial artist with a ninth-degree black belt, and Norris was one of his instructors. Norris, who learned martial arts while serving in the Air Force in Korea, soon began to compete professionally. In 1969, *Black Belt* magazine named him "Fighter of the Year." His first starring role was in the 1977 film *Breaker! Breaker!*

If your home burns down, rescue the dogs.
At least they'll be faithful to you.

LEE MARVIN, *during his celebrated 1971 "palimony" suit*

If only God could create a lawyer who could make a deal in ten minutes.

MARCELLO MASTROIANNI

People in the film industry have long complained about how long it takes to put a deal together, and lawyers often get the blame. Douglas Adams, author of *The Hitchhiker's Guide to the Galaxy*, expressed the complaint in vivid metaphorical language: "Getting a movie made in Hollywood is like trying to grill a steak by having a succession of people coming into the room and breathing on it."

If you cast wrong, you are in a lot of trouble.

PAUL MAZURSKY

If we'd had as many soldiers as that, we'd have won the war.

MARGARET MITCHELL

Mitchell made this remark after seeing the huge number of Confederate soldiers in the 1939 film *Gone With the Wind*, based on her 1936 novel.

If you achieve success, you will get applause,
and if you get applause, you will hear it.
My advice to you concerning applause is this:
Enjoy it but never quite believe it.

ROBERT MONTGOMERY

If I saved all my bad notices, I'd need two houses.

ROGER MOORE

If I died today, they might write on my tombstone:
"Here lies Paul Newman, died at 43, a failure because his eyes turned brown."

PAUL NEWMAN,
in a 1969 Playboy *interview*

If it works, *that's* The Method.

JACK NICHOLSON, *on Method acting*

If there's anything disgusting about the movie business,
it's the whoredom of my peers.

SEAN PENN

If a film is successful, it is commercial; if it isn't, it is art.

CARLO PONTI

If it's not fun, it's not worth doing.

ROBERT REDFORD

Redford said this in a 2007 documentary as he reflected on the essence of his and Paul Newman's careers. He added, "And it doesn't have to be silly. It can be hard work and it can be edgy. It can be a lot of things. But it can also be fun."

If a writer is sensitive about his work being treated like Moe, Curly and Larry working over the Sistine Chapel with a crowbar, then he would do well to avoid screenwriting altogether.

TERRY SOUTHERN

Southern wrote the screenplays for many films and received Oscar nominations for two film classics: *Dr. Strangelove* (1963) and *Easy Rider* (1969).

If a person can tell me the idea in twenty-five words or less, it's going to make a pretty good movie. I like ideas, especially movie ideas, that you can hold in your hand.

STEVEN SPIELBERG

If I have to diet, I'm gonna diet.
If I have to work out, I'm gonna work out.
If I have to sleep upside-down like a bat
so I don't look like a basset hound, that's what I'm gonna do.

SHARON STONE, *on what it takes to succeed in Hollywood*

If a man is pictured chopping off a woman's breast, it only gets an "R" rating; but if, God forbid, a man is pictured kissing a woman's breast, it gets an "X" rating.

SALLY STRUTHERS

Struthers added: "Why is violence more acceptable than tenderness?"

If someone's dumb enough to offer me a million dollars to make a picture, I am certainly not dumb enough to turn it down.

ELIZABETH TAYLOR

On the money paid by film producers, actress Glenda Jackson said in 1985: "If all the system can offer its talent is the crap it does, then producers should pay through the eyes, ears, nose, mouth—any orifice you can think of."

If you have the power to put your name on the screen, your name on the screen is meaningless.

IRVING THALBERG

Thalberg's point is clear: If you have the power to determine whose names appear on screen credits, you're not going to be concerned about whether your name is on the list. In F. Scott Fitzgerald's final novel *The Last Tycoon* (1941), Hollywood mogul Monroe Stahr (the character inspired by Thalberg) says: "I don't want my name on the screen because credit is something that should be given to others. If you are in a position to give credit to yourself, then you do not need it."

If you lose weight to keep your ass, your face goes. But if the face is good, forget the ass. I'll choose the face.

KATHLEEN TURNER

Turner, whose fabulous face, sultry voice, and smoldering sensuality came together in the 1981 film *Body Heat*, also had great comedic talent, which she showed off in the 1984 film *Romancing the Stone*.

If it were not for villains, there'd be no heroes.

PETER USTINOV

**If I want to pursue the art of painting—or music or writing or sculpture—
it requires only my time and a few dollars for materials.
If, however, I want to produce a motion picture
I have to go out and raise a million dollars!**

ORSON WELLES

If I asked for a cup of coffee, someone would search for the double meaning.

MAE WEST

If you're going to tell people the truth, be funny or they'll kill you.

BILLY WILDER

15

If You Aren't Fired with Enthusiasm, You'll Be Fired with Enthusiasm

BUSINESS & MANAGEMENT

As the nineteenth century turned into the twentieth, J. P. Morgan was one of the most familiar names in America's business community. The son of a prominent American banker, he used his father's firm as a launching pad to establish J. P. Morgan & Company, America's most influential private banking house. Morgan was one of America's great dealmakers, helping arrange mergers that led to the formation of firms like General Electric and the United States Steel Corporation. He was also an early corporate raider, so successful in reorganizing floundering businesses that his turnaround efforts were referred to as *Morganization*.

Morgan was also one of Manhattan's most familiar faces. A large man with massive shoulders, he had a ruddy, bulbous nose caused by the chronic skin disease rosacea. Despite his wealth, the problem was left untreated and became worse over time, his face eventually taking on a purplish hue and becoming grotesquely deformed. The condition clearly bothered Morgan, who had all his formal portrait photographs retouched. The tycoon was also frustrated by the many newspaper photographers who followed him around, and he was often seen angrily waving his cane at photographers trying to get a close-up shot.

Morgan used his great wealth to support a lavish lifestyle. He had a private suite on the *RMS Titanic*, and would have been on the maiden voyage were it not for a last-minute change of plans. His Manhattan residence was the first private home in America to be fully powered by electricity. He also owned several state-of-the-art yachts, including *The Corsair*, a boat so technologically advanced that it was purchased by the U.S. government and used in the Spanish-American War.

Morgan's interest in yachting resulted in his most famous remark. According to legend, while showing off his yacht to a fellow millionaire, Morgan was asked, "How much did it cost?" He replied:

If you have to ask the price, you can't afford it.

The saying is also sometimes attributed to Cornelius Vanderbilt, but it is not certain that either man made the remark in exactly this way. In her 1999 biography, *Morgan*, Jean Strouse tracked down a similar—but less impressive—reply Morgan made when he was asked about the price of his yacht: "You have no right to own a yacht if you ask that question." During her research, Strouse developed a sympathetic view of Morgan, but her admiration did not extend to his verbal skills. Regarding his ability to come up with the quip that is so closely associated with him, she wrote: "Morgan was a singularly inarticulate, unreflective man, not likely to come up with a maxim worthy of Oscar Wilde."

Morgan's famous reply, whether accurate or not, is often mentioned in tandem with that of another American business tycoon, J. Paul Getty. When Getty died in 1976, he was routinely described as "the richest man in the world." The son of a man who had made millions in the Oklahoma oil fields, Getty built an empire on the foundation his father had established, and he went on to became one of the first Americans to be described as a billionaire.

He made most of his money in the oil business, as the owner of the Getty Oil Company, but he was extremely well-diversified and is said to have held a controlling interest in over 200 companies. Getty once offered an observation that has become a classic in business circles:

If you can actually count your money, then you're not really rich.

When I hear people say "I'm not really interested in business," I believe they fail to appreciate the drama, excitement, and intrigue in the corporate world. Fortunately, much of that complexity has been captured in memorable observations. A few years ago, I was discussing brand loyalty with several CEOs. When one of them asserted that Harley-Davidson was unrivaled in customer loyalty, another quoted a line from one of his B-school professors:

If you can persuade your customer to tattoo your name on their chest, they probably will not ever switch brands.

Many word and language lovers don't associate great quotations with the world of business, but this is a view that is not supported by the evidence—as you will see with the many ifferisms to be found in the remainder of the chapter.

If you pay peanuts, you get monkeys.

ANONYMOUS SAYING,
first appearing in the 1960s

If you think you can, you're right.
And if you think you can't, you're right.

MARY KAY ASH

This observation from the cosmetics legend was inspired by a famous

Henry Ford thought: "If you think you can or think you can't, you're probably right."

If I had to do it over, I'd buy every square foot on the island of Manhattan.

JOHN JACOB ASTOR, *on his deathbed in 1848*

If stock market experts were so expert,
they would be buying stock, not selling advice.

NORMAN AUGUSTINE

If you had to identify, in one word, the reason why
the human race has not achieved, and never will achieve,
its full potential, that word would be "meetings."

DAVE BARRY

If a person can't do something, go back to goal setting.
If a person won't do something, reprimand.

KEN BLANCHARD

If you look for the best in your employees, they'll flourish.
If you criticize or look for the worst, they'll shrivel up.
We all need lots of watering.

RICHARD BRANSON

If past history was all there was to the game,
the richest people would be the librarians.

WARREN BUFFETT, *on the game of investing*

The worst rule of management is "If it ain't broke, don't fix it."
In today's economy, if it ain't broke,
you might as well break it yourself, because it soon will be.

WAYNE CALLOWAY, *former Pepsi-Cola CEO*

If you would be a favorite of your king, address yourself to his weaknesses. An application to his reason will seldom prove very successful.

LORD CHESTERFIELD *(Philip Dormer Stanhope)*

This recommendation, made in a 1753 letter to his son, looks like an early observation in the now-popular literature about "managing your boss."

If you think you've got it, then you've got it.
If you think you don't have it, even if you've got it, then you don't have it.

HERB COHEN, *on power*

In *You Can Negotiate Anything* (1980), Cohen also offered these wise words: "If you have something difficult to negotiate—an emotional issue, or a concrete item that can be stated numerically, such as price, cost, interest rate, or salary—cope with it at the end of a negotiation, after the other side has made a hefty expenditure of effort and a substantial time investment."

If the automobile had followed the same development cycle as the computer, a Rolls-Royce would today cost $100, get one million miles to the gallon, and explode once a year, killing everyone inside.

ROBERT X. CRINGELY

Robert X. Cringely was the pen name of Mark Stephens, who wrote a "Notes From the Field" column for *InfoWorld* magazine from 1987 to 1995.

If you want creative workers, give them enough time to play.

JOHN CLEESE

If you underrate him he will bitterly resent it or impute to you the deficiency in brains and knowledge you imputed to him.

PETER DRUCKER, *on managing your boss*

Drucker began by saying: "Never underrate the boss! The boss may look illiterate. He may look stupid. But there is no risk at all in overrating a boss."

If you have too many problems, maybe you should go out of business. There is no law that says a company must last forever.

PETER DRUCKER

If you have a radical idea . . . don't be radical in how you carry it out. Become a right-wing conservative in carrying out a left-wing idea.

J. PRESPER ECKERT

Eckert and colleague John Mauchly invented the first electronic digital computer, the ENIAC (forerunner of the first commercial computer, the UNIVAC).

If you have a job without aggravations, you don't have a job.

MALCOLM FORBES

Forbes, an avid quotation collector, was likely aware of a similar thought from Dr. Samuel Johnson: "If therefore the profession you have chosen has some unexpected inconveniences, console yourself by reflecting that no profession is without them."

If you ride a horse, sit close and tight,
if you ride a man, sit easy and light.

BENJAMIN FRANKLIN, *from*
Poor Richard's Almanack *(1734)*

If you would know the value of money, go and try to borrow some.

BENJAMIN FRANKLIN,
from The Way to Wealth *(1758)*

If thy business be perplexed, divide it, and look upon all its parts and sides.

THOMAS FULLER, M.D.

This 1731 recommendation about breaking down a problem into its component parts is early advice about taking an analytical approach to solving business problems.

If you have a reputation for always making all the money there is in a deal, you won't make many deals.

J. PAUL GETTY, *quoting his father*

The elder Getty began by saying, "You must never try to make all the money that's in a deal. Let the other fellow make some money too."

If you wish in this world to advance,
Your merits you're bound to enhance;
You must stir it and stump it,
And blow your own trumpet,
Or, trust me, you haven't a chance.

W. S. GILBERT, *in the comic opera*
Ruddigore *(1887)*

To blow your own trumpet means "to boast about one's accomplishments" (the American expression is *to blow your own horn*). From ancient times, the arrival of royalty was announced by the blowing of trumpets. The sentiment also shows up in a famous biblical passage (Matthew 6:2): "So whenever you give to the poor, don't blow a trumpet before you as the hypocrites do . . . so that they will be praised by people." A favorite saying of the Canadian-British entrepreneur William Maxwell Aitken (Lord Beaverbrook) was, "If you don't blow your own trumpet, no one else is going to blow it for you."

If you assign people duties without granting them any rights,
you must pay them well.

JOHANN WOLFGANG VON GOETHE

If I see something I like, I buy it; then I try to sell it.

LORD LEW GRADE

If you make a product good enough
even though you live in the depths of the forest,
the public will make a path to your door, says the philosopher.
But if you want the public in sufficient numbers,
you would better construct a highway.
Advertising is that highway.

WILLIAM RANDOLPH HEARST

Hearst, the American newspaper magnate, here makes an allusion to the famous "If you build a better mousetrap" line from Ralph Waldo Emerson. That full quotation—and the story behind it—appears in the Classic Ifferisms chapter.

If you can make people feel it's OK to enjoy themselves,
you've got a winning product—whatever it is.

HUGH HEFNER

If you want to know whether you are
destined to be a success or failure, you can easily find out.
One test is simple and infallible. Are you able to save money?

JAMES J. HILL

If you don't profit from your investment mistakes, someone else will.

YALE HIRSCH

If I had to sum up in one word what makes a good manager, I'd say decisiveness.

LEE IACOCCA

If economists were any good at business, they would be rich men instead of advisers to rich men.

KERKOR "KIRK" KERKORIAN

Born to struggling Armenian immigrants, Kerkorian went from eighth-grade dropout to one of the principal architects of the city of Las Vegas. In 2008, *Forbes* magazine called him the world's forty-first richest person. A related observation on economists has been attributed to the father of modern economic theory, John Maynard Keynes: "If economists could manage to get themselves thought of as humble, competent people on a level with dentists, that would be splendid."

If you want to kill any idea in the world today, get a committee working on it.

CHARLES F. KETTERING

Kettering, a towering figure in American industry, invented the electric ignition that made hand-cranking of automobiles obsolete. His name appears on over 300 patents, including ones for car radios, automotive air conditioning, and colored paint for cars. When his company, A. C. Delco, was acquired by General Motors in 1920, Kettering became GM's head of research, a post he held for twenty-seven years. Committees have been lambasted in many ways over the years, and some of the best indictments have been expressed ifferistically:

If Columbus had had an advisory committee,
he would probably still be at the dock.

ARTHUR J. GOLDBERG

If you see a snake, just kill it—don't appoint a committee on snakes.

ROSS PEROT

**If hard work were such a wonderful thing,
surely the rich would have kept it all to themselves.**

LANE KIRKLAND

Kirkland, the president of the AFL-CIO, said this after becoming annoyed with wealthy fat cats who were extolling the value of hard work to low-paid employees.

**If institutions need to be rescued like banks,
they should be regulated like banks.**

PAUL KRUGMAN,
during the 2008 Wall Street meltdown

If you are able to state a problem, it can be solved.

EDWIN H. LAND

**If you have a lot of what people want and can't get,
then you can supply the demand and shovel in the dough.**

MEYER LANSKY

Lansky and boyhood friends Lucky Luciano and Bugsy Siegel put this principle—often called "Lansky's Law"—into practice during Prohibition. When liquor became legal in the 1930s, their crime syndicate turned to gambling.

**If you are planning on doing business with someone again,
don't be too tough in the negotiations.
If you're going to skin a cat, don't keep it as a house cat.**

MARVIN S. LEVIN

If you aren't fired with enthusiasm, you'll be fired with enthusiasm.

VINCE LOMBARDI

This is one of the most popular observations from one of the most famous coaches in football history. The remark, which is now far more popular in the business arena than in the sports world, is especially favored by no-nonsense managers and others who adopt a hard-nosed approach to management.

If you want a man to be for you, never let him feel he is dependent on you. Make him feel you are in some way dependent on him.

GEORGE C. MARSHALL

If you get to thirty-five and your job still involves wearing a name tag, you've probably made a serious vocational error.

DENNIS MILLER

If you go through life convinced that your way is always best, all the new ideas in the world will pass you by.

AKIO MORITA, *founder of Sony Corporation*

If Aristotle Ran General Motors

TOM MORRIS

This was the title of a 1997 bestseller that advised business leaders to heed the advice of ancient thinkers. Morris, a Notre Dame philosophy professor, argued: "If we let the great philosophers guide our thinking, and if we then begin to become philosophers ourselves, we put ourselves in the very best position to move towards genuine excellence, true prosperity, and deeply satisfying success in our businesses, our families, and our lives." In 2006, Morris came out with a sequel: *If Harry Potter Ran General Electric.*

If we ever have a plan, we're screwed.

PAUL NEWMAN

Newman made this the official motto for *Newman's Own*, a specialty food company that he and A. E. Hotchner founded in 1982 to support their favorite charities. Since its founding, the company has donated over $220 million dollars to charity. When the two friends founded the company, they agreed that the point was to have as much fun as they could while doing good work. Newman also once said, "If we stop having fun, we're closing up shop."

If the marketplace has gone bonkers, you better have a bonkers organization. Straightlaced folks are not going to make it in a world that's not straightlaced.

TOM PETERS

If you suspect a man, don't employ him;
and if you employ him, don't suspect him.

CHINESE PROVERB

If a man works for you, you work for him.

JAPANESE PROVERB

If fools went not to market, bad wares would not be sold.

SPANISH PROVERB

If you speak the truth, have a foot in the stirrup.

TURKISH PROVERB

The truth of this ancient proverb shows up in a modern saying that has become very popular in business circles: "If you tell your boss the truth, the truth shall set you free."

If you do business with somebody you don't like, sooner or later you'll get screwed.

HARRY QUADRACCI

Quadracci, whose Quad/Graphics printing firm did such large-volume runs as *Time*, *Sports Illustrated*, and *Playboy*, was well known for his plain-speaking style. He preceded this observation by saying: "One of our iron-clad rules is 'Never do business with anybody you don't like.' If you don't like somebody, there's a reason. Chances are it's because you don't trust him, and you're probably right."

If your only goal is to become rich, you will never achieve it.

JOHN D. ROCKEFELLER

J. C. Hall, founder of Hallmark Cards, said similarly: "If a man goes into business with only the idea of making money, the chances are he won't."

If you think you're too small to have an impact, try going to bed with a mosquito.

ANITA RODDICK

Roddick was the founder of The Body Shop, an environmentally friendly cosmetics company. This saying, a personal motto that captured her determination to take on the giants of the cosmetics industry, eventually appeared on all company vehicles. About her firm's socially responsible orientation, Roddick said, "If I can't do something for the public good, what the hell am I doing?"

If you want to build a ship, don't herd people together to collect wood and don't assign them tasks and work, but rather teach them a yearning for the endless immensity of the sea.

ANTOINE DE SAINT-EXUPÉRY

If we hadn't put a man on the moon, there wouldn't be a Silicon Valley today.

JOHN SCULLEY, *in 1992*

If you love what you are doing, you will be successful.

ALBERT SCHWEITZER

Schweitzer preceded this observation by writing: "Success is not the key to happiness. Happiness is the key to success."

If you bet a horse, that's gambling.
If you bet you can make three spades, that's entertainment.
If you bet cotton will go up three points, that's business.

WILLIAM F. "BLACKIE" SHERROD

If you do it right 51 percent of the time you will end up a hero.

ALFRED P. SLOAN

If asked when you can deliver something, ask for time to think. Build in a margin of safety. Name a date. Then deliver it earlier than you promised.

ROBERT TOWNSEND

This advice appeared in Townsend's 1970 business classic *Up the Organization*. As president of Avis Rent-a-Car, Townsend introduced the famous "We Try Harder" slogan and built the company into a major industry player. He was also a critic of the way businesses were typically run. In another observation from the book, he wrote: "If you're the boss and your people fight you openly when they think you're wrong—that's healthy. If your men fight you openly in your presence—that's healthy. But keep all conflict eyeball to eyeball."

If you don't do it excellently, don't do it at all.

ROBERT TOWNSEND

This comes from *Further Up the Organization*, the 1984 sequel to Townsend's 1970 bestseller. He added: "If it's not excellent, it won't be profitable or fun, and if you're not in business for fun or profit, what the hell are you doing there?"

If you're going to be thinking anyway, you might as well think big.

DONALD TRUMP

Trump offered this thought in *The Art of the Deal* (1987). He revealed yet another aspect of his business philosophy when he once observed, "If people screw me, I screw back in spades."

If you're going to have a breakfast meeting,
it should be in bed with a beautiful woman.

GORDON WHITE

White, an English business tycoon who moved to America in 1973, became one of the era's most successful corporate raiders. A ruthless businessman, he was also notorious for his fun-loving ways. He introduced this observation by saying, "A breakfast meeting is the most uncivilized idea I've ever heard of."

If Christmas did not exist it would be necessary to invent it.

KATHERINE WHITEHORN, *on the importance of holiday shopping to a nation's economy*

If you don't bet on a few losers, you'll never bet on a winner.

DAVID WICKINS

**If you want to understand entrepreneurs,
you have to study the psychology of the juvenile delinquent.**

ABRAHAM ZALEZNICK

Zaleznick, a practicing psychoanalyst who also taught at the Harvard Business School, said this in a 1992 *U.S. News & World Report* article. His point was that entrepreneurs are not like traditional business people, but more like delinquents—who are noted for their poor impulse control, questionable judgment, and reckless habits.

**If two men on a job agree all the time, then one is useless.
If they disagree all the time, then both are useless.**

DARRYL F. ZANUCK

If you're sincere, praise is effective. If you're insincere, it's manipulative.

ZIG ZIGLAR

16

If You Add to the Truth, You Subtract from It

OXYMORONIC & PARADOXICAL IFFERISMS

In 1953, a twenty-nine-year-old advertising copywriter named Joseph Heller awakened one morning with an idea for a novel based on his experiences as a B-25 bombardier in World War II. He kept the key ingredients of the idea in his mind as he hurriedly dressed and took the subway to his job at a small Manhattan advertising agency. For the next several hours, he hunched over his desk as he wrote the entire first chapter in longhand. As the months went by, he continued to work on the project, occasionally at work, but mainly in a small writing area in his apartment on West End Avenue.

In early 1955, Heller submitted the first chapter of his book to *New World Writing* magazine under the title "Catch-18." He was delighted when he received a check for twenty-five dollars and an agreement to publish the chapter. Few people noticed the publication of the piece later that year, and there was some doubt in Heller's mind if the entire novel would ever be published.

Two years later, in 1957, a draft of the complete novel landed on the desk of Candida Donadio, a twenty-eight-year-old former secretary who had just been promoted to her first job as a literary agent. Donadio immediately recognized the book's potential and began shopping it around. She and Heller were elated when Simon & Schuster offered a $1,500 advance and agreed to publish the book.

It took Heller a few more years to finish the project, and the book was finally published in 1961—but not with the original "Catch–18" title. As the book neared completion, it was learned that writer Leon Uris was coming out with a novel titled *Mila 18*. Concerned about a confusion of titles, Donadio and Heller considered other numbers, including 11 (rejected because of the 1960 film *Ocean's Eleven*) and 17 (rejected because of Billy Wilder's 1953 film *Stalag 17*). They settled on 22, in part because Donadio's birthday was on October 22, 1929.

Catch-22 received mixed reviews. *The Nation* called it "the best novel to come out in years," but *The New York Times* said it was "repetitive and monotonous." Hardback sales during the first year were respectable but not spectacular. A British version of the book, published a year later, did extremely well, and when an American paperback version came out in 1962, it became a bona fide best seller. Movie rights were also sold in 1962—although the film would not appear for eight more years—and Heller was on his way to fame and fortune. The book went on to sell well over ten million copies and is now regarded as a great literary achievement. In 1998, Modern Library ranked it number seven on their list of the hundred best novels of the twentieth century.

In 1975, *Playboy* magazine selected Heller for an interview. As journalist Sam Merrill prepared for the meeting, he was astonished to discover that the now-wealthy writer was still teaching fiction and even grading student papers at the City College of New York. When he asked, "Have you considered giving up teaching so you could spend more time on your writing?" Heller gave a legendary reply:

If I gave up teaching, I would have no time at all for writing.

On the surface, Heller's reply makes no sense. After all, logic would suggest that giving up teaching would give him more time for writing. But Heller wasn't speaking logically, he was speaking paradoxically. And in the fascinating world of paradox, things are not as they appear on the surface. In his cleverly worded reply, Heller was communicating a paradoxical truth: More time to do what we want often makes us less productive, not more.

Paradoxical sayings are fascinating because they are true and false at the same time. A perfect example is "less is more" (authored by Robert Browning, but popularized by the German-born architect Ludwig Mies van der Rohe). From a logical point of view, the saying makes no sense. But in architecture, writing, art, and many other fields of endeavor, a final product is almost always improved when nonessential or extraneous elements are removed. "Less is more," like all oxymoronic and paradoxical sayings, is literally false but figuratively true.

I explored the nature of paradoxical thinking in my 2004 book, *Oxymoronica*. When most people think of an oxymoron, they think of simple two-word constructions, like jumbo shrimp, pretty ugly, or old news. An oxymoron is formed when two incompatible words are conjoined, creating a *compressed paradox*.

The most impressive examples of oxymoronica don't contain a simple contradiction in *terms*, but rather a contradiction in *ideas*. Some of history's most famous sayings are oxymoronically phrased, like "The more things change, the more they remain the same." When people first encounter a contradiction in ideas, their initial reaction is often to feel puzzled. An observation from the New Zealand–born writer Katherine Mansfield nicely illustrates the point:

If you wish to live, you must first attend your own funeral.

We cannot literally attend our own funerals, but we can do it figuratively, by imagining what will be written about us in obituaries and what will be said in eulogies. Only after we have done something like this, according to Mansfield, can we truly live. In some of history's most intriguing observations, opposing ideas cooperate with one another to express a truth or make a point:

**If you would be a real seeker after truth,
it is necessary that at least once in your life you doubt,
as far as possible, all things.**

RENÉ DESCARTES

If a man has a strong faith, he can indulge in the luxury of skepticism.

FRIEDRICH NIETZSCHE

**If you wish to forget anything on the spot,
make a note that this thing is to be remembered.**

EDGAR ALLAN POE

If you would civilize a man, begin with his grandmother.

VICTOR HUGO

The underlying notion in this last observation is that a human being cannot be civilized in one lifetime, but only—if it is going to happen at all—after several generations. Oliver Wendell Holmes, Sr., was thinking along the same lines when he wrote in *The Autocrat of the Breakfast Table* (1849): "A child's education should begin at least one hundred years before he was born."

Word and language lovers have always been intrigued by oxymoronic sayings. Some come from history's deepest thinkers:

If people never did silly things, nothing intelligent would ever get done.

LUDWIG WITTGENSTEIN

And some come from anonymous sources, like a modern classic addressed to know-it-alls who think they can assemble a product or operate a machine without as much as a glance at the operating manual:

If all else fails, read the instructions.

Oxymoronic observations have long been a staple of humorists, as when George Carlin once asked:

If you try to fail and succeed, what have you done?

Or when P. J. O'Rourke observed:

If you think health care is expensive now,
wait until you see what it costs when it's free.

Or when the writers of *The Simpsons* had Homer Simpson say to his children:

If you really want something in life, you have to work for it.
Now quiet, they're about to announce the lottery numbers.

Someone once said that a paradox is a truth standing on its head to get our attention. As you peruse the many oxymoronic ifferisms that follow, notice how often your thinking is stimulated by logical falsehoods and paradoxical truths.

If you listen carefully,
you get to hear everything you didn't want to hear in the first place.

SHOLEM ALEICHEM

Often called "The Yiddish Mark Twain," Aleichem's stories and characters, such as Tevye the Milkman, inspired the 1964 musical *Fiddler on the Roof.*

If I am doing nothing, I like to be doing nothing to some purpose.

ALAN BENNETT

If the animals had reason, they would act just as ridiculous as we menfolks do.

JOSH BILLINGS *(Henry Wheeler Shaw)*

**If there are obstacles,
the shortest line between two points may be the crooked line.**

BERTOLT BRECHT

If you wish to live wisely, ignore sayings—including this one.

HEYWOOD BROUN

If you live in New York, even if you're Catholic, you're Jewish.

LENNY BRUCE, *in 1992*

New York City has the largest population of Jews outside of Israel, and Bruce's remark captures how deeply Jewish life is embedded in the city's culture.

"If the Phone Doesn't Ring, It's Me"

JIMMY BUFFETT

This was the title of a song from Buffett's 1985 album, *Last Mango in Paris*. After the song aired, it became one of the most popular "break-up" lines of the 1980s.

If a lot of cures are suggested for a disease, it means the disease is incurable.

ANTON CHEKHOV

If a woman likes another woman, she's cordial.
If she doesn't like her, she's very cordial.

IRVIN S. COBB

If a cause be good,
the most violent attack of its enemies will not injure it so much
as an injudicious defense of it by its friends.

CHARLES CALEB COLTON

If you don't go to other men's funerals, they won't go to yours.

CLARENCE DAY

A similar observation ("Always go to other people's funerals; otherwise they won't go to yours") is attributed to Yogi Berra, but the original sentiment was authored by Day. It first appeared in his 1935 best seller *Life with Father*, a portrait of nineteenth-century family life in New York City. In another well-known—and much-copied—oxymoronic thought, Day wrote: "If your parents didn't have children, there's a good chance that you won't have any."

If we want everything to remain as it is,
it will be necessary for everything to change.

GIUSEPPE DI LAMPEDUSA

This is one of the twentieth century's most famous sayings, but the author is unknown to most present-day readers. Lampedusa was a wealthy Sicilian prince whose posthumously published 1958 novel *The Leopard* was the best-selling novel in Italian publishing history (it also became a big international hit after it was translated into English in 1960). In 1963, the novel was adapted into an epic film starring Burt Lancaster, Claudia Cardinale, and Alain Delon.

If you want total security, go to prison.
There you're fed, clothed, given medical care, and so on.
The only thing lacking . . . is freedom.

DWIGHT D. EISENHOWER

If you've had a good time playing the game,
you're a winner even if you lose.

MALCOLM FORBES

If you want to be true to life, start lying about it.

JOHN FOWLES

If you accept your limitations you go beyond them.

BRENDAN FRANCIS

If man could have half his wishes, he would double his troubles.

BENJAMIN FRANKLIN

This observation, from a 1752 issue of *Poor Richard's Almanack*, explores an age-old oxymoronic theme: Be careful what you wish for, it might come true.

If you feel that you have both feet planted on level ground,
then the university has failed you.

ROBERT GOHEEN

Goheen, then the president of Princeton University, said this to undergraduates in a 1961 speech. His point was clever, unexpected, and clear: The purpose of a liberal education is to challenge people's beliefs and, if anything, unsettle them.

If Roosevelt were alive today, he'd turn over in his grave.

SAMUEL GOLDWYN

A Hollywood legend, Goldwyn is now known for his fractured English, often called "Goldwynisms." In two other examples, he said: "If I look confused it's because I'm thinking" and "If I could drop dead right now, I'd be the happiest man alive."

It's a very ancient saying,
But a true and honest thought,
That "If you become a teacher,
By your pupils you'll be taught."

OSCAR HAMMERSTEIN II

This comes from the 1951 musical *The King and I* (music by Richard Rodgers, lyrics by Hammerstein). The words are spoken by Anna in the song "Getting to Know You."

If there is a 50–50 chance that something can go wrong, then nine times out of ten it will.

PAUL HARVEY

If the truth were known, the most disagreeable people are the most amiable.

WILLIAM HAZLITT

If you mean to keep as well as possible, the less you think about your health the better.

OLIVER WENDELL HOLMES, SR.

Holmes may have been influenced by an earlier thought from Goethe: "If you start to think about your physical or moral condition, you usually find that you are sick."

If you suffer, thank God! It is a sure sign that you are alive.

ELBERT HUBBARD

This is a nice reminder that only the dead are free from suffering. Hubbard also explored another oxymoronic theme when he wrote, "If you want work well done, select a busy man; the other kind has no time."

If you want to get rid of somebody, just tell him something for his own good.
FRANK MCKINNEY "KIN" HUBBARD

If writers were too wise, perhaps no books would get written at all.
ZORA NEALE HURSTON

Here, Hurston provides a new wrinkle on an old oxymoronic theme: Too much of a good thing is not necessarily desirable, and can even become a bad thing.

If from infancy you treat children as gods,
they are liable in adulthood to act as devils.
P. D. JAMES

If you don't risk anything, you risk even *more.*
ERICA JONG

This saying originally appeared in *How to Save Your Own Life* (1977), the sequel to *Fear of Flying* (1974), the phenomenal best seller that introduced Isadora Wing, Jong's pleasure-seeking protagonist. Near the end of the sequel, Isadora begins to question her hedonistic ways and thinks about leaving her comfortable life as the wife of a psychiatrist to pursue a committed relationship with a younger man she loves. In a conversation about what to do, Isadora's good friend Hans says to her: "Do you want me to tell you something really subversive? Love *is* everything it's cracked up to be. That's why people are so cynical about it." And then he adds, "It really *is* worth fighting for, being brave for, risking everything for. And the trouble is, if you don't risk anything, you risk even *more*." In a 1991 *Vanity Fair* article, actress Geena Davis offered this variation on the theme: "If you risk nothing, then you risk everything."

If you think you are not conceited, it means you are very conceited indeed.

C. S. LEWIS

**If you don't want to work,
you have to work to earn enough money so that you won't have to work.**

OGDEN NASH

If one does not have a good father one should furnish oneself with one.

FRIEDRICH NIETZSCHE

The point is that people can choose surrogate fathers to replace their inadequate or absent biological ones. Nietzsche, who was six years old when his own father died, adopted a number of intellectual and emotional father figures, some from previous centuries (such as Montaigne and Voltaire) and some contemporaries (the philosopher Arthur Schopenhauer and the composer Richard Wagner). In another oxymoronic ifferism, Nietzsche wrote, "If married couples did not live together, happy marriages would be more common."

If you are in a hurry, you will never get there.

CHINESE PROVERB

**If the rich could hire other people to die for them,
the poor could make a wonderful living.**

YIDDISH PROVERB

If I've told you once, I've told you a thousand times: Resist hyperbole.

WILLIAM SAFIRE

This is a self-contradictory rule—a directive that contradicts the principle it is stating. In 1979, Safire published three such "perverse rules of grammar" in his "On Language" column in *The New York Times.* He eventually published many more in *Fumblerules: A Lighthearted Guide to Grammar and Good Usage* (1990). In another example, he wrote: "If you reread your work, you will find on rereading that a great deal of repetition can be avoided by rereading and editing."

If one hides one's talent under a bushel,
one must be careful to point out the exact bushel under which it is hidden.

SAKI (H. H. MUNRO),
from The Unbearable Bassington *(1912)*

If we are polite in manner and friendly in tone,
we can without immediate risk be really rude to many a man.

ARTHUR SCHOPENHAUER

If he has failed, he has failed magnificently.

PIERRE SCUDO, *on Hector Berlioz*

If thou art rich, thou art poor.

WILLIAM SHAKESPEARE

In this passage from *Measure for Measure,* the Duke prepares Claudio to face death. He goes on to compare a wealthy man to a jackass that is heavily burdened with gold ingots. For such an animal, he suggests, death will finally bring relief from the great load he has carried.

If ever I utter an oath again,
may my soul be blasted to eternal damnation!

GEORGE BERNARD SHAW,
in St. Joan *(1923)*

This comes from the character Captain La Hire. The humor resides in the fact that the audience is aware of the contradiction while La Hire is not.

If we are all in agreement on the decision, then I propose we postpone further discussion of this matter until our next meeting to give ourselves time to develop disagreement and perhaps gain some understanding of what the decision is all about.

ALFRED P. SLOAN

This observation shows that Sloan, a pioneer in American management, recognized the danger of "groupthink" and the need for creative disagreement.

If you wish to preserve your secret, wrap it up in frankness.

ALEXANDER SMITH

If you are too careful, you are so occupied in being careful that you are sure to stumble over something.

GERTRUDE STEIN

If you shut the door to all errors, truth will be shut out.

RABINDRANATH TAGORE

If you add to the truth, you subtract from it.

THE TALMUD

If I knew for a certainty that a man was coming to my house with the conscious design of doing me good, I should run for my life.

HENRY DAVID THOREAU

This passage from *Walden* is a warning about the harm that can be done by do-gooders and reformers. Thoreau even suspected his own motives, writing earlier in the book, "If I repent of anything, it is very likely to be my good behavior."

If we had more time for discussion
we should probably have made a great many more mistakes.

LEON TROTSKY

In this passage from *Diary in Exile* (1935), Trotsky asserts the opposite of what is normally believed: that more discussion leads to fewer mistakes. As a general rule, it *is* a good idea to discuss things fully, but history has shown that people can engage in so much discussion they overplan, go down blind alleys, and even set traps for themselves. Thomas Hobbes applied the idea to reading: "If I had read as much as other men, I would have been as ignorant as they are."

If I only had a little humility, I would be perfect.

TED TURNER

This saying was popular long before a 1977 *New York Times* article attributed it to Turner. It was one of Turner's favorite sayings, though, and it captured the brash and flamboyant manner that had earned him the title "Mouth of the South."

If some great catastrophe is not announced every morning,
we feel a certain void.
Nothing in the paper today, we sigh.

PAUL VALÉRY

If there is anything the nonconformist hates worse than a conformist
it's another nonconformist who doesn't conform
to the prevailing standard of nonconformity.

BILL VAUGHAN

If you want to rise in politics in the United States there is one subject you must stay away from, and that is politics.

GORE VIDAL

If you are desirous to prevent the overrunning of a state by any sect, show it toleration.

VOLTAIRE *(François Marie Arouet)*

This is an example of a counterintuitive truth, since the natural tendency of people in power is to destroy threats, not allow them open expression.

If you don't execute your ideas, they die.

ROGER VON OECH

When we execute people, they die; but according to von Oech, the well-known creativity expert, it works in exactly the opposite way with ideas.

If you're there before it's over, you're on time.

JAMES J. "JIMMY" WALKER, *who was notoriously unpunctual*

If we desire to secure peace . . . it must be known that we are at all times ready for war.

GEORGE WASHINGTON, *in a 1790 speech*

Washington introduced the idea by saying, "If we desire to avoid insult, we must be able to repel it." The sentiment goes back to the Roman writer Vegetius, who wrote in the fourth century: "Let him who desires peace prepare for war."

If one tells the truth, one is sure, sooner or later, to be found out.

OSCAR WILDE

If a man has no vices, he's in great danger of making vices about his virtues, and there's a spectacle.

THORNTON WILDER

If I am to speak for ten minutes, I need a week for preparation; if fifteen minutes, three days; if half an hour, two days; if an hour, I am ready now.

WOODROW WILSON

Blaise Pascal was the first to express the oxymoronic insight that the shortest things require the lengthiest preparation. He wrote in a 1657 letter, "I have made this letter longer than usual, because I lack the time to make it short."

If I say, "Oh nice," about seven times in the same show, things aren't going well.

OPRAH WINFREY

17

If Your Head Is Wax, Don't Walk in the Sun

METAPHORICAL IFFERISMS

In May 2007, Queen Elizabeth and Prince Philip made a trip to the United States to celebrate the 400th anniversary of the Jamestown Settlement in Virginia. During their visit, they spent two days in Washington, D.C., where they were officially welcomed by President Bush in a ceremony on the lawn of the White House. Speaking before a crowd estimated at 7,000 people, the American president stumbled over his words—a not uncommon occurrence—and came dangerously close to suggesting that the English monarch had visited the United States in 1776.

The president immediately recognized his gaffe and, with a trace of a smile on his face, looked over at the Queen and gave her a big wink. It was a natural thing for an American to do, especially one known for his informality, but by British standards, it was a major breach of etiquette. The Queen returned the president's warm-hearted wink with an icy glare. (Press photographers captured the moment, and the next day newspapers throughout England prominently displayed the photographs.) President Bush was not shaken by the expression of regal disapproval, however. He even quipped later that the Queen "gave me a look that only a mother could give a child."

In 1983, during a previous trip to America, Queen Elizabeth and her husband also received many tributes, including a gala White House dinner hosted by President Reagan and a Frank Sinatra serenade while in California. A few days before the royal couple began the West Coast leg of their journey, a piece on the upcoming visit appeared in the *Los Angeles Times*. The article pointed out that Americans have always had a special fascination with royal appearances, especially when they come from English monarchs. But it also acknowledged that Americans have long struggled with the intricacies of royal etiquette. It went on to offer a remarkable piece of advice:

If you find you are to be presented to the Queen, do not rush up to her.
She will eventually be brought around to you,
like a dessert trolley at a good restaurant.

To some, comparing a regal queen to a dessert trolley might seem shocking, but the process of describing one thing by relating it to something else is the essence of a longstanding human tradition called *metaphorical thinking*. It's what Shakespeare was doing when he wrote, "All the world's a stage." And it is what countless people have done over the centuries when they've made a connection between two things that, at first, don't appear to have anything in common with each other.

I explored the nature of metaphorical thinking in *I Never Metaphor I Didn't Like*, a 2008 book in which I focused my attention on the three superstars of figurative language: *metaphors*, *similes*, and *analogies*. In metaphors—like "all the world's a stage"—one thing is described as being the same as something else (A is B). If Shakespeare had written "all the world is like a stage," he would have said that one thing is similar to something else (A is like B), creating a simile. And if the thought were to be expressed in an analogy (A is to B as C is to D), Shakespeare would have had to say something like, "People are to the world as actors are to the stage."

Throughout history, certain individuals have been blessed with what Aristotle called an eye for resemblance. These individuals, called "masters of metaphor" by the great Greek philosopher, have a special ability to discern a relationship between things that initially seem quite unlike each other (such as a queen and a dessert trolley). Benjamin Franklin, a true master of metaphor, had an exceptionally keen eye for resemblance and he demonstrated it countless times:

If your head is wax, don't walk in the sun.

In this observation from a 1749 issue of *Poor Richard's Almanack*, Franklin suggests that a human head can be made of wax, which he knows is not literally true. In the world of human discourse, we make allowances for such metaphorical flights of fancy by calling them *figuratively true*. Like leaps of faith in religion, people using metaphors make leaps of logic—asserting something is true, even when they know it is literally false.

When we examine Franklin's "head is wax" line, we learn something else about metaphorical observations: The meaning may not be completely obvious, and often becomes apparent only after a little thought. In the grand tradition of indirect communication, many writers express themselves obliquely, challenging their readers to figure out the meaning of a saying. In Franklin's case, he was suggesting that weak and soft-headed people should stay away from heated disputes, much as Harry Truman suggested in his famous line, "If you can't stand the heat, stay out of the kitchen." Ralph Waldo Emerson was also writing metaphorically, and communicating indirectly, in an 1841 observation:

If the hive be disturbed by rash and stupid hands,
instead of honey, it will yield us bees.

On the surface, this looks like an observation about beekeeping and honey gathering, but in reality it is a larger observation about what happens when important tasks are attempted by inept people. Instead of getting the desired result, they end up getting stung by their own lack of competence. A century later, Dale Carnegie picked up on Emerson's observation when he wrote:

If you want to gather honey, don't kick over the beehive.

In another example of indirect communication, Ann Landers wrote:

If you want to catch trout, don't fish in a herring barrel.

Was the famous columnist dispensing advice about fishing here? No, not at all. This was simply her metaphorical way of telling single female readers that going to bars was not an effective way to meet high-quality men.

Lest you think that metaphorical thinking is always elegant or profound, let me mention that the attempt to speak in such a way often backfires. A common mistake is to mix metaphors together in a way that is ludicrous or comical—the dreaded mangled metaphor. The British politician Ernest Bevin offered a classic:

If you open that Pandora's Box,
you never know what Trojan Horses will jump out.

The Canadian politician Robert N. Thompson offered another priceless example:

If this thing starts to snowball,
it will catch fire right across the country.

In the remainder of the chapter, though, we'll feature only those metaphorical observations that make sense—and only those that are beautifully expressed.

**If you wish to succeed in life,
make perseverance your bosom friend, experience your wise counselor,
caution your elder brother, and hope your guardian genius.**

JOSEPH ADDISON

**If you put a small value on yourself,
don't expect the world to raise your price.**

ANONYMOUS

**If a man be gracious and courteous to strangers,
it shows he is a citizen of the world,
and that his heart is no island cut off from other islands,
but a continent that joins to them.**

FRANCIS BACON

This topographical metaphor, from Bacon's *Essays* (1597), is a compelling image in its own right, but it may have also inspired one of literature's most quoted passages, John Donne's 1624 "no man is an island" sentiment.

**If you haven't had at least a slight poetic crack in the heart,
you have been cheated by nature.**

PHYLLIS BATTELLE

**If we have not quiet in our minds, outward comfort
will do no more for us than a golden slipper on a gouty foot.**

JOHN BUNYAN

An allegory is an extended metaphor, and Bunyan is the author of one of the most famous allegories of all time. *The Pilgrim's Progress* is a 1678 story about a character named Christian who encounters many obstacles—such as Vanity Fair and Giant Despair— on a journey through life that ultimately takes him to The Celestial City (that is, Heaven). After the Bible, *The Pil-*

grim's Progress was the favorite book used by proselytizing missionaries in the eighteenth and nineteenth centuries.

**If I try to seize this self of which I feel sure,
if I try to define and to summarize it,
it is nothing but water slipping through my fingers.**

ALBERT CAMUS, *on describing the elusive quality of "self"*

**If you set to work to believe everything,
you will tire out the believing-muscles of your mind,
and then you'll be so weak
you won't be able to believe the simplest true things.**

LEWIS CARROLL, *in an 1864 letter to eleven-year-old Mary MacDonald*

**If facts are the seeds that later produce knowledge and wisdom,
then the emotions . . . are the fertile soil in which the seeds must grow.**

RACHEL CARSON

**If I were called on to define briefly the word "art,"
I should call it the reproduction of what the senses perceive in nature,
seen through the veil of the soul.**

PAUL CÉZANNE

If we do not plant it when young, it will give us no shade when old.

LORD CHESTERFIELD *(Philip Dormer Stanhope), on knowledge, in a 1748 letter to his son*

**If the ladder is not leaning against the right wall,
every step we take just gets us to the wrong place faster.**

STEPHEN COVEY

If you don't know history, then you don't know anything.
You are a leaf that doesn't know it is part of a tree.

MICHAEL CRICHTON

This is the way the line is mistakenly presented on numerous internet quotation sites, but Crichton's original line was slightly different in his 1999 novel, *Timeline*: "Professor Johnston often said that if you didn't know history, you didn't know anything. You were a leaf that didn't know it was part of a tree."

If the Confederacy fails,
there should be written on its tombstone: *Died of a Theory*.

JEFFERSON DAVIS, *in 1865*

If I had my hand full of truth, I would take good care how I opened it.

BERNARD DE FONTENELLE

If one considered life as a simple loan, one would perhaps be less exacting.
We possess actually nothing; everything goes through us.

EUGÈNE DELACROIX

If I were personally to define religion,
I would say that it is a bandage that man has invented
to protect a soul made bloody by circumstance.

THEODORE DREISER

If my father was the head of our house, my mother was its heart.

PHILIP DUNNE

Dunne was the screenwriter who turned Richard Llewellyn's 1939 best seller *How Green Was My Valley* into a screenplay. In the 1941 film—considered one of director John Ford's finest films—the words were delivered by the voiceover narrator Rhys Williams. The saying does not appear in the original novel.

If a man will kick a fact out of the window,
when he comes back he finds it again in the chimney corner.

RALPH WALDO EMERSON

If you would cure anger, do not feed it.

EPICTETUS

The first-century Greek philosopher added, "Say to yourself: 'I used to be angry every day; then every other day; now only every third or fourth day.' When you reach thirty days, offer a sacrifice of thanksgiving to the gods."

If there is on earth a house with many mansions, it is the house of words.

E. M. FORSTER

If you would reap Praise you must sow the Seeds,
Gentle Words and useful Deeds.

BENJAMIN FRANKLIN

If passion drives, let reason hold the reins.

BENJAMIN FRANKLIN

The nineteenth-century English preacher C. H. Spurgeon described the problem of unbridled passion in a memorable metaphor: "A man in passion rides a horse that runs away with him." Franklin, in this 1749 observation from *Poor Richard's Almanack*, suggests a solution to the dilemma: When in the grip of passion, muster as much human reason as you can to keep it under control.

If a man empties his purse into his head, no man can take it away from him. An investment in knowledge always pays the best interest.

BENJAMIN FRANKLIN,
on the value of education

If society fits you comfortably enough, you call it freedom.

ROBERT FROST

If thou maketh *Bacchus* thy chief God;
***Apollo* will never keep thee Company.**

THOMAS FULLER, M.D.

This warning about the danger of drink comes from *Introductio ad Prudentiam* (1731). In Greek mythology, Bacchus was the god of wine and drink, and Apollo the god who represented humankind's greatest achievements. Bacchus inspired the word *bacchanalian*, an adjective describing orgies fueled by drunken revelry.

If you're not using your smile,
you're like a man with a million dollars in the bank and no checkbook.

LES GIBLIN

This comes from Giblin's motivational classic *How to Have Power and Confidence in Dealing with People*, first published in 1956. Giblin also wrote, "A smile is the million-dollar asset in your human relations inventory."

If you reveal your secrets to the wind,
you should not blame the wind for revealing them to the trees.

KAHLIL GIBRAN

If you miss the first buttonhole, you can't ever get fully buttoned up.

JOHANN WOLFGANG VON GOETHE

If you drive nature out with a pitchfork, she will soon find a way back.

HORACE, *in* Epistles *(1st century B.C.)*

The point here is one that stern moralists have ignored for centuries: The use of scare tactics to drive away natural desires will almost always fail.

If a man's fortune does not fit him, it is like the shoe in the story; if too large it trips him up, if too small it pinches him.

HORACE

If you haven't struck oil in the first three minutes, *stop boring!*

GEORGE JESSEL

In this observation, Jessel relates speech making to oil drilling—and playfully puns upon both meanings of the word *boring*. In my view, this is the best advice ever offered to platform speakers and others who are asked to "say just a few words." In the middle of the twentieth century, Jessel was a popular comedic actor and one of America's most celebrated after-dinner speakers (he was often called "The Toastmaster General of the United States").

If you cannot be gold, be silver.

JUAN RAMÓN JIMÉNEZ

If a man makes himself a worm, he must not complain when trodden upon.

IMMANUEL KANT

If poetry comes not as naturally as the leaves to a tree, it had better not come at all.

JOHN KEATS, *in an 1818 letter*

If Enterprise is afoot, wealth accumulates whatever may be happening to Thrift;

and if Enterprise is asleep,
wealth decays whatever else Thrift may be doing.

JOHN MAYNARD KEYNES

If you hit a pony over the nose at the outset of your acquaintance,
he may not love you,
but he will take a deep interest in your movements ever afterwards.

RUDYARD KIPLING,
in Plain Tales from the Hills *(1888)*

If you only knock long enough and loud enough at the gate,
you are sure to wake up somebody.

HENRY WADSWORTH LONGFELLOW

Longfellow began by writing: "Perseverance is a great element of success."

If dating is like shopping,
being engaged is like having a guy put you on layaway.
Like saying, "I know I want it.
I just want to delay taking it home as long as possible."

KRIS MCGAHA

If you torture data sufficiently, it will confess to almost anything.

FRED MENGER

If a man happens to find himself . . . then he has found
a mansion which he can inhabit with dignity all the days of his life.

JAMES A. MICHENER

If you surrender to the wind, you can ride it.

TONI MORRISON

Morrison may have been influenced by an observation from another celebrated female writer, Anne Morrow Lindbergh: "If you surrender completely to the moments as they pass, you live more richly those moments."

If you want the rainbow, you gotta put up with the rain.

DOLLY PARTON, *offering a time-honored saying*

If the horse is dead, get off it.

TERRY PAULSON, *on the questionable practice of beating a dead horse*

Many idioms are metaphorical, and this cleverly worded observation plays off a popular American one—beating a dead horse—that means to continue to do something long after it ceases to be productive. The saying is based on an English idiom, flogging a dead horse, that goes back to the 1870s.

If a window of opportunity appears, don't pull down the shade.

TOM PETERS

Milton Berle was thinking similarly a few generations earlier when he remarked: "If opportunity doesn't knock, build a door."

If you refuse to be made straight when you are green, you will not be made straight when you are dry.

AFRICAN PROVERB

If the camel gets his nose in a tent, his body will soon follow.

ARAB PROVERB

If you see the lion's teeth, do not think he is smiling at you.

ARAB PROVERB

If you scatter thorns, don't go barefoot.

CHINESE PROVERB

If you lie down with dogs, you will get up with fleas.

ENGLISH PROVERB

This warning about associating with bad company is based on an ancient Latin saying: "They who lie with dogs will rise with fleas." A 1721 book of Scottish proverbs explained the saying this way: "If you keep Company with base and unworthy Fellows, you will get some Ill by them."

If two ride a horse, one must ride behind.

ENGLISH PROVERB

The saying is usually applied to partnerships and joint collaborations, where it is typically suggested that one person must be prepared to defer to the other.

If you do not sow in the spring, you will not reap in the autumn.

IRISH PROVERB

If speaking is silver, then listening is gold.

TURKISH PROVERB

If the family were a container, it would be a nest,
an enduring nest, loosely woven, expansive, and open.

LETTY COTTIN POGREBIN

This comes from Pogrebin's 1983 book *Family and Politics*. In the following passage, also from the book, she continued in a figurative vein, exploring a variety of additional metaphors for family life:

> *If the family were a fruit, it would be an orange, a circle of sections, held together but separable—each segment distinct. If the family were a boat, it would be a canoe that makes no progress unless everyone paddles. If the family were a sport, it would be baseball: a long, slow, nonviolent game that is never over until the last out. If the family were a building, it would be an old but solid structure that contains human history, and appeals to those who see the carved moldings under all the plaster, the wide plank floors under the linoleum, the possibilities.*

If you keep your feathers well oiled,
the water of criticism will run off as from a duck's back.

ELLEN H. RICHARDS

Richards wrote this in a letter to a female student. In 1870, Richards was the first woman to be admitted to the Massachusetts Institute of Technology, and in 1879 its first female instructor. She was a respected chemist, influential educator, and a pioneer in the field of home economics.

If you are squeamish
Don't prod the beach rubble.

SAPPHO *(7th century B.C.)*

This fragment from history's first great female writer could also be expressed this way: If you're offended by bad odors, don't rummage around in the trash.

If cheerfulness knocks for admission,
we should open our hearts wide to receive it,
for it never comes inopportunely.

ARTHUR SCHOPENHAUER

If men were selected for breeding
on the same criteria as farmyard animals,
most would go to the slaughterhouse.

RICHARD M. SHARPE

Dr. Sharpe, an English reproductive biologist, said this in 1992. Earlier in the century, W. R. Inge, the English theologian and dean of St. Paul's Cathedral, made a related observation about humans and animals: "We tolerate shapes in human beings that would horrify us if we saw them in a horse."

If the other planets are inhabited,
they must be using this earth as their insane asylum.

GEORGE BERNARD SHAW

If you cry because the sun has gone out of your life,
your tears will prevent you from seeing the stars.

RABINDRANATH TAGORE

If there be
A devil in man, there is an angel too.

ALFRED, LORD TENNYSON

If your ship doesn't come in, swim out to it.

JONATHAN WINTERS

18

If You Can't Annoy Somebody, There Is Little Point in Writing

THE LITERARY LIFE

In 1923, three-year-old Isaac Asimov arrived in America with his Russian Jewish immigrant parents. After passing through Ellis Island, the Asimov family settled in Brooklyn and opened a small general merchandise store that was favored by neighborhood children for their many inexpensive candies. Young Isaac was a gifted child, although that designation would not be invented for another half-century. He quickly picked up the English language and became an avid reader. By age five, he was devouring the science fiction magazines that were stocked on a magazine rack in the family store.

As he grew older, Asimov was roused by his father every morning at six o'clock to begin his daily regimen: a newspaper delivery route before school and, after school, work at the family store until bedtime. The precocious young student thrived under the grueling schedule. With superior scholastic aptitude to match his determined work ethic, he skipped several grades and received his high school diploma at age fifteen.

Asimov's father, who was always a little leery of his son's interest in science fiction, was relieved when his boy was accepted at Columbia University. While majoring in chemistry as an undergraduate, Asimov began writing science fiction stories (his first was published in 1938, when he was eighteen). Three years later, in 1941, the twenty-one-year-old Columbia graduate submitted a story called "Nightfall" to *Astounding Science Fiction*, the nation's top sci-fi magazine. The story was quickly hailed as a work of genius, and three decades later was honored by the Science Fiction Writers of America as the best science fiction story ever written. Asimov's early writing success didn't affect his academic pursuits, however, and except for nearly four years of war-related service, he continued his studies at Columbia, ultimately getting his Ph.D. in chemistry in 1948.

In 1949, Asimov was hired to teach biochemistry at Boston University's School of Medicine. He recalled in an interview twenty years later, "I didn't feel impelled to tell them that I'd never had any biochemistry. By 1951, I was writing a textbook on biochemistry, and I finally realized the only thing I really wanted to be was a writer." A year after taking the Boston University job, Asimov published a legendary collection of sci-fi stories titled *I, Robot*. In the next three years, he came out with a trio of classic sci-fi books that are now called *The Foundation Trilogy*.

By 1958, Asimov had become so successful that he stopped teaching in order to devote himself exclusively to writing (he continued his association with BU's School of Medicine, though, and was made a full professor in 1979). From 1958 to his death in 1992 (from AIDS contracted from a blood transfusion during bypass surgery in 1983), Asimov was one of history's most prolific writers, authoring nearly 500 books. A self-described "compulsive writer," his range was breathtaking: In addition to science fiction novels, he wrote college textbooks, mystery novels, a book on Shakespeare, guides to the Old and New Testaments, and books on Greek mythology, space travel, history, mathematics, and astronomy. (It is often said that Asimov contributed books to nine of the ten categories of the Dewey

Decimal System.) He once said, "I write for the same reason I breathe—because if I didn't I would die." In a 1984 article in *Life* magazine, he offered an even more dramatic observation:

**If my doctor told me I had only six minutes to live,
I wouldn't brood. I'd type a little faster.**

While Asimov wrote primarily to inform and to educate, many other writers say they are motivated by a desire to stimulate and to challenge—and maybe even ruffle a few feathers along the way. In a 1971 interview, British writer Kingsley Amis was quoted as saying:

**If you can't annoy somebody with what you write,
I think there's little point in writing.**

In 1992, English writer A. N. Wilson echoed the Amis sentiment and carried it further: "If you know somebody is going to be awfully annoyed by something you write, that's obviously very satisfying, and if they howl with rage or cry, that's honey." Around the same time, Woody Allen was saying something similar about his cinematic efforts:

If my film makes one more person miserable, I've done my job.

Annoying people with one's literary or cinematic efforts is not without its risks. Voltaire, who was banished from his native France for speaking his mind, expressed the dilemma this way: "It is dangerous to be right in matters on which the established authorities are wrong." These days, however, the greatest danger comes less from established authorities than it does from religious fanatics. In 1989, Salman Rushdie bluntly observed:

If Woody Allen were a Muslim, he'd be dead by now.

Rushdie's point was that Allen was fortunate to be expressing his views in the democratic West, where irreverence and the expression of unpopular views have historically been tolerated, and even encouraged. The Indian-born Rushdie was a respected English novelist, but not widely known around the world, when he came out with his fourth novel, *The Satanic Verses*, in 1988. Within a month of publication, Muslim extremists all around the world were burning the book, which they considered blasphemous (in part because it suggested the Koran was not divinely inspired).

In early 1989, Iran's Ayatollah Khomeini issued a fatwa against Rushdie and put a $1.5 million bounty on his head. With the help of British authorities, Rushdie went into hiding, ultimately living in thirty separate houses over the next decade. His Japanese translator was killed, his Italian translator stabbed, and his Norwegian publisher shot three times in the back (after recovering, his first major publishing decision was to reprint the book). The fatwa was lifted in 1998 and Rushdie, ever-vigilant about his safety, continued to write novels, essays, and short stories. He also began speaking out on the danger of religious fanaticism. In one oft-quoted observation, he said, "If I were asked for a one-sentence sound bite on religion, I would say I was against it."

From ancient times, writers and poets have reflected on their vocation, dispensed advice about how to write more effectively, commented on other writers, and offered opinions about almost every aspect of the literary life. In this final chapter of the book, you will see that some of their most fascinating observations have been expressed in a very familiar way.

If you are going to be a writer, there is nothing I can say to stop you; if you're not going to be a writer, nothing I can say will help you.

JAMES BALDWIN

Baldwin said this in a 1953 *Paris Review* interview. He added: "What you really need at the beginning is somebody to let you know that the effort is real."

If you want to read a perfect book there is only one way: Write it.

AMBROSE BIERCE

Bierce suggests here that all authors engage in a form of self-deception, with many believing that all books are imperfect except the ones they write.

If a writer is true to his characters they will give him his plot.

PHYLLIS BOTTOME

If a theme or idea is too near the surface,
the novel becomes simply a tract illustrating an idea.

ELIZABETH BOWEN

If anyone asks me whether I like being a popular writer,
I ask them whether they think I'd rather be an unpopular writer.

BARBARA TAYLOR BRADFORD

Beginning with *A Woman of Substance* (1979), which went on to sell more than thirty million copies, Bradford has written twenty-four novels, all of which became best sellers in both England and America.

If I could I would always work in silence and obscurity,
and let my efforts be known by their results.

EMILY BRONTË

If Jane Austen were alive today she'd probably be writing books
called things like *Sex and Sensibility* and *Pride and Passion*.

JULIE BURCHILL

Here, Burchill suggests that titles like *Sense and Sensibility* and *Pride and Prejudice* would be much too bland for a modern audience.

If a book come from the heart, it will contrive to reach other hearts.

THOMAS CARLYLE

Aldous Huxley famously disagreed, writing, "A bad book is as much of a labor to write as a good one; it comes as sincerely from the author's soul."

If writers were good businessmen, they'd have too much sense to be writers.

IRVIN S. COBB

If you want to be a writer—stop talking about it and sit down and write!

JACKIE COLLINS

If you find a lot of explaining necessary,
something is wrong with your material or with your approach to it.

JAMES GOULD COZZENS

Cozzens was talking about prose, but the American poet Archibald MacLeish made the same point about poetry: "If the poem can be improved by its author's explanations, it never should have been published."

If I read a book and it makes my whole body so cold
no fire can ever warm me, I know *that* is poetry.
If I feel physically as if the top of my head were taken off,
I know *that* is poetry.

EMILY DICKINSON

This is one of Dickinson's best-known observations, first offered in an 1870 conversation with the American critic Thomas Wentworth Higginson. It was their first meeting, even though they had corresponded for many years (she had written him eight years earlier, asking for his opinion of her work). After the meeting, which took place in Dickinson's Amherst home, the critic was so impressed with this observation that he immediately recorded it. He later shared the details of the meeting—including the quotation—in a letter to his wife.

**If there is a special Hell for writers,
it would be in the forced contemplation of their own works,
with all the misconceptions, the omissions,
the failures that any finished work of art implies.**

JOHN DOS PASSOS

**If you have that unconquerable urge to write,
nothing will stop you from writing.**

THEODORE DREISER

Dreiser wrote this in a 1929 letter to a friend. He added: "You will write whether it is convenient or inconvenient, whether you are rich or poor, whether you are lonely or your life is filled with friends or frivolity."

If a poet writes to save his soul, he may save the souls of others.

RICHARD EBERHART

If you want to write poetry you must earn a living some other way.

T. S. ELIOT

W. H. Auden agreed, writing in the foreword to *The Dyer's Hand* (1962), "It is a sad fact about our culture that a poet can earn much more money writing or talking about his art than he can by practicing it."

**If a writer has to rob his mother, he will not hesitate;
the *Ode on a Grecian Urn* is worth any number of old ladies.**

WILLIAM FAULKNER

Faulkner said this to Malcolm Cowley in a *Paris Review* "Writers at Work" interview in 1956. He began by saying: "The writer's only responsibility is to his art. He will be completely ruthless if he is a good one." His point was that great writers can become so consumed by their craft that everything else, including family relationships, will be sacrificed. The idea is not original to Faulkner. Nor was he first to express it conditionally. In the essay "Wealth" in *The Conduct of Life* (1860), Ralph Waldo Emerson wrote, "Art is a jealous mistress." He then added, "If a man have a genius for painting, poetry, music, architecture, or philosophy, he makes a bad husband and an ill provider."

If a writer has anything witty, profound, or quotable to say, he doesn't say it. He's no fool. He writes it.

EDNA FERBER

The point of this observation is clear. When writers think they've created a gem of an idea or a spectacular phrase, they're not going to squander it in a conversation and possibly run the risk that another writer might steal it.

If you would not be forgotten, as soon as you are dead and rotten, either write things worth reading, or do things worth the writing.

BENJAMIN FRANKLIN

If I didn't have writing,
I'd be running down the street hurling grenades in people's faces.

PAUL FUSSELL,
on writing as sublimation

If any man wishes to write in a clear style, let him first be clear in his thoughts; and if any would write in a noble style, let him first possess a noble soul.

JOHANN WOLFGANG VON GOETHE

If we wish to know the force of human genius, we should read Shakespeare. If we wish to see the insignificance of human learning, we may study his commentators.

WILLIAM HAZLITT

Shakespeare is held in such esteem among writers and poets that he has become a kind of literary deity, or at least a secular saint. Indeed, Ralph Waldo Emerson once observed: "If we tire of the saints, Shakespeare is our city of refuge."

If I had to give young writers advice, I'd say don't listen to writers talking about writing or themselves.

LILLIAN HELLMAN

If you are lucky enough to have lived in Paris as a young man, then wherever you go for the rest of your life, it stays with you, for Paris is a moveable feast.

ERNEST HEMINGWAY, *the epigraph to* A Moveable Feast *(1964)*

In 1921, the twenty-two-year-old Hemingway moved to Paris. In the next two years, he cemented his reputation as a journalist and began his career as a novelist. By the end of the decade, with such novels as *The Sun Also Rises* and *A Farewell to Arms*, he was often described as the greatest writer of his generation. During his years in Paris, he rubbed shoulders with some of the century's most influential writers and artists, including James Joyce, Pablo Picasso, F. Scott Fitzgerald, Ezra Pound, and Gertrude Stein. When Hemingway's memoirs of his years in Paris were posthumously published in 1964, they were titled *A Moveable Feast*. It went on to become one of literary history's most famous book titles.

If a line of poetry strays into my memory,
my skin bristles so that the razor ceases to act.

A. E. HOUSMAN

If you want to be a psychological novelist and write about human beings,
the best thing you can do is keep a pair of cats.

ALDOUS HUXLEY

If we are imprisoned in ourselves, books provide us with the means of escape.
If we have run too far away from ourselves,
books show us the way back.

HOLBROOK JACKSON

If you don't have the time to read, you don't have the time or the tools to write.

STEPHEN KING

If a novel reveals true and vivid relationships,
it is a moral work, no matter what the relationships may consist in.

D. H. LAWRENCE

If you have a burning, restless urge to write or paint,
simply eat something sweet and the feeling will pass.

FRAN LEBOWITZ

This comes from Lebowitz's 1978 book, *Metropolitan Life,* in which she introduced the recommendation this way: "Very few people possess true artistic ability. It is therefore both unseemly and unproductive to irritate the situation by making an effort." She also offered this related ifferism: "If you are of the opinion that the contemplation of suicide is sufficient evidence of a poetic nature, do not forget that actions speak louder than words." Lebowitz might have been influenced by a well-known quip from the French writer

André Gide: "If a young writer can refrain from writing, he shouldn't hesitate to do so."

If you want your writing to be taken seriously,
don't marry and have kids, and above all, don't die.
But if you have to die, commit suicide. They approve of that.

URSULA K. LE GUIN, *offering tongue-in-cheek advice to aspiring female writers at a 1986 conference*

If I have something I want to say that is too difficult for adults to swallow, then I will write it in a book for children.

MADELEINE L'ENGLE

In the late 1940s, L'Engle was about to abandon her dreams of becoming a successful novelist when she was introduced to the ideas of Albert Einstein. Inspired by his breathtaking notions of time and space, she began writing an allegorical science fiction novel about children who rescue their father from a planet where individuality has been outlawed. Her manuscript was rejected by more than two dozen publishers, with most acquisition editors saying the tale was too difficult for children and too fantastical for adults. The book, finally published in 1962 under the title *A Wrinkle in Time*, went on to win the Newberry Medal and establish L'Engle as a serious writer.

If it sounds like writing, I rewrite it.

ELMORE LEONARD

If a book and a head knock against each other
and there is a hollow sound, is it always the book?

G. C. LICHTENBERG

If you want to change the world, pick up your pen.

MARTIN LUTHER

In 1517, the thirty-four-year-old Luther, a devout Roman Catholic monk and a professor of theology, began to question many of the practices of the church. (He was especially outraged over the selling of indulgences to poor people and the ludicrous suggestion that such purchases would reduce their time in purgatory.) After writing ninety-five theses attacking such practices, he nailed them to the front door of his church in Wittenberg, Germany—and changed the world.

If you would be thrilled by watching the galloping advance of a major glacier, you'd be ecstatic watching changes in publishing.

JOHN D. MACDONALD

If you want to get rich from writing, write the sort of thing that's read by persons who move their lips when they're reading to themselves.

DON MARQUIS

If you can tell stories, create characters, devise incidents, and have sincerity and passion, it doesn't matter a damn how you write.

W. SOMERSET MAUGHAM

If you steal from one author, it's plagiarism; if you steal from many, it's research.

WILSON MIZNER

This saying is usually attributed to Mizner, but he may have simply popularized a line that has been around since the early days of the twentieth century.

If good books did good, the world would have been converted long ago.

GEORGE MOORE

If a writer proclaims himself as isolated, uninfluenced, and responsible to no one,

he should not be surprised if he is
ignored, uninfluential, and perceived as irresponsible.

CHARLES NEWMAN

If we had to say what writing is,
we would define it essentially as an act of courage.

CYNTHIA OZICK

If I didn't know the ending of a story, I wouldn't begin.
I always write my last line, my last paragraphs, my last page first.

KATHERINE ANNE PORTER

If the word *arse* is read in a sentence, no matter how beautiful the sentence is,
the reader will react only to that word.

JULES RENARD

In England and many other parts of the British Empire, *arse* is the vulgar term for the buttocks; in the United States, *ass* has always been the preferred term.

If you're a writer there will come at least one morning in your life
when you wake up and want to kill your agent.

BERNICE RUBENS

Rubens was the author of two dozen novels and the winner of the 1970 Booker Prize for Fiction for *The Elected Member*. Her 1962 novel *Madame Sousatzka* was made into a 1988 film starring Shirley MacLaine.

If a book is worth reading, it is worth buying.

JOHN RUSKIN

If you do not write for publication, there is little point in writing.

GEORGE BERNARD SHAW

If you would be pungent, be brief; for it is with words as with sunbeams—the more they are condensed, the deeper they burn.

ROBERT SOUTHEY

In the nineteenth century, Southey was a critic of the elaborate style of writing so popular at the time, and a passionate advocate of a lean and vigorous style. A century later, George Orwell echoed Southey's advice, and he also did it succinctly: "If it is possible to cut a word out, cut it out."

**If the public likes you, you're good.
Shakespeare was a common, down-to-earth writer in his day.**

MICKEY SPILLANE

When Spillane's *I, The Jury* was published in 1947, the *New York Times* described it as "a spectacularly bad book" and the *New York Herald Tribune* called the author "an inept vulgarian." The book, which introduced the private eye Mike Hammer, sold only modestly in hardcover, but when the paperback came out with one of the most sexually suggestive covers ever printed, there was a huge explosion of interest. In the next twenty years, Spillane wrote a dozen more Mike Hammer novels and saw many of them turned into films, including one in which he also played the role of his hard-boiled detective. Spillane's books have sold more than 225 million copies (in 1980, seven of the fifteen all-time best-selling fiction titles in America had been written by him). According to *Life* magazine, Spillane wrote books that "no one likes except the public." And about himself, the mystery writer said, "I don't have fans. I have customers."

**If you're a singer you lose your voice. A baseball player loses his arm.
A writer gets more knowledge, and if he's good,
the older he gets, the better he writes.**

MICKEY SPILLANE

If you would shut your door against the children for an hour a day and say:
"Mother is working on her five-act tragedy in blank verse!"
you would be surprised how they would respect you.
They would probably all become playwrights.

BRENDA UELAND

This appeared in Ueland's *If You Want to Write* (1938). She was advising mothers who longed to write but complained that their child-rearing responsibilities gave them no time to do it. On the role writing played in her life, Ueland wrote, "If I knew for certain that I would never have anything published again, and would never make another cent from it, I would still keep on writing."

If art doesn't make us better, then what on earth is it for?

ALICE WALKER

Walker introduced this thought by writing: "Deliver me from writers who say the way they live doesn't matter. I'm not sure a bad person can write a good book."

If you are in difficulties with a book, try the element of surprise:
Attack it at an hour when it isn't expecting it.

H. G. WELLS

If we should ever inaugurate a hall of fame,
it would be reserved exclusively and hopefully for authors who,
having written four bestsellers,
***still refrained* from starting out on a lecture tour.**

E. B. WHITE

This is from White's *Every Day Is Saturday* (1934). On the same topic,

Dr. Joyce Brothers wrote, "If Shakespeare had to go on an author tour to promote *Romeo and Juliet*, he never would have written *Macbeth*."

If you force yourself to think clearly you will write clearly.
It's as simple as that.
The hard part isn't the writing; the hard part is the thinking.

WILLIAM ZINSSER

Acknowledgments

My deepest gratitude goes to my wife, Katherine Robinson, a partner in every aspect of my life. I would also like to express my deep appreciation to Terry Coleman, Linnda Durré, and Carolanne Reynolds, who provided invaluable proofreading and editing assistance. My heartfelt thanks also go to my many friends at HarperCollins, especially Bruce Nichols and Kate Antony, and to my agent, George Greenfield of CreativeWell, Inc.

Many subscribers to my weekly e-newsletter (*Dr. Mardy's Quotes of the Week*) have provided assistance with quotations and attributions, but nobody has helped more than Don Hauptman and Bob Kelly.

The contributions of the following people also deserve a special mention:

Joel Anderson, Karé Anderson, Derm Barrett, Carla Beard, David Bevans, Parminder Bhachu, Amy Brennan, Dan Brook, Donald Brown, Pam Bruce, Roger Burke, Robert Byrne, Jerry Caplin, Gardin Carroll, John Chamberlain, Adam Christing, Jim Clark, Martha Davey, Maya Debus, Bill Duncan, Mike Dineen, Ross Eckler, Loren Ekroth, Howard Eskin, Susan Evans, Carl Faith, Dan Ferris, David Fieldhouse, Alan A. Fleischer, Frank Forencich, Leonard Roy Frank, Marti Franks, Anu Garg, Leonard Geifman, Don Groves, William B. Hackett, Tasha Halpert, Fran Hamilton, Dan and Linda Hart, David Hartson, Lee Hatfield, Blair Hawley, Art Haykin, Jeff Jacoby, Chuck Jambotkar, Norman, Miki, and Gary Kaplan, Harron Kelner, Derm Keohane, Ed Kirkpatrick, Amit Kothari, Sylvia Lange, Richard Lederer, Milton Lewin, Phil Linker, Ken Logsdon, Carole Madan, John Mc-

Call, Erin McKean, Scott McKenzie, Mike Morton, John McCall, Bill Nye, Brenda Orndorff, Marlene and Barney Ovrut, Kalman Packhous, Dr. Emily Palik-Killian, Stan Pickett, Richard Raymond III, Wes Reynolds, Dennis Ridley, Bob Rosenberg, Peter Ross, Carky Rubens, Don Ruhl, Terry Scurr, Lee Sechrest, Phil Silverman, Ed Sizemore, Ed Schneider, Ralph Stewart, Lee Tilson, Art Tugman, G. Armour Van Horn, Dennis Vargo, Mike Wagner, J. Bruce Wilcox, and Joseph Woods.

index